THE CRESCENT

BY
FRANCIS BRETT YOUNG

CHAPTER I

I

When I stepped on to the platform at Nairobi I hadn't the very least idea of what I was in for. The train for which we were waiting was due from Kisumu, bringing with it a number of Indian sepoys, captured at Tanga and Jasin, whom the Belgian advance on Taborah had freed. It was my job to see them into the ambulances and send them off to hospital. But when I got to the station I found the platform swarming with clerical hats and women who looked religious, all of whom couldn't very well have been swept into this degree of congregation for the sake of an odd sepoy's soul. These mean and ill-dressed people kept up a chatter like starlings under the station roof. It was a hot day in November, and the rains were due. Even six thousand feet of altitude won't stimulate you then. It had all the atmosphere of a sticky school treat in August at home. . . . Baptists on an August Bank Holiday. That was how it struck me.

And anyway it was a nuisance: I couldn't get my ambulances on to the platform. "You see, sir, it isn't a norspital train," said the military policeman, "only a nordinary passenger train from the lake."

I asked him what all the crowd was about.

"They say," he replied cautiously, "as the missionaries is coming down. Them that was German prisoners."

So that was it. And a few minutes later the clumsy train groaned in, and the engine stood panting as though it were out of breath, as do all the wood-fuel engines of the Uganda Railway. The shabby people on the platform sent up an attempt at a cheer. I suppose they were missionaries too. My wounded sepoys had to wait until these martyrs were disgorged.

Poor devils. . . . They were a sad-looking crowd. I don't suppose Taborah in war-time had been a bed of roses: and yet . . . and yet one couldn't help feeling that these strange-looking creatures invited persecution. The men, I mean. Oh yes, I was properly ashamed of myself the next moment: but there's something about long-necked humility in clerical clothes that stirs up the savage in one, particularly when it moves slowly and with weak knees. Now to the cheers tears were added. They wept, these good people, and were very fluttered and hysterical: and the prisoners, poor souls, looked as if they didn't know where they were. It wasn't they who did the crying. I dare say, after all, they were quite admirable people and felt as sick at being slobbered over by over-emotional women as I did watching the progress. Gradually all of them were whipped off into cars that were waiting outside and conveyed, no doubt, to Christian homes where the house-boys come in for evening prayers. All of them except one. . . .

I had noticed her from the first: principally, I imagine, because she seemed horribly out of it, standing, somehow, extraordinarily aloof from the atmosphere of emotionalism which bathed the assembly as in weak tea. She didn't look their sort. And it wasn't only that her face showed a little tension—such a small thing—about the eyes, as though the whole thing (very properly) gave her a headache. And I think that if she hadn't been so dreadfully tired she would have smiled. As it was, nobody seemed to take any notice of her, and I could have sworn that she was thankful for it. But that wasn't the only reason why I was interested in her. In spite of the atrocious black clothes which she wore, and which obviously hadn't been made for her, she was really very beautiful, and this was a thing which could not be said of any other woman on the platform. But the thing which most intrigued me was the peculiar type of beauty which her pale face brought back to me, after many years. This girl's face, happily unconscious of my gaze, was the spring of a sudden inspiration of the kind which is most precious to those who love England and live in alien lands: it brought to me, suddenly and with a most poignant tenderness, the atmosphere of that sad and beautiful country which lies along the March of Wales. Other things will work the same magic: a puff of wood smoke; a single note in a bird's song; a shaft of sunlight or a billow of cloud. But here the impression was inconceivably distinct; so distinct that I could almost have affirmed the existence of some special bond between her and that country, and said: "This woman comes from the Welsh Marches somewhere between Ludlow and Usk, where the women have pale skins of an incredible delicacy, and straight eyebrows and serious dark eyes, and a sort of woodland magic of their own. And their voices . . ." I was certain that I knew what her voice would be like: so certain that I took the risk of disappointment and passed near her in the hopes that soon somebody would speak to her and then she would answer. I didn't have to wait long. A bustling female who oozed good works drew near. She held out her hand in welcome as she advanced.

"Well, my dear, are you Miss Burwarton?"

And my girl shivered. It was a little shiver which I don't suppose anyone else noticed. But why should she have shivered at her own name?

She said: "Yes, I'm Eva Burwarton."

I was right. Beyond doubt I was right. The "i" sound was deliciously pure, the "r" daintily liquid. Oh, I knew the sound well enough. My vision had been justified.

The bustling woman spoke:

"My dear, Mr. Oddy has been telling me about your poor dear brother. So sad . . . such a terrible loss for you. But the Lord . . ."

I didn't hear what precisely the Lord had done in this case, for a group of Sisters of Mercy in pale blue uniforms and white caps passed between us, but I saw the appropriate and pious gloom gathering on Mrs. Somebody's face, and in the face of Eva Burwarton not the shadow of a reply, not the faintest gleam of sympathy or remembered grief.

Good Lord, I thought, this is an extraordinary girl who can't or won't raise the flicker of an eyelid when she's being swamped with condolences about a brother to whom something horrible has evidently happened. And then the busy woman swept her away, and all the length of the platform I watched her beautiful, pale, serious face. And with her going that sudden vision, that atmosphere which still enwrapped me, faded, and I turned to the emptier end of the platform, where the wounded sepoys were squatting, looking as pathetic as only sick Indians can. And I was back in Nairobi again, with low clouds rolling over the parched Athi Plains, and the earth and the air and every living creature athirst for rain and the relief of thunder. A funny business . . .

But all that day the moment haunted me: that, and the girl's white face and serious brows, and the extraordinary incongruity of her ill-made, ill-fitting dress with her pale beauty. And her name, Eva Burwarton, which seemed somehow strangely representative of her tragic self. At first I couldn't place it at all. It sounded like Warburton gone wrong. And then when I wasn't thinking of anything in particular, I remembered that there was a village of that name somewhere near Wenlock Edge. And once again with a thrill I realised that I was right.

And after that I couldn't help thinking of her. I can't exactly say why. I don't think it was for the sake of her physical attractions: indeed, when I came to speak to her, when in the end she was driven, poor thing, into a certain degree of intimacy with me, I believe this aspect of her was quite forgotten. No . . . I think the attraction which she exercised over me was simply due to the curious suggestiveness which clung to her, the thing which had set me dreaming of a place or an atmosphere which it was an ecstasy to remember, and the flattering discovery that I had something more than imagination on which to build. And then, when my friendliness, the mere fact that we had something, even if it were only a memory, in common had surprised her into getting the inexpressible story off her mind, the awful spiritual intensity of the thing was so great that everything else about her was forgotten; she became no more than the fragile, and in glimpses the pathetic, vehicle of the drama. Nothing more: though, of course, it was easy enough for anyone who had eyes to see why poor old M'Crae (alias Hare) had fallen in love with her.

II

But at first, as I say, it was nothing more than the flavour of the country-side which she carried with her that held me. When next I saw her she had shed a little of that tender radiance. She had been furnished by some charitable person with clothing less grotesque. She certainly wasn't so indefinitely tragic; but now that she was less tired her country complexion—so very different from the parched skins of women who have lived for long in the East African highlands—made her noticeable.

She had been dumped by Mr. Oddy's friend (or wife, for all I know) into the Norfolk Hotel, the oldest and most reputable house in Nairobi, and it was in the gloomy lounge of this place that I was introduced to her by the only respectable woman I was privileged to know in the Protectorate. She said: "Cheer her up . . . there's a good fellow. She's lost her brother, poor thing! A missionary, you know."

And I proceeded to cheer up Eva Burwarton. My methods didn't answer very well. It was obvious that she wasn't used to the kind of nonsense which men talk.

3

She took me very seriously, or rather, literally. I thought: "She has no sense of humour." She hadn't . . . of my kind. And all the time those frightfully serious dark eyes of hers, which had never yet lost their hint of suffering, seemed full of a sort of dumb reproach, as if the way in which I was talking wasn't really fair on her. I didn't realise then what a child she was or a hundredth part of what she had endured. I knew nothing about M'Crae (alias Hare) or Godovius, or of that dreadful mission house on the edge of the M'ssente Swamp. And if it hadn't been for that fortunate vision of mine on the station platform I don't suppose that I should ever have known at all. The thing would have passed me by, as I suppose terrible and intense drama passes one by every day of one's life. An amazing thing. . . . You would have thought that a story of that kind would cry out to the whole world from the face of every person who had taken part in it, that it simply couldn't remain hidden behind a pale, childish face with puzzled eyes.

But when we seemed to be getting no further, and whatever else I may have done, I certainly hadn't cheered her at all, I brought out the fruits of my deduction. I said:

"Do you come from Shropshire or Hereford?"

Suddenly her whole face brightened, and the eyes which had been gazing at nothing really looked at me. Now, more than ever, I was overwhelmed with their childishness.

"Oh, but how do you know?" she cried, and in that moment more than ever confirmed me. I know that inflection so well.

It was Shropshire, she said. Of course I wouldn't know the place; it was too small. Just a little group of cottages on a hilly road between the Severn and Brown Clee. I pressed her for the name of it. A funny name, she said. It was called Far Forest.

I told her that veritably I knew it. Her eyes glowed. Strange that so simple a thing should give birth to beautiful delight.

"Then you must know," she said, "the house in which I was born. I can't believe that I shall see it again. I sometimes feel as if I've only dreamed about it. Although it was so quiet and ordinary, it's just like a dream to me. The other part is more real . . ." And the light went from her eyes.

But I think it did her good to talk about it. She was cheering herself up. And between us we pieced together a fairly vivid picture of the scattered group of houses above the forest of Wyre, where the highroad from Bewdley climbs to a place called Clows Top, which is often verily in cloud. There, we agreed, a narrow lane tumbles between cider orchards to a gate in the forest, that old forest of dwarf oak and hazel; and there the steep path climbs to a green space at the edge of a farm, where there is a duck-pond and a smooth green in which great stones are embedded, and nobody knows where the stones came from. And from this green you can see the comb of

Clee, Brown Clee and Titterstone in two great waves, and hear, on a Sunday evening, the church bells of Mamble and Pensax, villages whose names are music in themselves. And if you came back over the crest at sundown the lane would bring you out on the main road exactly opposite to the little house in which her father kept the general shop. Over the door there was a weather-beaten legend: "Aaron Burwarton, Licensed to Sell Tobacco"; and if it were summertime as like as not Aaron Burwarton himself would be sitting at the door in a white apron, not smoking, for he disapproved of tobacco, even though he sold it, and the westering sun would light up his placid, white-bearded face. People live easy lives in those parts . . . the quietest under the sun. All the walls of the house were beaten and weathered by wind and driving rain; and inside you would inhale the clean provocative odours of the general shop: soap, and bacon, and a hint of paraffin. She was delightfully ingenuous and happy about it all, and I was happy too. We sat and talked, in the gloomy Norfolk lounge; and outside the tropical night fell: the flat banana leaves stirred against the sky, the cicalas began their trilling chorus, and on the roof of the verandah little lizards stole quietly about. It was a surprising thing that we two should be sitting there talking of Far Forest. I said so. I said: "Why in the world are you here? What were you doing in German East?"

Now I could see she was not afraid of letting me into her confidence. I am not sure that she wasn't glad to do so. Even if it didn't "cheer her up." It was a long story, she said, beginning, oh, far away at home. The whole business had followed on quite naturally from a chapel service at Far Forest when she was quite a child. Her brother James was a little older than herself. And her father (this not without pride) was an elder of the chapel. A Mr. Misquith, she said, had driven up from Bewdley to preach about foreign missions: about Africa. Father had driven him up in the trap, and he had stayed to dinner. James, she said, had always been a clever boy and very fond of books. It had been father's great wish that James should some day enter the ministry. Not that he would have influenced him for a minute. Father held awfully strong views on that sort of thing. He believed in a "call." I wondered if she did too. "No, I don't think I was born religious," she said. But James was . . .

We were launched into a detailed recital of James' childhood, and it gave me the impression of just the queer, centripetal, limited sort of life which you could imagine people living at Far Forest, a life that sought ideals, but ideals of such an incredible humility. I don't think I had ever realised the horizons of an average Nonconformist family in a remote hamlet before. Old Burwarton himself was very far removed from that, and as for the children. . . . No; it was in relation to the events that came afterwards, the story that was gradually and in the simplest manner shaping before my imagination, that the environment of the Burwartons' childhood struck me as humble and limited. People who are brought up in that way don't usually find themselves forced into a highly coloured tropical melodrama, or, what is more, take their places in the scheme of it as if they had been specially created for that purpose. It was for this reason that I was content to consider James in some detail.

He had been, she said, a delicate child; but always so clever. Such a scholar. That was how she seriously put it. The little glazed bookshelf in the parlour had been full of his school prizes, and the walls with framed certificates of virtue and proficiency and God knows what else. And at quite an early age he had learned to play the harmonium. . . . "We had an American organ." I don't know what an American organ is, but I was quite satisfied with the picture of James playing Moody and Sankey hymns, which, if I remember rightly, deal mainly with The Blood, on Sunday afternoon, while old Mr. Burwarton sat by the fireside with a great Bible in his lap. Later she showed me a photograph of James: "He was supposed to be very like me," she said. And perhaps he was. . . . Yes, he certainly had the same straight brows, the same colouring of ivory and black; but his mouth was wholly lacking in that little determined line which made Eva's so peculiarly attractive. And I am almost sure that James had adenoids as a child, for in the photo his lips were parted, his nose a little compressed, and the upper lip too short. And later, she told me, because of the headaches which came with "too much study," he had to wear glasses; but in the photograph which she showed me you could see his dark eyes, the distant eyes of a visionary. I suppose in the class from which he came there are any number of young men of this kind, born mystics with a thirst for beauty which might be slaked in any glorious way, yet finds its satisfaction in the only revelation that comes their way in a religion from which even the Reformation has not banished all beauty whatsoever. They find what they seek in religion, in music (such music! . . . but I suppose it's better than nothing), in the ardours of love-making; and they go out, the poor, uncultured children that they are, into the "foreign mission field," and for sheer want of education and breadth of outlook die there . . . the most glorious, the most pitiful of failures. That, I suppose, is where Christianity comes in. They don't mind being the failures that they are. Oh yes, James was sufficiently consistent . . .

From school, the existence of a "call" having now been recognised, James had passed to college—the North Bromwich Theological College. Theology means Hebrew and New Testament Greek, a timid glance at the thing they call the Higher Criticism, and a working acquaintance with the modern pillars of Nonconformity. From the study of Theology James had issued in the whole armour of Light, ready to deal with any problem which human passion or savage tradition might put to him.

One gasps at the criminal, self-sufficient ignorance of the people that sent him to Central Africa, at the innocence of the man himself, who felt that he was in a position to go; for forlorner hope it would be impossible to imagine. Here, as in other cases of which I have heard, there was no shadow of an attempt at adjustment. James Burwarton went to Luguru to battle with his personal devil—and he hadn't reckoned with Godovius at that—very much as he might have gone to a Revival meeting in the Black Country. Fortified with prayer. . . . Oh, no doubt. But I wouldn't mind betting he went there in a collar that buttoned at the back and a black coat with flapping skirts. To Equatorial Africa. I've seen it. One of Eva's friends from Taborah was wearing one. Nor was that the only way in which I imagine his hope forlorn. He had gone there with the wrong sort of religion: with the wrong brand, if you like, of Christianity. You can't replace a fine exciting business of midnight n'gomas and dancing ceremonies by a sober teaching of Christian ethics without any exciting ritual attached, without any reasonable dilution with magic or mystery. The Roman missionaries in Africa know all about that. But James was prepared simply, to sit down in his black coat while a sort of reverent indaba of savages drank in the Sermon on the Mount, and forthwith proceeded to put it into practice. Ritual of any kind was abhorrent to him. Personality, example . . . those were the things that counted, said James. Personality! Compare the force of his personality with that of Godovius. Think of him dashing out milk and water ethics to the Masai, and then of Godovius with his deep knowledge of the origins of religion in man, with his own crazy enthusiasms added to a cult the most universal and savagely potent of any that has ever shaken humanity. I wish that James were not such a pathetic figure. I can't help seeing his pale face with Eva Burwarton's eyes. It's the very devil . . .

III

And so to Africa. In the ordinary way Eva would not have gone with him; but it so happened that only a month before he was due to sail the old general shopkeeper died, and everybody seemed to think that it would not be the right thing to leave the girl behind. Far Forest, they said, was not the place for a single young woman, implying, one supposes, that the Luguru mission was. And it would be so much better for James, they said, delicate, and a favourite, with all the makings of a martyr in him, to have someone to look after him; presumably to put on a clean collar for him before he went out converting the heathen. And so Eva went. She just went because she hadn't anywhere else to go. There wasn't any fine Apostolic fervour about her venture, nor even, for that matter, any great sisterly affection. She admitted to me that she had never understood James. If she hadn't been convinced that it was her duty to love him I think she would really have disliked him. But she too, for all her fine frank naturalness, had been brought up in the school of the old man Burwarton at Far Forest: it was partly that which made her so attractive—the spectacle of an almost constant conflict between instinct and education going on behind those dark eyes of hers. But then, of course, no one in the world can have seen that in the same way as Hector M'Crae . . . Perhaps that was partly the reason why he fell in love with her.

At any rate brother and sister embarked at London, steerage, on some Castle or other, for Durban. They went by the Cape. It was a very hot passage, and the boat, which called at St. Helena, was slow. She didn't really enjoy the voyage. In the steerage there were a lot of low-class Jews going out to Johannesburg. Even then she disliked Jews. Besides these there were a number of young domestic servants travelling in charge of a sort of matron, an elderly woman who was paid for the work by the society which arranged the assisted passages. Eva rather liked her; for she was kind and excessively motherly. What is more, she took her work seriously. "Some of these young persons are so simple," she said. "And the fellers . . . Well, I suppose there's nothing else to do on board." A human and charitable way of looking at the problem to which she owed her office. It was she, as a matter of fact, who relieved Eva of the attentions of the third engineer, who habitually sought diversions in the steerage. They were passing through the oily seas about the Equator. The nights were languid, and Jupiter shed a track over the smooth waves almost like that of the moon. The third engineer was rather nice, she said, at first. His uniform. Until one night . . . but the Emigrants' Matron had put him in his place. "Your brother should be looking after you by rights," she said. "But then, what does he know about that sort of thing?" On Sundays glimpses of heaven, as typified by the First Saloon, were vouchsafed to them. Indeed, James, who was the only parson aboard, had taken the service and even preached a short sermon. He was rather flattered by the politeness of the First-Class people, who took it all in with innocence and serenity. "They were nice to us," said Eva, "because they wanted to assure their own souls that they weren't mean in despising us. I knew . . ."

And from a stuffy coasting steamer that paused as it were for breath at every possible inlet from Chindi to Dar-es-Salaam they were thrust panting into Africa, into the sudden, harsh glories of the tropics, into that "vast, mysterious land." Mysterious . . . that was the adjective which people always used in talking about Africa . . . I beg their pardon . . . the Dark Continent—and to my mind no word in the language could be less appropriate. There is nothing really mysterious about Africa. Mystery is a thing of man's imagining, and springs, if you will, from an air which generations of dead men have breathed, emanates from the crumbled bricks with which they have builded, from the memory of the loves and aspirations of an immemorial past. But this land has no past: no high intelligence has made the air subtly alive with the vibrations of its dreams. And another thing which the word mysterious implies is the element of shock or surprise, while in Africa there is nothing more rare. From the Zambesi to the Nile a vast plateau, rarely broken, spreads; and on its desolation the same life springs, the same wastes of thorny scrub, the same river belts of perennial forest, the same herds of beasts, the same herds of men.

Into the centre of this vast monotony the Burwartons were plunged. By rail, for a hundred miles or so up the Central Railway to the point where the missionary whom they were relieving met them. He might have waited at Luguru to see them into the house, they thought. But he was in a hurry to get away. He said so: made no attempt to disguise it. Eva said from the first: "That man's hiding something." But James wouldn't have it. They had talked a little about the work. A stubborn field apparently . . . and yet such possibilities! So many dark souls to be enlightened, and almost virgin soil. James thrilled. He was anxious to get to work. The things which Bullace, the retiring minister, had told him had set fire to his imagination, so that for days on end he moved about in a state of rapt emotion.

But Eva wasn't going to leave it at the stage of vague enthusiasms. She wanted to know about the house. Mr. Bullace had been unmarried: his housework had been done by two native boys of the Waluguru tribe. Their names were Hamisi and Onyango. Oh yes, good boys both of them. Excellent boys, and Christians, of course. He had to confess that the house wasn't up to much. The garden? . . . He feared the garden had been rather neglected. But then the work . . . He hoped, hoped with rather an exaggerated zeal, she thought, that they would be happy. It would be strange for a white woman to live at Luguru: such a thing had never happened before.

She wanted to know about neighbours. Well, strictly speaking, there weren't any there, except Herr Godovius, a big owner of plantations. He didn't seem to want to talk about Godovius; which was quite the worst thing he could have done, for it made her suspicious. For James. That was always the funny part of her: she wasn't really fond of James (she admitted as much), and yet she always regarded herself in some sort as his protector, and was quick to scent any hostility towards him in others or even by any threat to his peace of mind. She regarded him more or less as a child. And so he was, after all . . .

Now she didn't give poor, shaky Mr. Bullace any peace. By hedging he had put her hot on the scent; she tackled him with that peculiar childish directness of hers.

"What's the matter with this Mr. . . . Mr. Godovius?"

Mr. Bullace couldn't or wouldn't tell her. "There's nothing really the matter with him," he said. "In some ways you'll find him . . . oh . . . kind—extraordinarily kind. I don't want to prejudice you against him."

"But that's what you are doing, Mr. Bullace," she said.

"I want you to start with a clean sheet, so to speak. I want you to be happy at Luguru. I don't see why you shouldn't, I don't really."

And by that she knew that he did. Indeed I pity little Mr. Bullace under Eva's eyes.

James was different, very different. He mopped up all that Mr. Bullace could tell him about the people: how this village chief was a reliable man; how another was suspected of backslidings; a third, regrettably, a thief. James took shorthand notes in a penny exercise-book. But he couldn't help noticing how ill and haggard Mr. Bullace looked.

"The work has told on you," he said.

Yes, Mr. Bullace admitted, the work had told on him. "But you," he said, "will not be so lonely. Loneliness counts for a lot. That and fever. Have you plenty of quinine?"

"I am ready to face that sort of thing," said James. "One reckons with that from the start." He even glowed in anticipation. He would have blessed malaria as a means to salvation. Eva, listening to his enthusiasms, and what she took to be Mr. Bullace's gently evasive replies, smiled to herself. She wondered where she came in.

CHAPTER II

I

Next morning Mr. Bullace left them. There wasn't really anything suspicious about his haste; for if he hadn't gone down the line that day he would have had to forfeit a month or more of his leave by missing the boat. From the railway the two Burwartons set off northward. Luguru was distant six days' safari: in other words, between seventy and eighty miles.

Of course this journey was very wonderful for Eva. I suppose there is no existence more delightful than that of the wanderer in Africa, in fair weather, particularly in these highlands, where the nights are always cool, and the grassy plains all golden in the early morning when most of the journeying is done. To these dwellers in the cloudy Severn valley was given a new intoxication of sunlight, of endless smiling days. And the evenings were as wonderful as the earlier hours; for then the land sighed, as with relief from a surfeit of happiness; when night unfolded a sky of unusual richness decked with strange lights more brilliant than the misty starshine of home. James Burwarton too was sensitive to the magnificence of these. From a friend at "college" he had picked up a few of the names of Northern constellations; but many of these stars troubled him by their strangeness. The brother and sister sat together alone in the dark watching the sky. Alone in the middle of Africa. James' imagination struggled with the idea. "To think," he said, "that even the stars are different. One might be in another world." Adventure enough for the most exacting of devotees! The sight of this starry beauty filled him with a desire to moralise. With Eva it was quite different. To her their loveliness and strangeness were self-sufficient. "I think," she said, "that I simply moved along in a sort of dream. I couldn't pretend to take it all in then, but now I seem to remember every step of it."

That was one of the characteristics of the girl which I quickly discovered: she had an almost infallible sense of country—a rare thing in a woman. Thanks to this, I have now almost as clear a conception of the Luguru mission and its surroundings as if I had been there myself. The lie of the whole land was implicit in her account of their first arrival there.

It was evening, she said—the sixth evening of their safari. All day long they had been pushing their way through moderately dense thorn bush. Awfully hot work it was, with the smell of an orangey sort of herb in the air: like oranges mixed with another scent . . . mint, or something of that kind. She was rather tired; for she had been walking most of the day, preferring that sort of fatigue to the sea-sickness of riding in a machila. All along the road the tsetses had been flicking at them as if they must bite or die, and Eva's ankles were swollen with tick bites.

And then suddenly, just as the evening grew calm and beautiful and the air cool, the bush began to thin a little, and the scent of that funny stuff (she said) began to thin too. They were approaching a well-defined ridge, and when they reached the crest they saw that the bush on the farther slope was far thinner and the trees bigger. "Just like an English park," she said. And that is what they call Park Steppe in German East. The slope in front of them shelved into a semicircle of low hills beyond which an unbroken line of mountain stretched, very solemn and placid in the evening air. A wide basin was this country of the Waluguru, clogged in its deepest concavity with dense blue forest and the brighter green of the M'ssente Swamp. Towards the ambient foothills, lips of the basin, the Park Steppe rose on either hand: and these lower hills were bare except for dark streaks of forest which marked the courses of winter torrents. On the western rim, part of which was already in shade, a white building shone in the middle of the bare hill-side. That was the mission.

I have written that all these lesser hills were bare but one. And this one, which was the highest of them all, overhung the sources from which the M'ssente river issued into the dark forest. It seemed, indeed, as if some special virtue in the moisture of the river's springs had tempted the forest, whose vast body lay dark in the valley's bottom, to swarm up its slopes and to clutch at the hill's conical peak. But towards the top the trees abruptly ended, and the volcanic form of the summit, the commonest of hill shapes in East Africa, showed pale against the mountains behind. On either side of this central peak the slopes of the hills were cultivated and planted with rubber and coffee. The sight of tilled earth and the homely green of the rubber-trees gave an aspect of cheerfulness and civilisation to the valley which helped one to forget the forest and swamps beneath. After all, it seemed as if life at Luguru need not be as strange as they had imagined. That night they encamped on the edge of the basin. Another evening of brilliant starshine, until a little later a crescent moon rose and hung above the peak of that wooded hill.

Next day, though it was much farther than they had imagined, they reached the mission. The place was sufficiently well ordered, and reasonably clean. Although in the distance the hill-side had seemed to be almost bare, they found that their home was set about with a number of scattered trees, a kind of croton, with slender twisted trunks and expanded crowns. By daylight these trees carried their green heads so high in the burning air that they gave no shade, and one was not conscious of them; but when the evening descended on Luguru and their branches stirred in a faint zodiacal glow they were most lovely creatures. Every evening, at sundown, they would awake to gracious life. Eva Burwarton grew to love them. All the open ground about their little compound was scattered with their fruit, which resembled that of the walnut.

By the side of the mission house lay the garden of which Bullace had spoken, hedged with a boma of sisal aloes, many of which had flowered so that their tall poles rose up like spears. Within the boma were untidy banana-trees with their ragged leaves; a corner of guava and citrus; beds of French beans and sweet potatoes over which a gourd had straggled. It was a little garden, and Eva was sure that soon she could reduce it to order. The prospect of doing so pleased her. Such labour would be very sweet in the blue evening when the croton-trees awakened. It was wonderful, in a way, to be thrown upon one's own resources for every comfort; and particularly in a country where nature did half the work, where the ancient soil was rich with the death of centuries, only waiting to give forth new life. Eva decided that in a little while she would have a treasure of a garden. But there were no flowers: that was the strange thing about it—there were no flowers.

At the end of the garden most distant from the house and under the spears of sisal stood a substantial banda, or hut, built of grass closely thatched. A thin partition divided this building into two chambers. In the outer a number of gardening tools were stored. The inner and smaller of the two was dark, the doorway of the partition being blocked with loose boards, and Eva, looking through the cracks between the boards, discovered that it was empty except for an immense pile of empty whisky bottles in one corner. Her thoughts returned quickly to her memory of Mr. Bullace's face, to his hands that trembled with nervousness. She wondered. . . . But her orderly mind soon realised that this inner room might be useful as a store for lumber, and that the outer, when once it had been cleaned and swept, would make her a sort of summer-house in which she might sit and read in the heat of the day. There, she decided, she would take her sewing. The banda should be devoted to her as the little arbour at the bottom of the garden at Far Forest had been her chief playground, the home of herself and her dolls, when she had been a child. Living there, by herself, she would be a child again. While she had this refuge James need never be disturbed at his studies. It would be such fun . . .

Indeed it seemed to her in those days that their life at Luguru must be almost idyllic, that they would live simply and at peace, unvexed by troubles of body or mind. I think she was naturally hopeful, and, if you like, ignorant. The idea of tropical violence didn't enter into a mind fascinated with tropical beauty. She didn't consider the menace of disease. She didn't realise anything of the savage life which struggled as it were to the surface in the depths of the M'ssente forests and the great swamp. She saw only their own sunny hill-side, and the pleasant plantations of Herr Godovius. Even when I came to know her she was only a child . . .

During these first few days James showed himself eager to get to work. As for the house and the garden and the little shamba behind the mission, where coffee and mealies were growing, he simply didn't seem to take them in. James was all for souls—seriously . . . and the practical details of life fell naturally to the lot of Eva. Goodness knows what would have happened to him if old Mr. Burwarton had not died and released Eva to look after him. I suppose he would have led a wild, prophetic sort of existence, depending for his sustenance on locusts and wild honey (there were plenty of both) or the ministrations of ravens . . . just until he discovered that a man can't live on nothing. In a way it was a misfortune that his physical wants were so completely provided for by Eva's care; it gave him a chance of such complete absorption in one idea as can be good for no man. In the end it gave him time for brooding on his difficulties. Of course, for all his fervour, he was exactly the wrong sort of man for missionary work; but, as Eva herself admitted, he was built for martyrdom. They didn't expect in those days how literally he would get it. Win it, he would have said.

II
It was not until their first Sunday, one of the great days, as James said, of his life, that they met Godovius. He came to the mission church. . . . Yes, Godovius came to church . . .

A rather astonishing introduction. He galloped up on a little Somali mule that somehow seemed to have got the better of fly. A Waluguru boy had run all the way by his side. When he handed over the mule to the boy, he stood waiting on the edge of the kneeling assembly. The service was nearly over; but he showed the least tinge of impatience at being kept waiting. James was quite unconscious of this. At home and on the voyage he had been taught a very fair smattering of mission Swahili, and the repetition of prayers in this exotic language by the lips of forty or fifty converts led by the mission boys, Hamisi the Luguru and Onyango, a stranger from the Wakamba country with filed teeth, was an incense to him. This oasis of prayer in the heart of an infidel desert . . .

But Eva, from the moment Godovius had ridden up, was conscious of his physical presence, and even more, in an indefinite way, of his spiritual immanence. He was, she reflected, their only neighbour; and it struck her that James' disregard of him, a white man, was a shade impolite. Besides, she had only just realised that the Luguru Christian, next to whom she knelt, exhaled a distinct and highly unpleasant odour. Of course that wasn't his fault, poor thing . . . but still . . . She noticed, too, that James was the only person in all that assembly who didn't realise Godovius's presence. The natives on either side of her gave a little movement which might have meant anything when he approached. She even heard one of them murmur a word . . . something like Saccharine . . . and wondered what it meant. Although they still muttered the formula which they had learned, Eva was certain that they were really thinking a great deal more of the dark man who stood waiting behind them. It was a funny impression; and the intuition vanished as quickly as it had come to her; for James finished his service, the crowd drifted away, and Godovius himself came forward with an altogether charming smile. He spoke English well: with more purity, indeed, than either of them. He said: "Mr. Burwarton? . . . I was told your name by the good Bullace. I am your neighbour . . . Godovius. We must be friends."

He held out his hand: James grasped it and shook it fervently.

He bowed to Eva. "Your wife?" he said. "My sister."

"How foolish of me . . . I should have known."

This is how Eva saw him: Tall, certainly taller than James, who himself was above middle height. And dark . . , perhaps that was only to be expected from the sun of those parts; but she had always imagined that Germans were fair. In no way did he answer to her ideas of Germanity. He was exceedingly polite: after all, she supposed most foreigners were that: but to the exotic grace which was the traditional birthright of Continentals there was here added strength. She had never met a man who gave such an impression of smooth capability. "He looked clever," she said. It doesn't seem ever to have struck her that Godovius was a Jew, even though she quickly decided that he wasn't typically German. Indefinitely she had been prejudiced against him; but now that she saw him she liked him. "You couldn't help liking him. He was really very handsome." The only thing about

13

which she wasn't quite sure was his eyes. They were dark . . . very dark: "Not the soft sort of dark," she said.

They all moved towards the mission house, Eva first, Godovius and her brother walking side by side. They were already talking of the Waluguru.

"You won't find them easy," Godovius said. "I think I may safely say that I know more about them than anyone else. No other settler has a shamba in their country. And it isn't a big country, although they're a fairly numerous tribe. Down there"—he pointed with the long thong of hippo hide which he carried as a whip to the dark forest beneath them, bloomed with quivering air—"down there, under the leaves, they live thickly. The life in that forest . . . human . . . sub-human . . . because they aren't all like men . . . the apes: and then, right away down in the scale, the great pythons. Oh . . . the leeches in the pools. Life . . . all seething up under the tree-tops, with different degrees of aspirations, ideals. Life, like a great flower pushing in the sun . . . Isn't it?"

James said yes, it was. He reined back Godovius to the business in hand: his business. Why, he asked, were the Waluguru difficult? Why? But the matter was ethnological. Mr. Burwarton was a student of ethnology?

James wasn't.

Godovius was quick with offers of help. "It's a habit with me," he said. "I can lend you books if you wish them. Perhaps you don't read German? Ah . . . all the best ethnology is German. But I have some English. Frazer . . . The Golden Bough. No doubt you have read that . . . if religion interests you."

James couldn't for the life of him understand what these things had to do with the gospel of Christ. To him religion was such a simple thing. And all the time Eva was listening, not because she understood what Godovius was talking about, but because she was conscious of the suppressed flame in him: just because, in fact, he interested her.

He came back to the Waluguru. They weren't, he said, a pure Bantu stock by any means. There were elements of a very different kind. Semitic. Of course there was any amount of Arab blood among the coastal Swahili; but the case of the Waluguru was rather peculiar: the way in which they were isolated by the lie of the land—the Mountains of the Moon to the north, the thick bush on the south. They'd developed more or less on irregular lines. Nobody knew how they'd got there. Physically they were very attractive . . . the women at any rate.

But none of these things would necessarily make them "difficult," James protested.

Godovius smiled. "Well, perhaps not . . . At any rate," he said, "you'll find my people interesting." He called them my people.

Eva noticed that: she always noticed little things, and remembered at the same time the way in which the Waluguru congregation had responded to his presence in the middle of James's prayers; but this impression was soon covered by her appreciation of the fact that he was talking all the time to her as much as to James: and that was for her an unusual sensation, for she had been accustomed for long enough to taking a back seat when James was present. This attitude of Godovius subtly flattered her, and she began to feel, rather guiltily, that she had allowed a first impression to influence her unfairly. She became less awkward, permitting herself to realise that their neighbour was really very good-looking in a dark, sanguine, aggressively physical way. She noticed his teeth, which were white—very white and regular as the teeth of an animal or of an African native: and then, suddenly, once again she noticed his eyes, deep brown and very lustrous. He was looking at her carefully; he was looking at her all over, and though she wasn't conscious of any expression in them which could allow her to guess what he was thinking, she blushed. It annoyed her that she should have blushed, for she felt the wave spreading over her neck and chest and knew that he must realise that she was blushing all over. "I felt as if I weren't properly clothed," she said.

Then Godovius smiled. He took it all for granted. He spoke to her just as if James had not been there: as if they had been standing alone on the stoep with nothing but the silence of Africa around them. He said:

"Do you realise that my eyes haven't rested on a white woman for more than five years?"

And she answered: "I'm sorry . . ." Why on earth should she have said that she was sorry?

That morning he spoke no more to her. He stood on the stoep, a little impatiently, slapping his leggings with his kiboko, and answering the anxious questions of James as if he had set himself a task and meant to go through with it. Eva, watching them, realised that if she were sorry, as she had said, for Godovius, she had much more reason to be sorry for James. The physical contrast between the two men was borne in on her so strangely. And a little later, feeling that she wasn't really wanted, she slipped into the house.

III
James and she discussed this surprising visit over their evening meal. They were sitting, as usual, upon the wide stoep which overlooked the valley and the forest and all that cavernous vista which the plantations of Godovius and the conical hill named Kilima ja Mweze dominated. James was rather tired with his day's work—the enthusiasm of the Sabbath always consumed him and left him weak and mildly excited—and it was with a sense of sweet relief that they watched the croton-trees stirring in an air that was no longer eaten out with light. They ate sparingly of a paw-paw which Hamisi had cut from the clusters in the garden, and Eva had picked a rough green lemon from one of her own trees that stood decked with such pale lamps of fruit in the evening light. Then they had coffee made from

the berries which Mr. Bullace had left behind: Mocha coffee grown in the plantations of Godovius.

James sipped his coffee and then said suddenly: "Do you like him?"

Eva knew whom he meant perfectly well, but found herself asking: "Who?"

"Mr. Godovius."

"I don't quite know," she said. "Do you think he is a good man?"

"Yes. . . . I think he is a good man. Here we cannot judge by the same standards as at home. Settlers live very isolated lives . . . far away from any Christian influences, and I think that very often they don't look with favour on missionary work. I've been told so. . . . One is fortunate to find them even—how can I put it?—neutral. He that is not against us is for us. He was kind, extremely kind. And then we have Mr. Bullace's word."

"Do you trust Mr. Bullace's word?" she said.

"If we can't trust our own people . . ." he began; but she was sorry for what she had said, and hastened to tell him that she didn't mean it, and that she really thought Godovius had been quite kind and neighbourly to have visited them so soon, and that, no doubt, he knew more about the Waluguru than anyone else and might be a great help to them.

He was only too happy to agree with her. "When you left us," he said, "he offered to help you with the garden, to explain to you all the things of which you probably wouldn't know the uses. Oh, he was most kind. And why did you run away from us?"

She could not tell him the real reason, principally because she did not know. But that was always the peculiar thing about her relation with Godovius: from the first an amazing mixture of repulsion and . . . something else to which she found it impossible to give a name.

That night when she had gone to bed, leaving James a lonely figure in the pale circle of light which his reading-lamp reclaimed from the enveloping darkness, she found herself curiously restless and disturbed. It was perhaps in part that she was still unused to the peculiar character of the African night, that tingling darkness in which so much minute life stirs in the booming and whiffling of uncounted wings, in the restless movements of so many awakening tendrils and leaves. This was a darkness in which there was no peace. But it was not only that. Godovius troubled her. The picture of him which abode with her that night was so different from that of reassurance in which he had left them. Now she could only be conscious of his sinister side; and the impression assailed her with such an overwhelming force that she wondered how in the world she could have been led into such a feeble acquiescence with James, who thought evil of no man, on the subject of their neighbour. For now, if she confessed the truth to herself, she was frightened of Godovius. She was convinced, too, that Mr. Bullace had lied to them. She conceived it her duty to tell James so. And thus, half sleeping or half awake, she found herself in the passage of the bungalow at the door of the room in which she had left her brother reading. He was not there. The vacant room lay steeped in moonlight of an amazing brilliance; she could read the sermon of Spurgeon which lay open on the table. It took her a few seconds to realise that the impulse which had forced her to set out upon this errand of disillusionment had come to her in sleep, flying into her consciousness like a dark moth out of the restless night: but for all that she could not at once persuade herself that she had been foolish, not indeed until she realised that her feet were cold upon the floor and that she had better beware of snakes and jiggers and other terrors of the earth. If she had been wearing slippers she would probably have wakened James. As it was, defenceless and bewildered, she moved out of the cold moonlight back to her room, where she fell into an uneasy sleep. For now, more than ever, she was conscious of the night's noises and a little later of one noise which resembled the fluttered beating of her own heart as she listened: the monotonous pulsations, somewhere down in the white mist of the forest, of an African drum.

CHAPTER III

I

Next day when she woke she had forgotten all about her questionings. It was one of the peerless mornings of that hill country in which the very air, faintly chilled by night, possesses a golden quality, which gives it the effect of sunny autumn days in Europe. Only once did she remember the shadow of her premonitions, and that was when she came singing into the room which she had last seen in the moonlight and found upon the table the book of Spurgeon's sermons open at the same page. But in this new and delightful atmosphere Eva could afford to laugh at her fancies. There were so many pleasant things to be done, and as the sun rose that vast, smiling country unfolded around her with a suggestion of spaciousness and warmth and leisure. A land of infinite promise in which the very simplicity of life's demands should make one immune from the menace of discontent: where, for a little labour, the rich soil should give great recompense. Indeed it seemed to her that in this place she might be very happy, for she asked very little of life.

Her first concern was Mr. Bullace's banda, and the tangled garden which seemed as though it had been long deserted and overgrown, although it had only been cumbered with the fierce growth of one season's rains. Here, in the golden morning, she would get to work with the two boys, Hamisi and Onyango, watching their happy, leisurely manner of husbandry. They worked until their black limbs were stained with warm red earth, and sometimes while they were toiling they would sing to each other strange antiphonal airs which made their labour seem like some delightful game of childhood. It was good to watch them at work, for they seemed so happy and human and unvexed by any of the preoccupations of the civilised man. Indeed it was very difficult to realise that they were really savages, and it came as a shock to her one day when she saw Hamisi, the M'kamba, with his splendid torso stripped, and noticed upon his chest the pattern of scars which the medicine-man had carved upon his living flesh in some barbaric rite. She grew fascinated with their patience and good nature and their splendid white teeth: and after a little while she was no longer distressed by their obvious laziness, for in the placid life of Luguru there was no conceivable need for hurry. She even went to the trouble of borrowing a green vocabulary from James' shelf and learning a few words of everyday Swahili which she would use with intense satisfaction. There was a new pleasure and a sense of power in the speaking of a strange tongue which she had never known before. When she spoke to the boys in Swahili they smiled at her: but this did not mean that they were amused at her flounderings: they were of a people that smiled at all things, even at suffering and at death.

One morning when they were working thus, and she sat watching them in the door of Mr. Bullace's banda, she was startled to hear them stop in the middle of one of their songs. With a sudden sense of some new presence she turned round, and found that Godovius was standing near her in the path. He raised his hat to her and smiled.

"I promised to come and help you," he said. "And here I am . . . quite at your service."

It was strange that in this meeting not one of her old doubts returned. His arrival had been too sudden to leave her time to think, and now, instinctively, she liked him. He seemed so thoroughly at ease himself that a strained attitude on her part was impossible: and in a very little time he convinced her that he was actually as good as his word and that his knowledge would be of great use to her. They walked round the garden together, and he told her the names of many things which she had not known, while he instructed her in the cooking of many strange delicacies.

"But these boys of yours aren't working properly," he said. "You can get a great deal more out of them."

"But I get quite enough," she protested. "In fact, I believe I rather like their way of work. It's . . . well, it's restful."

He laughed at her: "That's all very well, Miss Burwarton; but it's bad for them . . . very bad for them. There's only one way of managing natives. I expect you'd think it a very brutal way. I'm a great believer in the kiboko. You can only get at an African through his skin. It's a very thick skin, you know. Nothing is so terrible as physical pain. But then . . . nothing is so quickly forgotten. On a mind of this kind . . . if you like to call it a mind . . . the impression fades very quickly. Fear . . . that is the only way in which we small communities of Europeans can rule these black millions. By fear. . . . It sounds cruel: but when you come to think of it that is the way in which your missionaries teach them Christian morals, by frightening them with threats of what will happen if they don't embrace them. I know that the good Bullace rather specialised in hell. But what is an indefinite hell compared with definite physical pain?"

She didn't fully understand what he was driving at. Life had never accustomed her to deal with abstractions; but he saw that she was puzzled and perhaps a little frightened.

So he stuck the kiboko, which he had been flourishing as he spoke, under his arm and smiled at her in a way that was almost boyish. "You don't like what I say?" he said. "Very well then. I will show you. We will apply the other kind of persuasion. So . . ."

Still smiling, he called to the two Africans. "Kimbia . . . Run!" he cried. They stood before him, and he spoke to them in swift, guttural Swahili. The foreigner from the Wakamba country stared at him dully; but the Waluguru boy, Hamisi, cowered beneath his words as though a storm were breaking over him. He fell to his knees, covering his head with his hands and shaking violently in every muscle, almost as if he were in the cold stage of an attack of fever. When Godovius stopped speaking the boy still trembled. Onyango, the M'kamba, turned and went sullenly back to his work, Godovius pushed the other with his foot. "Get up . . . quenda," he said. Then Hamisi staggered on to his legs. He rubbed his eyes, those brown-veined African eyes blotched with pigment, as though he wanted to obliterate some hallucinated vision, and Eva saw that they weren't like human eyes at all, but like those of an animal full of terror. Again Godovius told him to go, and he murmured, "N'dio Sakharani," and stumbled away.

Sakharani. . . . Eva remembered the whisper which had spread through the Waluguru congregation on the morning when Godovius had ridden up on his little Somali mule. She was startled and at the same time instinctively anxious to appear self-possessed. She said:

"Sakharani. . . . Is that a name that they give you?"

He laughed. "Why, of course. They are funny people. They always invent names for us. I expect they have given you one already. They are generally descriptive names, and pretty accurately descriptive, too."

"Then what does 'Sakharani' mean?" she asked.

"Well now," he said, "you are making things very awkward for me. But I will tell you. 'Sakharani' means 'drunken.'"

All this he said very solemnly, and Eva, taking the matter with a simple seriousness, looked him up and down with her big eyes, so that he burst out laughing, slapping his leggings in that most familiar gesture with his whip.

"Then you are shocked. . . . Of course you are shocked. You think I am a drunkard, don't you?"

She told him truthfully that he didn't look like one; for the skin of his face beneath the shade of the double terai hat of greyish felt was wonderfully clear, and those strange eyes of his were clear also: besides this, she could see that he was still intrigued by the joke.

"You think that I am one who is drunk with whisky like your reverend friend Mr. Bullace. No . . . you're mistaken. You English people have only one idea of being drunk—with your whisky. But there are other ways. You do not know what it is to be drunk with the glory of power—was not Alexander drunk?—or to be drunk with beauty . . . you have no music . . . or to be drunk, divinely drunk, with love, with passion. Ah . . . now do you know what 'Sakharani' means?"

Rather disconcerted by this outburst, for she had never heard anything of this kind in Far Forest, she told him that she thought she knew what he meant.

"But you don't," he said. "Of course you don't. What can an Englishwoman know of passion? Nonsense! . . . Of course you don't." And then, seeing her bewilderment, his manner suddenly changed. "Forgive me my . . . my fit of drunkenness," he said. "It is much better that you should be as you are. You are beautifully simple. A woman of your simplicity is capable of all. Forgive me . . ."

And with this he left her feeling almost dazed in the sunny garden, in the fainting heat of the tropical midday in which all things seem to be asleep or in a state of suspended life. When he had gone the whole of that land around seemed uncannily still, there was no sound in it but the melancholy note of hornbills calling to one another in dry recesses of the thorn-bush, and it seemed to her that even their voices drooped with heat . . .

II

That evening a Waluguru boy came over from Njumba ja Mweze with a great basket of strange flowers, great orchids horned and blotched with savage colour. When she took them out of the basket and placed them straggling in a wide bowl upon the table in their living-room she was almost afraid of them, for their splendour seemed to mock the meanness of the little house almost as if the forest itself with all its untamed life had invaded their quietude, asserting beyond question its primeval, passionate strength. Before she had finished arranging them James came into the room.

"How do you like them?" she said.

He fingered the fleshy petals of a great orange flower.

"They are marvellous," he said. "All this hidden beauty of creation. . . . Where did you get them?"

"I didn't get them. Mr. Godovius sent them."

"It was kind of him to think of us," he said; but his face fell, and she knew that he was suddenly questioning the propriety of the gift, suspecting in spite of his own words that they had been sent to her and yet ashamed of his suspicions. She knew James so well.

But she did not show him the card she found in the bottom of the basket, which was written in a pointed, foreign hand with many flourishes, and said:

"You have forgiven me? For you they should have been violets."

All that evening the presence of these flowers worried her. It seemed to her as if Godovius himself were in the room, as if those extravagant blooms were an expression of his sanguine, sinister personality: and when James, who was tired with a long day of tramping in the heat, had gone to bed, a strange impulse made her want to take the fleshy flowers and crush their petals to a pulp. She hated them.

"If I were to crush them," she thought, "they would be wet and nasty and bleed, as if they were alive." And so she left them where they were.

But he sent many other flowers, and several times he came himself, nearly always in that hour of the level sunlight. He would come into the garden and stand over her, saying little, but all the time watching her from beneath his grey slouch hat. In all these days he never returned to the subject of the name the natives had given him or allowed himself to be led into such another outburst of passion. Instead of this, he nearly always talked to her of herself, subtly, and with a very winning friendliness, inducing her to do the same. He had been in England a good deal, it appeared; but there was nothing remarkable in that, since he had been everywhere. And yet even so, they had little in common; for the England which he knew was nothing more than the West End of London, with which he assumed an impressive familiarity and which she did not know at all. It did not seem to have occurred to him that there was any other England, and he listened with a sort of amused tolerance to her stories of Far Forest and those Shropshire days now so incredibly remote. Of these things she would talk happily enough, for to speak of them mitigated without her knowledge a home-sickness to which she would not have confessed. The remembrance of many green days in that country of springing rivers had the power of soothing her almost as gently as the music of their streams, so that speaking of her love of them she would forget for a moment all that vast basin of Luguru. And then, no doubt, that look of tender wistfulness which I myself had seen would steal into her eyes, giving them an aspect peculiarly soft and . . . vernal: there is no other word. It was not strange that Godovius, caressing her ideal innocence, should have told her that her voice was soft when she spoke of her home. And this frightened her. Why should he have noticed her voice? She became, with an alarming suddenness, stiff and awkward and unnatural: which made Godovius smile, for he saw that he had read her very thoroughly and that the workings of her mind were plain to him. It amused him to see the adorable shyness with which she shut the opened doors of her heart and flattered him that he should have guessed the way in which they might be opened without her knowing it. She was scared; but it was very certain that however she felt towards him, and however she might have been repelled by sudden glimpses of his strange personality, she could not deny that he had been kind.

One day it happened that she disclosed to him that her name was Eva. "A beautiful name," he said, "and one that perfectly suits you."

She asked him "Why": and in reply he told her, as one might tell a child, the story of the Meister-singers, of the love of the handsome Walther for her namesake in the opera, and of the noble resignation of Hans Sachs.

"You are like the music of Eva," he said.

She smiled at him: for it seemed to her ridiculous that music of any kind could be like a living woman. Indeed she thought him rather silly, and extravagant as usual, and was amazed to see the seriousness with which he proceeded to explain what seemed to her a very ordinary story.

"One day," he said, "you will come to my house and I will play to you some Wagner, and then you will see for yourself that I am right. Of course music is not natural to the English . . ."

After this he would often ask her: "When are you coming to see me . . . you and your brother?" so often that at last she was compelled to ask James when he would take her.

III

But for all that she did not visit the House of the Moon for many weeks. James could not find time to go there with her. With an almost desperate enthusiasm he had thrown himself into the task of Christianising the Waluguru. He could not treat the business in a measured, leisurely way. Every morning Eva would watch him setting out from the stoep over the scattered park-land which sloped to the forest and the great swamp, a bizarre, pathetic figure, threading his way between the flat-topped acacias. In a little while the thin shapes of innumerable trees would close around him and for the rest of that day he would be lost to her, for he always carried a small parcel of food and a water-bottle with him into the forest. Just about the time of their sudden sunset he would return, in the hour when the fine noises of night begin: and then he would fling himself down, tired out, on the lounge-chair in their little room, with his feet on the long wooden foot-rest stained with the intersecting circles of Mr. Bullace's glasses. When he came home at night he was always exhausted, sometimes too tired even to eat, and Eva, who felt unhappy about him, would try to persuade him to take things more easily. She knew as well as he did that it was not usual for Europeans to work themselves to death in the neighbourhood of the Equator: she had seen for herself the man's stormy, precarious childhood and knew how delicate he was. When he had been working at "college" a nervous breakdown had thrown him back on Far Forest for four months, and she felt that soon something of the same kind must happen here. But it was useless to argue with James. She realised that from the beginning. In the Burwarton family his distinguished vocation had always made him a law to himself; her part in his career had been limited to respectful admiration, and it was impossible that their change of surroundings should alter the relation. Whatever she might say, James believed he knew best: and there was an end of the matter.

It is difficult to visualise the kind of life which James was leading amongst his Waluguru. Entering the forest by one of those tawny paths of sand which trickled down to it from the dry bush, he must have passed into the still outer zone of their retreat, moving through the green gloom far beneath the crowns of those enormous trees like some creature struggling among thickets of seaweed in the depths of the sea. In these profundities no sound disturbed the heavy air: the trailing tangles of liana never stirred, and into their gloom there penetrated none of the fragrance and light and colour which trembled in an ecstasy of sunlight above the roofs of those green mansions. Not easily did one attain to the haunts of the Waluguru. Two stinking creeks were to be crossed by the trunks of forest trees which had been felled by fire—the only bridges the Waluguru know—and next a reach of dazzling river, where the forest fell away and sunlight burst through with the pride of a conqueror, flashing back from the smooth sheets of yellow water. Then one came to a zone in which tree trunks had been felled on every side, where often a smouldering fire might be seen in the heart of a doomed but living tree: and in the spaces between the Waluguru had planted vast groves of the plantains on which they live: for they are a forest people, and the maize which feeds so great a part of Africa will not flourish in the dank air which they breathe. Between the groups of plantains they had dug pits in that black soil which is nothing but the mould of green things which had thrived and died and rotted in the same gloom, and in the bottom of these pits lies the black water of the M'ssente Swamp, breeding the fever of which many of them die.

Serpentine paths trodden in the oozy earth by the flocks of goats which the Waluguru tend threaded these groves: and by following one of them James was certain to arrive at a little clearing in the forest and a group of huts with pointed roofs of reeds. These oases, miserable, and sunless, were the field of his labours. In them he would find a number of women decked in rings of copper wire and small pot-bellied children who stared with open mouths. The men he would seldom see, for all of them who could stagger beneath a load were toiling as slaves in the airy plantations of Godovius, wearing for the symbol of their servitude a disk of zinc on which a number and the brand of their master, the crescent moon, were stamped. On the whole, I imagine that theirs was a far happier existence than that of the women who languished in the great swamp. They, at any rate, might sometimes see the sun, even if the sunlight were cruel. Most of the women seemed to James to be very old; but it was impossible for him to guess at their real age, and they could not tell him, for lengths of years is not a thing to be treasured among the Waluguru. It is probable that none of them were really aged, but only emaciated by labour and poor feeding and disease. Nor were there many children. The Waluguru know well enough that it is a tragedy to be born. Most of the small creatures which he saw lolling their great heads were scabbed with yaws and tragically thin. An atmosphere of hopelessness descended on him as soon as he set foot within their clearings. It seemed to him that in these sinister recesses some devil had been at work trying malignantly to stamp out the least flicker of humanity in the souls or bodies of these people, and beneath this intangible menace he was powerless. There was no more hope for these creatures than for any pale weed struggling to catch a glimpse of light in the bottom of one of their black pits. Everywhere the swarming green stole from them the life of the air: and when they still struggled miraculously upward a winged death, whining in the dank air, must sow their blood with other hungry parasites. It was all hopeless . . . hopeless. It would have been better, he was sometimes tempted to think, if a great fire should consume all this damnable green, a purging fire that should sweeten where it destroyed, and give the ashes of humanity a chance to make a new start. But even if his wish had not been impious, he knew that its fulfilment was impossible: for he remembered the living trees in whose heart a dull fire smouldered, just as the fire of fever smouldered in these people's blood.

It was necessary to make a beginning: and so James set himself to learn the language, Kiluguru; and this he rejoiced to find less difficult than he supposed, for the tongue was scattered very thickly with Arabic words, more thickly even than the coastal Kiswahili. To these were added the Bantu inflective prefixes with which he was already fairly familiar. The consciousness that in this he was gradually drawing nearer to these people cheered him, although he knew that even when he had made himself master of their speech he must find himself faced with the merest outposts of the enemy. And so with an aching heart he settled down to the first steps of a most exhausting campaign. No man with a small or faltering faith could have faced it; but there was never any doubt but that James was of the stuff of which heroes, and martyrs, are made.

All day he moved among the people of Godovius, and little by little he began to think that he was getting nearer to them. Their squalor, their loathly diseases, the very grotesqueness with which their faces were modelled—things which in the beginning had filled him with bewilderment rather than distaste—became so familiar that he thought no more of them. They were so near to the beasts that any token of humanity smiled suddenly at him with the effect of a miracle. He was even surprised into finding strange revelations of beauty . . . beauty . . . no less . . . in their black masks. In the gloom of the evening, when the sun which bathed the hills in amber light could no longer penetrate the thick curtains of the forest, when the thin song of innumerable mosquitoes thrilled the air and the liquid trilling of frogs arose from every creek and cranny of the swamp, he would leave them and set out for the mission with a sense of exaltation in the work accomplished and horrors overpast. The mere physical relief of emerging into the open air of the thin bush, scattered with slades of waving grasses in which herds of game were grazing, coloured his mood. Sometimes, indeed, he would be so overwhelmed with their poignant contrast that he would ask himself whether after all it wasn't his duty to leave the mission and live altogether with the Waluguru, and wonder why he, any more than they, should be entitled to the luxury of light. For the most part he was too richly contented to consider his own fatigue: but once or twice, in the midst of this bland mood, he found himself arrested and thrown back upon despair by a sudden sound which mocked him from the recesses of the swamp behind him. This was the sound which had troubled Eva on the night which she had visited his moonlit study: the rhythmical beating of a drum. It seemed to him not merely a mysterious symbol of some darkness to which he had not penetrated, but rather malignant and challenging. He realised that there was more in the forest than he had bargained for;

that he was opposed to powers of whose existence and strength he was ignorant. An imaginative man, it seemed to him that these distant, insistent pulsations were like the beating heart of the forest, an expression of its immense and savage life. When he heard it he would do the simple thing which seemed most natural to him. There, in the tawny sand of the bush path, he would kneel down and pray; and later, comforted in some mysterious manner, he would move on his way.

CHAPTER IV

I

There came a day of cruel, intolerable heat. All the morning Eva lay in a long chair within the shade of the banda in the garden under the sisal hedge. There was no sun, but the light which beat down from the white-hot sky seemed somehow less bearable than sunlight. Little by little she had realised her idea of turning this grass hut into a sanctuary for herself, and though the thatching of the reeds gave her less protection from the sky than the roof of the house would have done, she was so far in love with this privacy that she preferred to lie there. Its shelter defied the heavy dews which settle in the night: and she had made the place homely with a couple of chairs and a table on which her work-basket stood. There was even a little bookshelf crammed with the paper novels which Mr. Bullace had left behind him and others which Godovius had sent down for her to read. But the day was far too hot for reading: the mere unconscious strain of living was enough. That morning after James had left her she had begun to write a letter in pencil to her aunt at Pensax, a village hidden in the valleys beyond Far Forest, and when she laid it aside she had fallen asleep in her chair and dreamed that she was back again in that distant March, walking through meadows that were vinous with the scent of cowslips. It was a pleasant day, with skies of a cool blue and fleets of white cloud sailing slowly out of Wales, a day on which one might walk through the green ways of the forest until one reached Severn-side above the floating bridge at Arley. This pleasant dream cooled her fancy. When she awoke it was afternoon and hotter than ever, and the awakening was less real than her dream. In the midst of the garden Hamisi and Onyango sprawled asleep in the full sunlight with bent arms sheltering their eyes. She wondered why they did not lie in the shade of the row of flamboyant acacias farther back. Now they were bursting into blood-red bloom, very bright against their rich feathery leaves. Beyond them the mission glared in the sun. A great bougainvillea had oversprawled the white corner of the house in a cascade of magenta blossom. It was all rather fantastically lovely, so lovely that she couldn't help feeling she ought to be happy. But she was too hot to be happy. . . . Even the voices of the hornbills calling in the bush drooped with heat.

That evening when James came home from the forest he would take no supper. She tried to coax him; but soon discovered that he was irritable and depressed. Even now, at sunset, the air trembled with heat. She said: "It's been a dreadful day. . . . I expect the heat has been too much for you. You don't take enough care of yourself."

"Heat? . . . What are you talking about?" he replied. "It's really rather chilly . . . quite chilly for Africa."

Of course it was no good arguing with James, so she left him sitting at his table with an open Bible before him. She went into the kitchen and busied herself with the distasteful job of washing her own dirty plates. On a day like this it was hardly worth while eating if the process implied such a laborious consequence. When she came back to the living-room, intending to finish her Pensax letter, she found her brother swathed in a blanket which he had fetched from his own bed.

"Why, whatever is the matter with you?" she cried.

"I told you it was chilly . . ."

"My dear boy, you must be ill."

He flared up in a way that was quite unusual for him.

"Ill? . . . Don't talk nonsense, Eva. . . . I'm never ill. I haven't time to be ill."

But a few minutes later he fell a-shivering, shaking horribly within his blanket.

"I believe there is something the matter with me," he said. "But it can't be fever. It can't possibly be fever. I've never missed taking my quinine, and you never get fever if you take quinine. My head aches. I'd better go to bed."

He stalked off to his room, a pitifully fantastic figure in his blanket. Eva brought him some hot milk. He complained that it tasted bitter, of the gourd, but she made him swallow it. Then she took his temperature and found that it was a hundred and four. The thermometer chattered between his teeth.

"I suppose it is fever," he said.

All that night she stayed near his bedside. James was not a pleasant patient. Even now he wanted all the time to make it clear that his illness was his own affair and that he was competent to deal with it. Now the blanket was too much for him. He wanted to throw off all the clothes and lie in his cotton nightshirt. His head still ached, but he was excited and talkative and would not let her sleep. His brain seethed with excitement and for the first time since they had been at Luguru he began to talk to her about his work under the leaves. He told her many things which seemed to her horrible: so horrible that she could hardly believe that they were anything more than imaginations of his enhavocked brain.

"Now you see what we are fighting against," he said; "and it's only the beginning . . . it's only the beginning. God give me strength to finish it, to go through with it."

In the middle of the night he prayed aloud.

That night there was no sleep for either of them. Eva lay wakeful on the stretcher bed in his room, listening now to the wandering talk of James and now to the howling of the hyenas over on the edge of the forest.

At half-past five in the morning, when the first light came, he pulled himself together. "I'm all right now," he said. "I've a big day in front of me. Will you help me to get up?"

She thought it best to let him try. When he got on to his feet he swayed and clutched at the bed to steady himself.

"What's the matter?" he cried. "Everything swims ... the whole room went round even when I shut my eyes. I must be ill. What can I do? ... What can I do?"

She was thankful that he had proved it for himself. "This is where I come in," she thought, convinced that she was going to have a bad time of it.

For four days James kept his bed; as long, indeed, as the fever had its way with him. At first he fought desperately; but in a little while, realising that he was powerless, he submitted to her tenderness. "Really," she said, "he was awfully good ... much nicer than when he was well." She found him patient and pathetic ... almost lovable, quite different from the acknowledged success of the family which he had been at home; and she discovered in him—in his tired eyes and even in his voice-an amazing hidden likeness to their mother which almost moved her to tears. It seemed as if the fever had suddenly made him a man instead of the incarnation of a spiritual force. Not even a man, but a frail, puzzled boy, with no pretensions in the world. He appealed to her dormant instincts of maternity, making her all tenderness. She wanted to kiss him as he lay there with the open unread Bible—always the Bible—on his bed.

When he was at his worst Godovius called to inquire. She wondered how Godovius knew he was ill, not realising that Godovius knew everything in Luguru. He met her on the stoep and cross-questioned her narrowly. How much quinine was he taking? Five grains a day? P'ff! ... Useless! That was the English method: Manson's method.... Proved useless long ago. The proper way of taking quinine was the German way, the only reasonable way—ten and fifteen grains on two successive days once a week. That was the only prophylaxis worth considering. He told her to look at himself, standing there in his fine, swart robustness, and looking at him she remembered the poor, transparent child whom she had left within. "And what about yourself?" he said. "You are looking tired, pale." She blushed in a way that removed the second accusation. "You must not wear yourself out for him—you who are young and vigorous and magnificently healthy." His interest confused her, and she slipped into the house to see if James would see Godovius.

He was greatly agitated. He, too, flushed.

"Herr Godovius?" he said. "Why does he come here when I am in bed? A man who has slaves! No . . . No . . ."

She protested that he had come with the kindest intentions.

"No . . . not that man," he said.

She made her excuses to Godovius. He looked at her in a way that revealed their hollowness, then laughed and rode away. "I am not a favourite of your brother? Now why is that? Mr. Bullace and I were the best of friends. Do you think we had more in common?" She felt that he had surprised her in a swift remembrance of Mr. Bullace's whisky bottles and was ashamed. "It is better that we should be friendly, don't you think so?" he said.

When he had gone she told James that she thought Godovius had been offended by the return which had been given him for his kindness. "I think he must have heard what you said . . . these wooden walls are so thin."

"I know," he said. "I'm sorry . . . very sorry. I'm not quite myself. I was thinking of those people in the forest. I'm afraid I couldn't help it." And then, after a long interval of thought, he said: "I will apologise to him. It was un-Christian."

She melted: humility on the part of this paragon always knocked her over. In these moments she very nearly loved him.

II
But when James recovered from his bout of fever this delightful atmosphere of intimacy faded. With diminished strength but with a greater seriousness than ever he set about his work. Eva found him increasingly difficult.

I suppose that he had expected to go back to his work as though nothing had happened, or even, in some miraculous way, to make up the time which he had lost. He didn't realise in the least how much the fever had taken out of him. The walk to the forest in the morning seemed twice as long: the upward path, in the evening, purgatorial. Even in the heart of the forest itself the atmosphere of hopelessness, of evil swarming like the wood's lush green seemed never to leave him. Perhaps it was that now he couldn't face it. All his day was comparable to those moments in which he had heard the menace of distant drums. Often, indeed, in the midst of his ministrations he would hear them, so distant that he couldn't be sure whether they were not some trick of his fancy, and he would ask the Waluguru women what was the meaning of the sound. They would shrug their shoulders, smiling their soft, deprecating smile of Africa with half-closed eyelids, and say that they did not know.

"N'goma," they would say . . . "a dance."

"N'goma gani?" . . . "What sort of dance?" he would ask. "A devil dance?"

At this they would only smile. There was no getting on with these people . . .

He determined that if they would not help him he must find out for himself: and so when next he heard the beat of drums in the forest he left the colony of huts in which he was working and set off in pursuit of the sound. Through endless mazy paths of the swamp he pressed, baffled by many changes of direction—for when he had struggled for a mile or two it seemed to him that all the forest was full of drums, as if the drummers were leading him a fool's dance and their noise no more than an elusive emanation of the swamp, a will-o'-the-wisp of sound.

It was a terrible quest, for he was already tired, and his eagerness carried him far beyond his strength. Several times the drumming ceased, leaving him in a silence of utter desolation, making him think that his struggles had been all for nothing. At others it seemed so close to him that he pushed through tangles of undergrowth which no sane man would have attempted, only to find that he was no nearer his goal.

He must have wandered many miles. In that part of the forest he found no villages, and all the time he never saw the sun; but experience had taught him that he must carry a compass, and by this he judged that under the leaves he was gradually approaching that part of the swamp which clung about the river at the point where it issues from a deep cleft in the conical hill on which Godovius's house was built. Time was pressing. Farther than this he dared not go, or darkness would overtake him, and in darkness he could not return.

He was on the point of giving up his search when the drumming burst out again, a little to the right. He crossed a creek, knee-deep in black mud, and pushed his way into a clear space where the smaller trees had been felled and the pointed roofs of bandas rose among the plantain leaves. As he set foot within the clearing the drum ceased. He heard a shriek that sounded scarcely human. Surely he had broken in upon some unspeakable torture. But when he came into the open space between the huts he saw nothing more than a little group of Waluguru women, who cried out in surprise at the invasion of this pale, bedraggled figure.

There were perhaps a dozen of them, and it seemed to him that they had been engaged in the crushing of sugar-cane for the making of tembo, their fermented drink, for they were grouped about two of the hollowed trunks in which the fibre is shredded with poles in the manner of a pestle and mortar. That was all that he could see, except for one old man, with an evil face, squatting in the doorway of the largest banda, staring straight before him, and one woman, a girl of sixteen or seventeen years, who lay almost naked on the ground with her arms clasped above her head, as though she were asleep or very ill.

James addressed them, and the old man gravely returned his salutation with a flat hand lifted to his brow. He blurted out rapid questions. He had heard a drum. Where was the N'goma?

They shook their heads and smiled. They knew of no N'goma.

He spoke to them of other things: of food and fever . . . life and death . . . the matters which most concerned them. They answered him politely, but with a tired tolerance. Food was scarce, and the devil of fever was among them; but it was always so.

He looked at his watch. It was getting late. He knew that he had failed again and that he must go. When James pulled out his watch he saw the eyes of the old man light up and heard a murmur among the women in which he caught the word Sakharani. Of course . . . Godovius, too, had a watch. No people, it seemed, were too remote to know Godovius. He wondered if Bullace had ever visited this village. He turned to go, and at the same moment the galloping triplets of another drum began in some neighbouring village. He saw the women smile, and this irritated him so much that he burst out into abuse of the old man, who still sat unsmiling in the door of his banda. And then a strange thing happened. The body of the girl who had lain motionless upon the ground in their midst was shaken by a sound that was like a sob, but somehow less human. Her hands, which had been sheltering her head, clutched at her breasts. Then, as the faint drumming continued, her head began to move in time, her limbs and her body were gradually drawn into the measure of the distant rhythm till, with a steadily increasing violence, each muscle of her slender frame seemed to be obeying this tyrannical influence, so that she was no longer mistress of herself, no longer anything but a mass of quivering, palpitating muscle. A horrible sight . . . very horrible. And then, when her miserable body was so torn that the tortured muscles could bear it no longer, there was wrung from her that ghastly, sub-human cry which James had heard in the forest as he approached. It was like the noise which a cat makes when it is in pain.

The others took no heed of her; they went on pounding tembo; but James, to whose disordered nerves the horror of the sight had become intolerable, could do no more. He burst out again into the forest, pushing his way blindly through vast tangles which he might have avoided, spending the remains of his strength in a futile endeavour to escape anywhere, anyhow, from that nightmare. The forest grew darker. Even in the open bush, when he emerged, the short twilight had come. For him it was enough to know that he was out of the forest. He lay down at the side of the path panting and trembling. Here, in the cool of the night, his reason gradually reasserted itself. He was humiliated and ashamed to realise that his faith had failed him, that terror had broken the strength of his spirit. And thus, being full of repentance, he seriously considered whether he should not turn back, pushing his way through the forest to that remote village, and see the business through. This time he would be certain not to fail. In the end he abandoned this test, which he would gladly have undergone; for he doubted if he could find the path again, and guessed that his purpose would probably be ruined by another attack of fever. But he determined that once again, in daylight, he would find that village and that woman, that he would strip bare the mysteries which it contained, and that by faith and prayer he would conquer them.

III
Of course he did not confide in Eva. To him she was never any more than the small girl who had watched his triumphs from the seclusion of the little shop at Far

Forest, to whom the privilege of dealing with his clothes, mired in the M'ssente swamps, was now entrusted. Indeed it was a pity that he left Eva out of his preoccupations; for nothing is more dangerous to the born mystic than isolation from his fellow men, and the conditions of the isolation which James endured in the forest were extreme. It is doubtful, too, whether the constant companionship of such fiery fellows as the prophets Isaiah and Ezekiel, to whom James resorted in the hours when he sat in loneliness with his open Bible, was good for him in his present state of unstable emotion. The directness, the simplicity, the common-sense of Eva would have helped him; but she knew better than to interrupt her brother when he was engaged with the prophets. In Far Forest they called it The Book.

So James went on his way, fighting for ever against the weakness to which his fever had reduced him in this visionary company. For sheer weakness he was forced to spend more time in the neighbourhood of the mission, busying himself with the education of Mr. Bullace's converts, whom he had rather neglected in his anxieties to break new ground. To break new ground. . . . His mind was always ready to play with words, and thinking of this familiar metaphor, he remembered one day how an old African planter had spoken with him on board ship; how he had told him that he should never dig a trench for storm water round his tent, because the act of breaking virgin soil released the miasma of fever inherent in the jealous earth. That, he thought, was figuratively what had happened to him. And finding that he had worked the metaphor to its logical conclusion, he was ashamed to think that his mind could have been diverted into such foolish byways.

He was so eager to assure himself that he had recovered his balance that he deliberately discounted things which at one time would have disturbed or frightened him. But one thing he could not persuade himself to dismiss from his thoughts, try as he might—there was scarcely a day in his life when he did not find it staring him in the face or lurking invisibly behind the disappointments that troubled him—and this was the influence of Godovius among the Waluguru. Whenever he found himself thwarted by some failure, often enough a small thing in itself, he was conscious of the man's imminence. The name of Sakharani was often the only word which he could recognise in whisperings that were not meant for his ear. When the shambas of Godovius needed tilling the mission classes must go. In every occurrence that balked him, in every mystery that baffled, the influence of Sakharani was betrayed. And as time went by he realised that the menace was a very real one. He felt that he was actually losing grip, so that a sense of insecurity invaded even the matters in which he had felt most confident. The fact had to be faced: the original congregation of the mission, the very existence of which had gladdened and strengthened his heart on Sundays, was undoubtedly dwindling; and what vexed him even more was to find that some of his favourite converts, men on whom he had felt he could rely and whose tongues were accustomed to the Christian formula, seemed to fail him as readily as the others. He was honestly and miserably puzzled.

Almost against his will he began to suspect the hand of Godovius in every trace of opposition which he encountered. Whenever he failed he grew to dread the mention of Godovius's name. And this was all the more troubling because Godovius came fairly frequently to the mission. When James returned in the evening he would find flowers from Njumba ja Mweze in his study, or hear from Eva that he had been helping her in the garden or lent her some new book. It distressed him. He never spoke of him to Eva; but for all that he would wait anxiously for her to mention his name, and that feeling of insecurity and grudging would come over him whenever the name appeared.

It was after many weeks that his growing distrust reached its climax. At the end of that time he set out early one day to visit the village to which he had penetrated in search of the heathen drums. That day the way seemed miraculously easy. He could scarcely believe that he was passing through those miles of tangled forest in which he had once struggled to exhaustion; but when he arrived there the little circle of huts was the same as ever; the same women were crushing sugar-cane for tembo; the same evil-faced man squatted in the mouth of the greatest banda. He talked to them, and they answered him happily enough until he came to question them about the girl who had then been lying on the ground and had only been recalled to consciousness by the thud of the distant drum. When he asked for her they dissembled, with their soft African smiles. He became suspicious and pressed them. Where was she? He would not go until they told him where she was. The women began to speak; but the old man in the mouth of the banda made them be silent.

James started to question him, asked him why he would not let them answer.

"It is Sakharani's business. That is enough," said the old man. "She has gone away."

Where she had gone he would not say, protesting that he did not know. He only knew that she had gone from them at the last new moon. Perhaps she would return. That was the business of Sakharani. More than this he could not say.

"I shall find out," said James. "You know you are deceiving me . . ."

The old man only shook his head and smiled.

Walking home that evening on the bush path James heard a scurry of hoofs and saw the big outline of Godovius cantering down on his Somali mule, with a Waluguru boy running at his stirrup. Godovius, too, spotted him, and waved him a cheery good-evening. James guessed that he had been up at the mission. He determined to speak to Eva.

When he reached home he found her busy laying the table for him. She seemed happy and well: she was humming to herself an old song that reminded him of Far Forest. He would speak to her now . . .

He said: "Has Mr. Godovius been here?"

"Yes . . . he has only just gone."

"Why does he come here?"

She wondered why he was asking this with such intensity. "Why on earth shouldn't he?" she said. "He is very kind."

"I don't wish him to come here. I don't think he is a good man. I don't think he is fit company for you. To-day—" He stopped, for it struck him that he might appear foolish if he went on. He said: "You like him?"

"No . . . I don't think I do, exactly. I don't mind him. He's . . . he's funny, you know. . . . I don't think I understand him."

"Has he been making love to you?" James asked in a whisper.

Eva blushed.

"Of course he hasn't. What an idea!"

She thought: "How very funny. . . . James is jealous. Father was like that."

He had felt sure that she would prevaricate. Her directness took the wind out of his sails. He felt rather ashamed of his suspicions.

"I'm sorry I asked you that question," he said. "I'm sorry. But don't forget that I warned you."

She laughed to herself. The idea of Godovius as a lover struck her as grotesque. Later she wondered why it had struck her as grotesque.

CHAPTER V

I

In those days James was never free from fever for long, despite the German method of quinine prophylaxis to which, in defiance of Manson, he had submitted. It seemed as if the tertian parasite—and there is none more malignant than that which the M'ssente Swamp breeds—had rejoiced to find a virgin blood in which it might flourish as long as life lasted. Every ten days or so Eva would find herself called upon to face a new attack. She became used to the succession of shivering and high fever; she began to know exactly when James should be bullied and when he should be left alone; to realise how the sweet submissiveness of the sick man merged into the irritability of the convalescent. Symptoms that once would have frightened her out of her life were now part of the day's work. She steadfastly determined that she would let nothing worry her. It was just as well to have one equable person in the house.

Godovius still came to the mission from time to time. Eva was glad to see him. She would have been glad to see almost any man; for the idea of being quite alone in those savage solitudes was frightening. She was not ignorant of the power of disease in that country. She knew perfectly well that some day "something might happen" (as they say) to James, and without definitely anticipating it she felt a little happier for having the strength of Godovius behind her. For he was strong, whatever else he might be. In his presence she was always conscious of that: and even if his strength seemed at times a little sinister, there were moments in which he struck her as wholly charming, almost boyish, particularly when he smiled and his beautiful teeth showed white against the ruddy swarthiness of his face. Seriously, too, he was ready to help her.

"Your brother is overworking," he said. "Do you think the unfortunate results to himself are balanced by any colossal success in his work? Do you? I think he should take a little alcohol . . . a sundowner . . . quite a good thing for Europeans."

Eva smiled. "He'd have a fit if I told him that."

"Would he? . . . In many ways your brother does not resemble the Good Bullace. And yet in others I think he deserves a little of my name . . . Sakharani." He laughed. "I believe, Miss Eva, you are still rather frightened of my name. Now how long is it since last you saw me drunk?"

Even though she protested, she wasn't altogether sure that he was joking.

"But you never know when I may break out," he said. "Now you witness nothing but my admirable self-control."

Every time that Godovius came to see her when James was in bed her brother would question her narrowly as to what he had said. His persistence annoyed her, because it seemed to her ungenerous that he should not take Godovius as he found him.

"I sha'n't tell you when next he comes," she said one day.

"That would be no good. . . . I know. . . . I have a feeling in my bones when he is here. It's like some people who shiver when a cat comes into the room even if they don't see it."

"I think it's rather horrid of you," she said. "Is it that you're jealous? . . . Or don't you trust me?"

"Oh, I trust you all right," he said bitterly.

In the intervals between his attacks he brightened up wonderfully. It was difficult to believe that he was the same man; but for all this he had lost a great deal of weight, and his face showed a blue and yellow pallor which alarmed her. And he was sleeping very badly. Eva became accustomed to the sound of his footsteps walking up and down his room at night, and to the whining voice in which he would recite long passages of scripture. She knew that some day there must come a big breakdown. Yes . . . it was good to have Godovius behind her.

II

Insidiously the occasion which she had looked for came. An ordinary attack of malaria, one of her brother's usual ten-daily diversions, flamed suddenly into a condition which she could not understand. The babble of a night of delirium died away, and in the morning, with cheeks still flushed and all the signs of fever with which she was familiar, Eva found him becoming drowsy and yet more drowsy. Usually in this stage of the disease she knew him to be exacting and restlessly active. This time when she came to give him food she had difficulty in rousing him. He lay huddled on his side with his legs drawn up and his face turned away from the light. Even when she had wakened him he fell asleep again. The warm milk which she had brought him went cold under a yellowish scum at his bedside. All that afternoon she did not once hear him praying.

She became anxious. Perhaps Godovius would come. She wished that he would; for she knew that he could help her: all the Waluguru bore witness how great a medicine-man he was. But Godovius did not come. "Just because I want him," she thought.

For a few moments in the afternoon James brightened up. He complained to her of the pain in his head, which he had clasped in his hands all day; but even as he spoke to her his mind wandered, wandered back into the Book of Kings and the story of the Shunammite's son. "And he said unto his father, My head, my head. And he said to a lad: Carry him to his mother," he muttered. Then he was quiet for a little. Eva sat by his side, watching. Now at last he seemed to be sleeping gently. She expected that this was what he needed, but in the early evening, when next she wanted to feed him, he would not wake. She spoke to him, and gently shook him. A terror seized her lest he should have died. No . . . he was still breathing. For so much she might be thankful.

Something must be done. In this extremity her mind naturally turned to Godovius. At James's desk she scribbled a note to him, and ran out into the compound at the back of the house to the hut of galvanised iron in which the boys slept. She called them both by name, but no answer came. The mouth of their den was covered with an old piece of sacking, which she pulled aside, releasing an air that stank of wood-smoke, and oil and black flesh. Almost sickened, she peered inside. Only one of the boys was sleeping there. He lay curled up in the corner, so that she could not see which of them it was, his head and shoulders covered with a dirty red blanket. She had to shake him before she could rouse him. He stared at her out of the darkness with dazed eyes. Then he smiled, and she saw by his filed cannibal teeth that it was Onyango, the M'kamba . . . just the one whom she didn't want. Hamisi, the Luguru, would have known the way to Godovius's house.

"Where is Hamisi?" she asked.

Onyango still rubbed his eyes. He did not know. She told him that Hamisi must be found. He shook his head and smiled. Hamisi, he said, could not be found. It was useless to try and find him.

Eva was irritated by his foolish, smiling face. Why had Hamisi gone away, just when he was wanted most? she asked.

Onyango mumbled something which surpassed her knowledge of Swahili . . . something about the new moon. What in the world had the new moon to do with it? . . .

Very well, then, she decided—Onyango must take Godovius's letter.

"You know the house of Sakharani?" she said. "Carry this barua to Sakharani himself . . . quickly . . . very quickly." She gave him the letter. Onyango shrank back into his corner. He wouldn't take the letter, he said. If he took the letter on this night the Waluguru would kill him. She didn't seem to understand, and he made the motion of a violent spear-thrust, then clutched at his breast. Eva tried to laugh him out of it, to make him ashamed at being afraid; but it was no good. Why should the Waluguru kill him? she asked.

It was the night of the new moon, he said.

She saw that it was useless to waste time over him. While they had been disputing the sun had set. It was a beautiful and very peaceful evening. The crowns of the croton-trees were awakening that soft zodiacal glow. She was very angry and worried, for she realised that she would have to go herself.

"Very well, then, you must stay with the bwana," she said: and Onyango, who still wanted to be ingratiating and was ready to do anything but face the new moon and the Waluguru, slunk into the house. She took a last look at James. There was no difference in his condition except that now he was obviously alive, breathing stertorously through his mouth, lying there with his eyes half opened. She wondered for a moment if she dared leave him. "Tell the bwana when he wakes," she said to Onyango, "where I have gone. Say that I will come back again." She feared to stay there any longer, for in a little while it would be dark. She comforted herself with the thought that the road through the forest to Njumba ja Mweze must be fairly well defined, since Godovius used it so often. She couldn't disguise from herself the fact that the adventure was rather frightening, but the thing had to be done, and there was an end of it.

So she took the forest road. In the open Park Steppe there were already signs of night: most of all a silence in which no voices of birds were heard, and other dry rustlings, which would have been submerged beneath the noises of day, heralded the awakening of another kind of life. In the branches of thorn-trees on every side the cicalas set up vibrations: as rapid and intense as those of an electric spark: a very natural sound, for it seemed to be an expression of that highly charged silence. In a wide slade of grasses a herd of kongoni were grazing. When they caught the scent of Eva they reached their heads above the grasses and after following her for a little with their eyes one of them took fright, and with one accord they flashed into the bordering bush, a flying streak of brown. An aged wildebeeste bull, vanquished in some old duel and banished from his own herd, stood sentinel to the kongoni, and when the others disappeared he held his ground, standing with his enormous shoulders firmly planted on his fore feet. Eva was rather frightened of him, for she knew nothing of the nature or habits of big game. As she passed across the opening of that glade he slowly turned, so that his great shoulders and lowered head were always facing her. Some unimaginable breeze must have been moving from her towards him, for he suddenly threw up his head, snorting, and stamped the ground. Then she picked up her skirts and ran, with his mighty breathing still in her ears. She saw that this night journey of hers was going to be no joke. In the night so many savage beasts were abroad. She remembered that less than a week before Godovius had shot a leopard on the edge of the forest. He had told her how the creature had been lying along the low branch of a tree, and how it had sprung into the midst of a herd of goats which a Waluguru boy was driving along the track. Godovius had been near and his second shot had killed it. He had offered her the skin. Now, for the very first time, she realised the savagery of that land. In the mission there had always dwelt a sense of homeliness and protection. She realised, too, the conditions in which James had been working. Poor James.... She couldn't help feeling that she herself was better qualified to deal with that sort of thing than her brother. She pulled all her courage together.

She had come to the edge of the forest. Black and immense it lay before her. If she made haste she might still borrow a little courage from the light. The sky above the tree-tops was now deepening to a dusky blue. As yet no stars appeared; but over the crown of that sudden hill a slender crescent of the new moon was soaring. A lovely slip of a thing she seemed sailing in that liquid sky. A memory of Eva's childhood reminded her that if she had been carrying money in her pocket she should have turned it for luck and wished.... What would she have wished?

It gave her a new assurance to find that under the leaves the path was well defined. She reckoned that she had at the most no more than three miles to go. At the end of three miles she would see the lights of Godovius's house and not be frightened any longer. She made up her mind to travel as fast as she could, looking neither to left nor right, for fear of eyes which might be watching her from the thickets. She comforted herself with the thought that it was here that the Waluguru lived; that they had lived here for centuries and were as unprotected as herself; that there were actually women and children living there in the heart of the forest. In the silence she heard the soft cooing of a dove, and a minute later a couple of small grey birds fluttered up from the path. "As harmless as doves," she thought. "You beautiful little creatures..." And she smiled.

As she penetrated farther into the forest the light failed her, and it was very still. The little fluttering doves were the last creatures that she saw for a long time. Of the people of the forest there was no sign, and she would have thought that there were no beasts abroad either but for an occasional distant sound of crashing branches made by some body bigger and more powerful than that of a man. By the time that the light of day had wholly faded from the sky she had come to a zone of the forest in which the trees were more thinly scattered: between their high branches stars appeared, in front of her a blurred outline, which she took to be that of Kilima ja Mweze, above which the crescent moon now whitely shone. A little later she found that the track was ascending. It had reached the slopes of the conical hill on which she knew that Godovius's house was placed. Here under a brighter starlight she could see that the whole hill-side was cut into terraces, like the stages of a wedding cake, along the face of which the track climbed obliquely. It reassured her to find that she was now within a definite sphere of human influence, that the most savage part of her pilgrimage was past: but the road made stiff climbing: the mantle of forest had concealed the lower slopes of the hill so completely that she had never realised how abruptly it rose from the swamp.

Suddenly, in the half light, she saw upon the terrace above her a building of stone. She stopped for a moment to regain her breath, for this must surely be one of the outbuildings of the House of the Moon. When she came abreast of it she was puzzled to find that it was nothing but a circular wall of rough stones piled one upon the other. All around it the forest trees had been cut down; and this seemed to her a great waste of labour, for the building could obviously be no more than a stone kraal for the protection of cattle. Now it was empty. The track which she was following passed close to the only breach in the circle of stone. She peered inside, and saw that the wall was double. In the centre of the circular space within rose a strange tower, shaped like a conical lime-kiln of the kind which she had known at home but more slender, and fashioned of the same rough stone as the double walls outside. As she looked within her presence disturbed another flight of doves, fluttering pale in the moonlight. She wondered whatever could be the meaning of this building, for the doves would not nest there if it were used by men and cattle; but her curiosity was overborne by her disappointment at finding that her journey was not yet over. From that clearing she passed once more into denser forest, under the shadow of which she climbed perhaps a dozen more of those steep terraces. Once more the forest trees gave way to an open space. A wave of sweet but over-heavy perfume came to meet her. Pale in the moonlight she saw the ghost of a long white house.

III

A length of white-washed stoep supported on slender pillars faced her, and from the stoep a flight of wide steps descended to the sandy path over which she had climbed out of the forest. There was no fence or boma to mark the transition from the desert to the sown; so that the House of the Moon was really set like any Waluguru village in a sudden clearing of the forest; and this seemed strange to Eva, for she had imagined that the house of Godovius would be more in keeping with his wealth and power. She had expected to find a garden carefully tended, an oasis of urbanity and fragrance. Fragrance indeed there was. The wave of perfume which had met her emerging from the forest path eddied gently in the garden space about the open cups of many moon-pale blossoms, blooms of the white moon-flower from which the scent named frangipani is distilled: and although she was happily unaware of this perfume's associations, Eva felt that she hated it, that its cloying sweetness robbed the air of life. Very pale and ghostly the flowers hung there in the faint moonlight, in so great a congregation that one was aware of their life, and thought of them as verily living creatures, silent only because they were entranced with their own sweetness. In the gloom of the long verandah no light shone. The windows within were unlighted. The long house seemed as empty as the building of circular stone which she had passed below.

Eva mounted the steps. Over the floor of white stone a big lizard moved noiselessly. There was a fluttering sound in the masses of bougainvillea above the porch, a clapping of wings, and a little flight of doves fluttered out above the moon-flower blossoms and vanished into the forest. "This place is full of doves," she thought. It was so quiet that she began to wonder if they were the only tenants.

She remembered that in Africa people do not wait for an invitation to enter the houses of their friends, nor for servants to announce their coming. No doubt Godovius would have expected her to open the door and walk into the house, and yet she hardly liked to do this, for the whole place seemed to be sleeping under some spell which it might be rash to break. For a moment she stood waiting on the threshold. It was a double door massively made, with panels of fine mosquito netting instead of glass. Inside it she imagined there must be a wide flagged passage, smelling of damp. She saw that the pillars supporting the lintel were of a different kind of stone from that of which the rest of the house was built: they were smooth, and their capitals were carved into the shape of the head of some bird of prey with hooked beak and staring eyes. While she hesitated she remembered the pitiful room of James, down at the mission, and the last that she had seen of James himself, lying on his back, with his mouth open, breathing stertorously, and clutching at his head with unconscious hands . . . thin, incapable hands.

She tried to open the door, and found it locked. So this was the end of her adventure. . . . An end so pathetic to the courage which she had screwed up that she wouldn't accept it. She beat upon the door with the palms of her hands.

A light appeared. Through the mosquito gauze she saw a small figure approaching, swathed in a white cloth and carrying a blizzard lamp. She thought it was that of a child, but a hand fumbled with the key in the lock and she saw that the lantern-bearer was an old and shrivelled woman who stared at her but did not speak.

Eva stammered over her Swahili. Was this the house of Godovius? . . . Was the bwana in?

The old woman only stared. Then, she remembered the name that she had been wanting—Sakharani. She repeated her question in that form. The old woman nodded. She opened wide her mouth and pointed with her finger. Eva saw a collection of hideous teeth and a purple stump that once had been a tongue. It was very horrible. And then the creature led her along the passage and pushed open the door of a long, low room. On the open hearth a wood fire flickered, from which she carried a light to a copper lamp that swung from the ceiling. When this was done she shuffled out of the room. The hanging lamp with its reflectors of copper shed a mellow light, and when Eva's first bewilderment was past she began to appreciate the embellishments of Godovius's room. It resembled no room which she had ever seen before: nor, for that matter, was it in the least like what she had imagined the room of Godovius would be. To begin with, the floor was covered

39

with a soft carpet in the pattern of which the lamplight illumined warm colours. On either side of the fireplace an immense divan upholstered in crimson lay. One of them was half covered with a barbarous kaross of leopard skins, the other piled deep with cushions of silk. The door by which she had entered was covered by a portière of heavy velvet of the same crimson colour with a wide hem of tarnished gold. Everywhere there were cushions, big, soft cushions. And there were no books. The air of the room seemed in keeping with its furniture, for even here the cloying scent of the moon-flowers had penetrated. Eva had an impulse to open the window, or at any rate to draw the crimson curtains; but the atmosphere of the place suggested that liberties must not be taken with it. She wondered why on earth they had lit a fire . . .

By this time, her eyes being more accustomed to the mild light, she began to regard the room in greater detail. She saw that the mantelpiece above the fireplace had been made out of the same smooth soapstone which she had noticed in the lintel of the outer door, and that the ends of the beams were carved with the same conventional figure of a bird's head. On the mantelpiece itself stood other pieces of soapstone carving: two small, quern-shaped cylinders chased with rings of rosettes; three smaller and more elementary versions of the original bird pattern. She supposed that they were curios of the country, but was rather puzzled to find the one symbol so often repeated. She decided that she would ask James about them. From these she passed to an examination of the pictures, in heavy frames of gold, which decorated the walls. They were not easily seen; for the copper reflector of the hanging lamp cast its rays downwards, leaving a colder light for the upper part of the room. The first that she came to was a painting in oils of the bust and shoulders of a Masai girl, her head thrown back, her lips smiling and eyes closed. From her ears hung crescent-shaped ornaments of gold, and a big golden crescent was bound across her forehead: a clever painting, with the suggestion of a shimmer of moonlight on her smooth shoulders. Eva wondered why her eyes were closed, and why she smiled. Would Godovius never come? . . .

On the opposite wall hung a large framed photograph. Eva stood on tiptoe to examine it. When she saw what it was, she was overwhelmed with a sudden and awful feeling of shame. She had never felt so ashamed in her life. She found herself betrayed into a funny childish gesture: she put her hands to her eyes. "Now I can never look at him again," she thought. . . . "Oh, dear, how terrible . . ."

But the Godovius of the picture was obviously not ashamed. He was younger than the Godovius that she knew: the face smooth and unlined, the full lips smiling. In this presentation, despite the German colonial uniform of white duck which he wore, one could not help seeing that he was of Jewish extraction. One hand clasped the hilt of his sword, the other arm was linked through that of a woman, a white woman with a stolid, eminently Teuton face. And the woman was naked . . . stark naked. To any English eyes the photograph would have come as a shock. And Eva was a simple country girl, who knew no more of life than the little shop at Far Forest had shown her. She couldn't get over it. She sat down among the downy cushions on the scarlet settee and blushed. She thought: "I must go. I can't stay in this dreadful house. I should die if I met him now. I can't. . . . I can't."

And then she thought once more of James.

Only it was all so difficult, so horrible, that she could have cried. Even as she sat with her back to it she was conscious of that photograph, of the lips of Godovius and that poor cow-like creature. The thing was subtly in keeping with the rest of the room, the soft carpet and the cushions, the lavish crimson and gold, the sickly scent of frangipani. She shuddered. In another moment she would have gone precipitately. She had even risen to her feet when the velvet portière swung back and Godovius himself entered the room.

He smiled and held out his hand: "At last, Miss Eva."

His smile resembled that of the man in the photograph; his cheeks were flushed; he looked far younger than usual. She forced herself to speak.

"James is ill . . . that is why I came. I can't understand him. I'm terribly distressed."

"At any rate you have come at last. . . . What is your brother's trouble?"

To Eva it was a tremendous relief to talk of it. She told him how she had left James; implored him to let her know if the condition were serious. He listened, a thought impatiently. "Quinine? He has had plenty of quinine? Then you can do nothing more. This cerebral type of malaria is not uncommon. To-morrow it is possible he will be better. To-morrow . . ."

"Then you can't do anything?" she asked. "Oh, can't you help me at all?"

"No . . . there is no other treatment," he said.

"I'm sorry to have troubled you. I was so distressed. I must get back quickly. Perhaps you will spare me one of your boys to show me the way."

"It was plucky of you to come alone . . . at this time of the day."

"There was moonlight . . ."

"Ah, yes . . . the new moon. You are a brave girl, Miss Eva. Why then are you frightened now?"

"I'm not frightened," she cried. "What made you think so?"

And of course she was horribly frightened. She couldn't quite say why. On other occasions the dread or distaste, or whatever the feeling might be, which the thought of him inspired had always vanished in his bodily presence. This time she felt it more acutely than ever, and since it was now reinforced by his physical imminence, it seemed harder to bear. It came to her suddenly that if he were once assured that she was really frightened of him it would be all up with her. That was why she lied so eagerly.

He stood leisurely surveying her, with the same smile on his flushed face. He took no notice of her denial. He was big and dark and smiling; and all the time she was appallingly conscious of the contrast of her own physical weakness, wondering how, if anything dreadful should happen, she might escape. It was as bad as that. He gave her an exaggerated bow.

"Very good, then. We will agree that you are not frightened. In that case there is really no reason why you shouldn't sit down and give me the pleasure, for a little, of your society. I beg you to be seated."

She thought: "If I sit down I sha'n't have a ghost of a chance; I shall feel he's right on the top of me. If I don't sit down he'll know just how frightened I am." As a compromise she placed herself on the arm of the long sofa. At this elevation she didn't feel quite so helpless. She made a determined effort to escape.

She began: "My brother . . ."

"Ah, yes . . . your brother . . ." He began to prowl up and down the room. "Your brother. . . . You need not worry yourself too much about him, Miss Eva. It is unkind of you to be so sparing of your devotion. Your brother is lonely? Well, there are other people as lonely as your brother. Do you remember my saying that my eyes hadn't rested on a white woman for more than five years? There are varieties of loneliness. Spiritual loneliness . . ."

All the while she was thinking of the photograph on the wall behind him.

He checked himself. The little flicker of passion which had found its way into his speech and made a mess of the last of his quite admirable English fell. Again he became polite. She would almost have preferred the other manner.

"But it appears you are not interested, Miss Eva. At least you will allow me to treat you as an ordinary guest . . . an honoured guest. You will taste my coffee: perhaps you will even permit me the pleasure of showing you my poor house. Visitors are so rare . . . so very rare. And there was some music that I had promised myself to play for you . . . the tenderest music that the noble mind of a man ever made: Eva's music . . ."

And all the time she felt that he was spinning words; that his quiet, caressing manners didn't in the least represent what was passing in the man's mind; that he was talking to gain time, and, while he talked, forming some plan or other which threatened her peace. She had an awful feeling that there was something mad and sinister forming within his mind. In what other wise could she explain the cool unreason with which he had almost ignored her appeal for help? It seemed as if he had put the question of James' illness aside from the first as something that didn't really matter; as if he wouldn't accept it as the reason for her coming. The illogical nature of the thing frightened her. And she, too, was not listening to what he said. She was thinking: "That woman in the picture . . . how did she come to be so degraded? What, in the end, became of her?"

He went on talking in the same smoothly persuasive tones. She didn't listen to him. She heard him laugh softly in the middle of what he was saying. She wondered if perhaps he were drunk. He came and stood close above her, putting his hand on her upper arm just below the shoulder. Through her cotton blouse she could feel the heat of it. It would have been less disturbing if it had been deadly cold.

"You are tired, you must rest a little," he said. "I would not have you tired. You will be quiet a little. Why shouldn't you sit down? The room is not uncomfortable. You will wait while I bring you some hot coffee. You should know how good my coffee is . . ."

He was still holding her arm. The fingers of his hand moved gently. She felt that he was permitting himself to caress it. She obeyed him. She let herself sink into the crimson cushions of the sofa. He seemed pleased with her acquiescence. "I shall not leave you for long," he said. "Then perhaps I will see you home."

He was gone.

She could not believe that he had left her. Somehow she had felt that she was cornered, that nothing but some extraordinary chance could save her from whatever might be the sequel of his suave, possessive manner. The opportunity of escape was presented to her so suddenly that she couldn't grasp its significance. She sat there, on the sofa, as lacking in volition as if the heavy perfume of the place had drugged her. If she were not drugged or hallucinated it was strange that Godovius should have left her. A moment of incredible length passed. "If I don't go now . . ." she thought. She lifted the heavy portiere. In the passage all was dank and sepulchrally quiet. She moved swiftly towards the outer door. A wave of perfume rose to meet her. Then she found herself running: the white ghost of that low house watching her from behind . . .

CHAPTER VI
I

Through the garden of the moon-flowers down those oblique paths which climbed the Sabæan terraces into the blackness of deep kloofs in which the track could only be felt. She was too overwhelmed by one fear to take count of any others. In her return she quite forgot the anxiety and fatigue which had marked her coming . . . she had almost forgotten James and the reason of her adventure. At length, not knowing why she did so, she stopped. Careless of what might be beneath her, she sat down, pressing her hands to her beating temples, alone in the middle of Africa. The sense of her solitariness came over her suddenly. She felt like a child who wakes from a strange dream in the middle of the night. She had to convince herself that it was silly to have been frightened. "I lost my head," she said to herself. "It was ridiculous of me. It doesn't do to lose one's head out here. It's a

43

wonder I kept to the road." She wished there had been a stream of water near: one of those little brooks which made her own land musical: for then she would have bathed her face and pulled herself together. She felt that if there were any more terrors to be faced she couldn't cope with them in her present dishevelled condition. But in all that forest there was no murmur of water short of the M'ssente River, that tawny, sinister flood which was many miles away, and which in any case she dared not have approached for fear of crocodiles; so she contented herself with putting up her fallen hair and wiping her face with her handkerchief. She only hoped that while she had been sitting down the siaphu ants had not got into her petticoats. She rose to her feet, a little unsteady but now immensely fortified. "I think I can manage anything now," she thought.

So she went on her way. The forest was very still, for whatever winds may have been wandering under the stars were screened from her by the interwoven tops of the trees. That there were winds abroad she guessed, for sometimes, in the air above her, she would hear the sound of a great sighing as the forest stirred in its sleep. There was one other sound which troubled her. At first she couldn't be certain about it; she thought that her disturbed fancy was playing her tricks; but at length she became convinced that some animal was moving through the undergrowth parallel with her path. She stopped to listen, and all was still. She moved on again and the faint rustling in the leaves returned. She did this several times. Without doubt she was being followed. A new pang of terror assailed her. Godovius . . . supposing that he had actually followed her. Even though his presence might be in some sense a protection, she would rather have had anything than that. She argued swiftly with herself. If it were Godovius, she thought, he would not need to slink through the forest beside the track; he wouldn't be afraid of coming into the open. Obviously it couldn't be Godovius. Nor, for that matter, could it be an African, for, as he had told her, the Waluguru are frightened of the dark. She decided that it must be an animal. She thought of the leopard which Godovius had shot; she remembered hunters' tales of the wounded buffalo which will follow a man for fifty miles, brooding upon a feud which must end with the death of one of the two. If it were something of that kind she hoped that the end would come soon. "I can't do anything!" she thought. "I must just go on as if nothing were going to happen. But it will happen . . ."

It happened suddenly. A greater rustling disturbed a patch of tall grasses in a patch of swampy ground a little ahead of her, and in the path the figure of a man appeared.

One cannot tamper with the portrait. Although it was never my luck to meet Hare, there must be very few among the older settlers and hunters and adventurers of equatorial Africa who have not known him: a sinewy, grave and eminently characteristic figure that was always to be found stalking through the gloom of the unknown countries that have opened before the successive waves of occupation from the south. The men who went to Rhodesia in trod in his footsteps. With the Jameson raiders he lay in Pretoria jail. When the Uganda Railway was struggling upwards through the thorn-bush about Tsavo he was shooting lions in the rolling country above the Athi Plains which is now Nairobi hill. Everybody in central

Africa knew him, not merely the English, but the Belgians, the Germans, the Portuguese, all of them, from the Zambesi to the Lorian Swamp. Everybody knew the face of Hare, everybody knew his fame as a shikari. And that was all; for his soul was as lonely as the solitudes into which he had so often been the first to penetrate. You may carry the simile a little further: it was of the same simplicity and patience and courage, if a country may be said to possess these attributes of a soul, and there are some people who think it can. In this solitude I have known of only one adventurer: and that was Eva Burwarton. Perhaps there had been one other many years before. I don't know. At least Hare, that figure of tragedy, was fortunate in this. And it was thus they met. You are not to imagine the figure of which the East African settler will tell you over his sundowner in the New Stanley. What Eva Burwarton saw upon this strange occasion was a thin brown man, a scarecrow in the dark wood path, and liker to a scarecrow because of his arms. The sleeve of one was empty: the other swung helplessly at his side in spite of the strips of drab cotton which he had torn from his shirt to keep it steady. All his clothes were torn: his beard red with the dust of Africa: his lips and eyelids black with the same dust caked and encrusted: the skin of face and brow of the colour of red ochre. The blackened dust on lips and eyelids relieved the brightness of his teeth and eyes. He was a figure at the same time savage and bizarre, and as he staggered into the path he addressed her, as well as his parched tongue would let him, in a ridiculous attempt at German. He spoke as though he were drunk or raving. No wonder that she shuddered.

"Ich.... Ich..." he said. "O ... nicht ... frightened sei. Wasser. Will nicht leiden. Helf mir. Verstehn?"

She hadn't tumbled to it that he was English, as anyone might have done who knew German. Brilliantly she stumbled into Swahili.

"Wataka maji.... Water. Oh, his arm's broken.... Do lie down ... you'll fall."

And he fell in the path at her feet. A minute later he smiled up at her. "You're English?" he said. "My apologies. I'm sorry to have frightened you." He still spoke thickly.

"You were speaking German to me? But you are English yourself   "

He said: "A Scotsman." For a moment he could say no more, and all the time Eva was realising what a pitiable creature he was, with his torn, dusty face, his empty left sleeve and the other dangling arm. As a matter of fact, this alarming introduction had come as a reassurance to both of them.

At last he spoke: "First of all, if you don't mind, water. I've had none for ... it's difficult to remember. The arm was ten days ago. If you can get a little ... water" (it came out like that) "I can manage. You can put it in my hat."

Now all her nervousness had gone. The forest, which had been a horror, became suddenly quite friendly. She took his greasy hat and walked away into the darkness; and in one of those poisonous creeks of the swamp she filled it with water that was as thick as coffee. On her return the black mouth greeted her with a smile that was altogether charming.

But it was a terrible thing to see him drink the filthy stuff. "You could feel," she said, "the dryness of his throat." He must have seen, for all the darkness, the pity in her eyes, for he hastened to explain that matters weren't nearly as bad as they might have been. "The arm," he said, "is nothing, a piece of bad luck. Time will mend it. But unless you are in some way a prodigy it is something of a handicap to have to do without hands." Although the position had been desperately serious, and he wasn't much of a hand at joking, he wanted to make a joke of it. He didn't know much about women . . . that sort of woman at any rate; and this made him unusually anxious to be gentle with her. Besides, a man who is on the point of dying with thirst in the middle of Africa at night does not expect to fall in with a woman walking hatless and unarmed. He knew that something unusual was doing; he knew that she too was in trouble. And obviously he was going to help her. In the middle of Africa people help one another without asking questions: in their relations there appears a certain delicacy which sits particularly well on such a villainous-looking person as Hare was then. So he asked her nothing of herself. In a moment or two, his strength reviving, according to its obstinate wont, like that of a cut flower that had been given water, he sat up in the path. She glowed to see him better; two sick men would have been rather a large order.

"This is the M'ssente Swamp?" he asked at length. She answered: "Yes."

"And the M'ssente runs into the Ruwu. Yes. . . . We're about a hundred miles from the railway. Up above there are rubber plantations. Yours, I suppose?"

She told him that they belonged to a German, Godovius.

"Godovius?"

She tried "Sakharani."

"Now I have it," he said slowly. "Of course. A Jew. I know all about Mr. Godovius. . . . I've heard from the Masai. Sakharani. . . . Yes. And you are living on his estate?"

She denied it hastily. There was a hint of pity in his question. All the time she was conscious of the scrutiny of his eyes from within their dark circles. She told him that she came from the Luguru mission, a mile or two away, and that her brother was there. She told him their name.

He said: "A minister?" as though he were uncertain whether the information suited his plans. It was ludicrous that a man in this extremity should pick and choose his host.

There followed a long silence. At last he spoke:

"Now I think I can manage. I mean I think I can walk as far as the mission. But I want to put the case to you, Miss Burwarton, for it's possible under the circumstances that you won't like me to come."

"Whatever the circumstances were," she said, "I couldn't let you go." She meant that ordinary humanity wouldn't let her turn him away; but I suspect that she was clutching also at the shadow of a strong man in him, because his gentleness had shown her already that he could help her. She could not have abandoned him if only for that reason.

"Well, don't be hasty . . . you shall judge," he said. "I'll be perfectly frank with you and I shall expect you to be the same with me. My name is Hare. If you had been longer in this country you'd have heard of me; and you wouldn't have heard much good. A fellow who makes his living as I do is not usually an exemplary person. No doubt a lady would be shocked by my way of living. I don't know any, so that is no odds to me. When your neighbour Godovius hears that I was here, and probably he will hear sooner or later, I shall find myself clapped into jail at Dar-es-Salaam. If only I had the use of my hands I could get out of this country. In B. E. A. they know me well enough. And I'm not "wanted" for anything I'm more than usually ashamed of. It's ivory poaching. I've never been a great believer in any game laws: and particularly German ones. But I realise that I'm done . . . more or less. There are only two alternatives: to shelter with you at Luguru and fight it out, or to throw in my hand on Godovius's doorstep. In either case I sha'n't starve: but the Germans have a long score to settle with me, and I doubt if they'll kill any fatted calves when they get me. The other is a fair sporting chance. If your brother can find it in accordance with his conscience to aid and abet a felon. . . . Well . . . that's all."

But already she was convinced that the felon was a man that she could trust. I think she would have trusted him if the crimes to which he had confessed had included a murder. "Whatever it had been," she said, "I couldn't have thrown him over. It was so pathetic to see such a strong, hard man as that absolutely beaten. It wouldn't have been fair. And I felt . . . I knew . . . that he had been somehow sent to help me." (She wasn't ashamed of the words.) "Even then I knew it."

Perhaps she did. I think most of the things which Eva Burwarton did were dictated to her by instinct rather than reason: but there was another factor which she possibly discounted, or did not realise, and this was the knowledge that this man too was an enemy of Godovius. It struck her that they were both in the same boat.

As for James . . . whatever James might think—and it was quite possible that he wouldn't countenance the protection of a man who was "wanted" by the German authorities as a matter of principle, if not for the protection of the mission's name—whatever James might think, she had determined to take this man and to hide him. After what had happened that night she felt that she couldn't take any risks of being left alone to deal with Godovius. For all she knew, James might be dead by the time she returned; and the mere presence of another man of kindred race had made her a little easier. It is in the way of a compliment to our race that she had so quickly decided that she could trust a gaunt and battered wreck of an adventurer—for that is what it came to—just because he was British. She clung to the happy chance of their meeting as if it were indeed her salvation. And she wanted from the first to tell him all her story, as a child might do to any stranger who sympathised with its loneliness. That was why she couldn't answer him at first. She didn't know where to begin.

He mistook the causes of her hesitation. "Very well then," he said. "I quite understand. I can shift for myself. And I am grateful for your kindness. I had no right to ask for more."

For answer she burst into tears. That was what she had been waiting for all the time since she had run out of Godovius's room, and the sudden sense of relief which his presence implied quite overwhelmed her. She was ashamed of her crying; but she couldn't help it. Through her tears she saw the ragged figure of Hare, squatting in the dark path and infinitely more embarrassed by this storm of feeling than herself. Indeed it was a strange setting for their first meeting. Under the same atmosphere of stress, within the same utter solitudes these two met and parted. In after time Eva always remembered this moment with a peculiar tenderness. Perhaps Hare remembers too.

At last she dried her tears.

"I'm all right now," she said. "Are you sure you can manage two miles? . . . I don't think it can be more. We will go slowly. And I will take your rifle."

And though he protested, partly because he would not have her burdened, and partly because it offended his instinct to be for a moment unarmed, she slipped the strap of the Mannlicher from his shoulders, guiding it gently over his helpless right arm. Her tears had so steadied her that she acted without any hesitation. It is not strange that Hare wondered at her.

II
When she thought about it in after times it often struck her as strange that she found herself equipped with a regular plan of concealment for the stranger. "I had never had to hide anything before in my life," she said, "and yet long before we got to the mission I knew exactly where I should have to put him: I'd even thought about his food, and bandages for his poor arm, and water for him to wash in. It was funny: it all came to me naturally. I suppose concealment and scheming of that kind are more natural to a woman than to a man. I couldn't ever have believed that I was so deceitful."

Of those first strange days she would always speak without reserve. I suppose that it is always a happiness for people to remember the beginnings of a relationship of that kind: and to have mothered a man who was so utterly helpless as Hare in secret, and to have shielded him from a positive danger, brought into her life a spice of romance which was hardly to be found in her daily endeavours to preserve the constitution of James from the menace of draughts or damp sheets. In those days she was very happy, and, above all, never lonely. Apart from any other appeal, the situation aroused her imagination. In this most serious business she was playing, just as she had played at houses when she was quite a little girl. And I am certain that she never once thought of the possibility of a passion more profound arising from her play.

It was in the inner chamber of her little banda in the garden that she had decided to place Hare. She felt that here, in the company of Mr. Bullace's whisky bottles, he would be reasonably safe; for the outer of the two rooms had always been sacred to her, and even the boy Hamisi never entered it. She knew that she could feed him there. In that country food need never be a serious problem, and after sunset she could always be sure of freedom from observation. If once she could make Hare comfortable she felt sure that all would be well. That night, indeed, she left him alone with a gourd full of milk and a plate of mealie meal porridge. He begged her not to worry about him, saying that he had often slept in rougher places than this. With his clasp-knife she unfastened two of the bales of sisal fibre, which she spread upon the floor for bedding. A third bale of the white silky stuff served him for pillow. He assured her that he wanted no more . . . or rather only one thing more: the loaded rifle which she had been carrying and which he could not bear to sleep without. "You could not use it without any hands," she said, smiling. "I must have it," he said; "you do not know how undefended I am." And she laid it by his side.

Returning to the house, she found the boy Onyango sleeping on the floor at the foot of James's bed, and James too sleeping so quietly and with such gently stirring breath that she began to wonder why she had ever been frightened or embarked on her amazing expedition to the house of Godovius. She saw now that Godovius had been right when he had said that there was nothing to worry about, that nothing terrible would have happened if she had stayed at home and never suffered any of the nightmare from which she was just emerging. The stark reality of that little room, the figures of the two sleepers, the symbolical pictures and texts on the walls, the glass of milk at James's bedside, recalled her with a variety of appeals to a normal world untroubled by vast emotional experience, and the shadow of the other world huge and fantastic faded from her mind until there was only one vestige of it left: the vision of a gaunt man with an empty sleeve and another broken arm lying asleep on the sisal in Mr. Bullace's banda. It was just as though this fragment of a dream had materialised and become fantastically embodied in the texture of common life.

Thinking of these things, she suddenly realised that for some moments her eyes had been interested in watching a big black Culex mosquito which had swooped down from the white mosquito net upon the transparent arm which James in his restlessness had slipped beneath its edge. And this awakened her. She roused the faithless watchman Onyango and sent him back to his shed. Then she tenderly replaced that pitiable arm of James beneath the shelter of his net. The slight movement roused him. He opened his eyes and stared at her lazily, without speaking. She became suddenly conscious of her own appearance. It seemed to her that all her night's experience, even the secret of Hare's concealment, must be written in her face. But the wondering eyes of James saw nothing. He, too, was returning from a strange land.

At last he spoke: "Is it night, Eva?"

She told him "Yes"; she didn't want him to look at her like that, and so with her hand she smoothed back the lank hair from his brow.

"I think I have been dreaming," he said. And then, again: "What day is it?"

She had to consider before she answered him. "It's . . . it's Saturday morning."

"Saturday. . . . Saturday. . . . To-morrow will be Sunday. I don't know. . . . I seem to have missed two days. I don't understand . . ."

"Don't try to understand now," she begged him.

He was wonderfully mild. "All right," he said, "I won't try to understand. It does hurt rather. I'm awfully thirsty too. And I want to tell you about my dream. A peculiar dream."

She gave him a cupful of milk, which he drank eagerly.

"Saturday morning," he said. "And Sunday to-morrow. That means that I shall have to be better by then. But to have dropped two days, two whole days. Where have I been during those two days?"

Literally, as one answers a child without thinking, she told him that he had been in that room and on that bed; and, curiously enough, her answer seemed to satisfy him. Then suddenly he started to laugh in a feeble, helpless way.

"My dream," he said, "while I remember it; for you were in it; we were both of us in it." He told her how he had dreamed that they were walking together on a Sunday afternoon in the country to the west of Far Forest. A beautiful day, and they were going hand in hand, as they used to do when they were children. The road along which they moved was a grass-grown track which had once been used by the Romans. That afternoon it was full of people; but all the people were moving in the opposite direction, so that at last he had begun to think that they were going the wrong way. So he had stopped an old man with a white beard who was running back as hard as he could go, and asked him if they were on the right road. "Yes," he said, "you are on the right road. But can you guess what the end will be?" Then suddenly, as he caught sight of James's face, he had made a gesture of terror and rushed away. James would have stopped others of that running stream of people, but as soon as they saw him they covered their eyes and ran. "And although they were sometimes near enough to brush us as they passed," he said, "it was just as if the whole thing were going on many miles away, and we were watching them from a distance: just as if they were in a different world or in a different patch of time." At last they had come to a little crest (Eva knew it well) where the green lane falls to a valley through the slant of a grove of beeches. All the time the moving stream of people with averted faces never ceased, and at the bottom of the hill, where, in reality, the grass lane cuts down beside a stream into a piece of woodland, a sudden change came over the scene. It was night. People were brushing past them in the darkness. And instead of Shropshire it was Africa; he could have been sure of that from the peculiar aromatic odour of brushwood in the air. Between the branches of the trees above the stream a new moon was shining: an African moon all the wrong way round. Perhaps Eva had never noticed that the moon was the wrong way round in Africa? A man whispered as he passed them: "Hurry up, or you'll be too late for the end." They hurried on. There was no sound in the wood but a crooning of pigeons. In a clearing there stood a little church of galvanised iron of the same shape and size as the mission church at Luguru. However it had got there James could not imagine. It never used to be there. From the narrow doors of this church people were pouring in a steady stream like the sand in an egg-boiler. Both he and Eva were hot and tired, but they pressed on: for they felt that after all they might not be in time: and when they came to the door the stream of people, who covered their eyes, divided on either side of them, so that they could easily have entered. "But I couldn't get you to go in," said James. "You told me that you couldn't bear to look at it. So I went in myself. A funny thing: the church smelt of Africans; it smelt like a Waluguru hut. And it was empty. Except for one man. And he was a European in black clothes—I couldn't see his face, for his head lolled over. He was stretched out on the front of the pulpit, hung there with big nails through his hands. I called to you; but as I shouted it went dark. I've never had a dream like that before. It isn't like me to dream. What tricks fever will play with a man!"

All the time she had scarcely been listening to him. "I don't think you'll dream again," she said. She knew that this sort of extravagance was not good for James. Still, it was better that he should be talking excited rubbish than lying there unconscious. She tried to make him comfortable with a sponge wrung out in water and eau-de-Cologne. While she was sponging him he still wanted to go on talking; but she knew that it would be wiser not to encourage him, and a little later he fell asleep.

She left him: tired as she was, she knew that it was no use trying to sleep herself. She went out on to the stoep and sat there in faint moonlight under the watery sky. The night was chilly and she wrapped herself in a blanket, and sat there, thinking of that strange night and of the doubtful future until the black sky grew grey and birds began to sing in some faint emulation of the chorus of temperate dawns. She listened to them for a little while, and then, sighing, with fatigue, but strangely happy, went into the house.

She could not tell how long she had sat there. It must have been several hours at least, for a heavy dew had drenched the blanket which she had wrapped round her.

CHAPTER VII

I

Now it was far too light for her to think of sleep, and so she went into the house to change her clothes and to make herself clean. When she saw her own reflection in the little mirror she was shocked, for it seemed to her a strange thing that she should have passed through so many hours of intense experience and show so little for it. Her blouse was torn and her skirt caked with black mud, but that was all. She would not have been surprised if she had found that her hair had turned white. But it hadn't: only, when she took it down, she was puzzled for a moment by an unfamiliar perfume which seemed to have been imprisoned in its folds. She shuddered, realising all at once that it was the scent of Godovius's room. But when she had bathed and changed her clothes and stepped out into the summery sunshine of early morning she felt as though she had really managed to wash that damnable atmosphere away. There wasn't really a vestige of it left. She just felt a little light-headed and nervous, as if her legs didn't quite belong to her. But she did realise that she had got her hands full.

In the first place, James. Several times she passed in and out of his room. He was still sleeping peacefully, and she did not disturb him; but somewhere about nine o'clock, when she had breakfasted, she found that he had wakened. He was lying on his back with his arms folded in front of his chest and his eyes wide open. He smiled at her.

"I think I'm all right now," he said. "It's been a funny time."

She was unfeignedly thankful. She washed him tenderly, and from time to time he asked her short questions which she thought it her duty to evade for fear of exciting him. And he was easily satisfied.

"I'm afraid you've been up all night with me," he said. "It was a strange night. Did I talk to you in the night? I seem to remember . . ."

"You told me a silly nightmare," she said, "that was all. You had been dreaming."

He laughed softly. "I'm always dreaming. Even when I'm awake. I don't remember anything about it. Everything at Luguru is like a dream."

And so she left him for a little. She had begun to wonder about her hidden guest. Now for the first time, in broad daylight, and removed from all the romantic circumstances of the night before, she realised the results of her hospitality. The possibilities were frightening. A law-abiding citizen, she was sheltering a felon; a modest young woman, she was hiding a strange man of whom she knew nothing at all. But there was no running away from it. She had taken on the job and must see it through. That was the way in which she looked at it, even in the face of a considerable anxiety. It struck her as strange that she hadn't for a moment counted the cost the night before. She smiled at herself, a little indulgently. "I always do things like that and think about them afterwards," she thought.

Meanwhile she had a great deal to be thankful for in the recovery of James. Freed of this anxiety, she was far more capable of tackling the problem which Hare presented. Godovius was her other concern, and it seemed to her providential that things had really come to a head at Njumba ja Mweze that night, for after what had happened there he couldn't very well pursue his attentions. She was thinking all the time of Godovius as a possible threat to her two protégés. For the sake of both of them it was essential that he should be kept away from Luguru. Nothing could have happened better. Now he couldn't have the face to come. That was all she knew about Godovius.

In this way, scheming for his protection, searching for every probable contingency which might threaten his safety, and arming herself against them with an unusual caution, she came to Mr. Bullace's banda. It was now midday and very hot. Close to the banda, dangerously close, the shamba boys were cutting down the poles on which the sisal spires had withered. They hacked at the pulpy poles with iron pangas, and sang to each other a queer antiphonal song which had lightened the labours of black men cutting wood for untold generations. Hamisi had climbed up the pole, and when the trunk was nearly severed he swung himself to and fro until the whole thing toppled over with a tearing sound. When the pole fell they shouted to one another and laughed; and one of them, a naked M'luguru who had sat in the garden path busily excavating a jigger from his toe, looked up and laughed too, as though the occasion were one for universal happiness. He was an ugly creature with shining cicatrices on either cheek and porcupine quills which he had picked up stuck through his hair, and as soon as he had done with his surgery he jumped to his feet and lolled up against the side of the banda.

It suddenly came to Eva that only the thin grass wall of the banda now separated him from the place where Hare was lying. Already her secret seemed on the point of being discovered. She remembered hearing Godovius tell her brother one day that the Waluguru, in common with other African races, could detect the presence of a white man by his smell. She was so frightened that she hurried to the side of the banda and pulled the lounging Luguru away. It was the first time in her life that she had handled a native roughly. The others, standing idle in their dirty red blankets, laughed. She felt that they were jeering at her; but if she had laid open their comrade's back with the cut of a kiboko they would have laughed in the same way. She called Hamisi, and told him to see to the other side of the hedge first. He said: "N'dio, Bibi," and smiled. She hated all their smiling. He was smiling, she thought, at her secret. Probably they all knew it by now. Soon Godovius would know . . .

The boys moved off to the other end of the garden and still she stood at the corner of the banda thinking. Around her the lazy life of the morning stirred. Among the aromatic herbs which had invaded that neglected garden with their ashen foliage and clustered flowers, purple and cinnabar, the restless butterflies of Africa hovered in mazy flight. Most of them were small and barred with cinnabar, like the little orange tips which brightened the Shropshire lanes in spring. A green lizard moved as quietly as a shadow at her feet. Through the green curtain of acacia a flight of honey-suckers passed with a whir of wings. She hated all this busy, mocking life, this land that smiled eternally and was eternally cruel. She felt that she had no part in it. It was all wrong.

She went into her banda and tapped at the partition. Hare answered her in a whisper. He said that he was quite comfortable. He had slept and was not hungry. All that morning he had lain listening to the chatter of the boys as they worked on the sisal hedge, and he had heard many curious things of which they would never have spoken if they had known that he was there. He wanted to know all about James, and seemed relieved when she told him of his calm awakening. "Now he should be all right," he said, and told her what to do in the matter of food and of quinine. "But you sound tired," he said. "You must rest yourself. The night of quiet and comfort has made all the difference to me. I'm afraid I'm an anxiety to you; and you have enough to worry about already."

Although this was almost an echo of her own thought, she denied it hastily.

"Ah, but I need not be an anxiety much longer," he said. "A day or two and I shall be able to fend for myself. I could hear that you were nervous when you spoke to the boys."

She wanted to explain herself; for suddenly, thinking of what life at Luguru would be like if he left her, she realised what the presence of the fugitive meant to her. But this was no time for talking, even in whispers. After sunset, when the Africans had gone to sleep.... She asked him if there was anything that he needed particularly. He told her that he only wanted two things, water to wash in and a pencil.

"But you can't use either of them," she said, "as you are now."

She heard him laugh softly. "You don't know how clever I am with no hands to speak of."

She moved away softly, and a little later she returned, bringing with her a gourd full of water, soap and a towel, and the pencil for which he had asked her. Very carefully she moved aside the partition and pushed them inside. But she did not see him, for the inside of the banda was dark and the sound of a step on the garden path made her close the open space hurriedly. And even though she found that her fancy had deceived her, this sort of thing was not over-good for her nerves.

II
In this manner, all through that day which was the first and the most trying, she hovered between her two anxieties. James was more than usually difficult and talkative. With the vanishing of his fever it seemed as if all the accumulated nervous energy which disease had beneficently drugged were suddenly released. He prayed aloud; he made plans, and in the intervals he would call to Eva to remind her of

some small thing that had happened at Far Forest many years before. It was all encouraging in a way, but tiring . . . very tiring. In the evening, about the time of sunset, he fell asleep over his Bible, and the relief to Eva was as great as if he had been delirious all day.

She sat on the stoep in that sudden interval of silence and relief, watching the hot sky grow cool and temperate, watching, a little later, the growing crescent of the young moon free itself from the topmost tangles of the forest and then go sailing, as if indeed it had been caught and were now released into a dusky sky. Almost before she had realised that the light was failing, it was night. The crescent now was soaring through the crowns of her own tall crotons. From every grassy nullah where water once had flowed the frogs began their trilling. She wondered if she would ever taste the long coolness of twilight again.

Then, when she had made a small meal and put aside some food for Hare, she lit a blizzard lantern and carried it to her banda. From the other end of the compound, where the Africans slept, she heard the twanging of a strange instrument. One of the boys was singing an interminable, tuneless native song. At any rate they were safe for the night.

Hare was waiting for her. She placed the lantern on her own side of the partition, so that only a wide panel of light fell within the inner chamber. He was sitting up on his bed of sisal fibre, making a savage but intensely pathetic figure. I don't suppose he knew for one moment what a ruffian he looked. For many years he had lived a life in which one does not consider appearances, but, for all that, he had tried to make himself as clean as he could with one imperfect hand. He had combed his long hair and even attempted to make a job of his beard. This was really the first time that Eva had properly seen him. The night before, in spite of his exhaustion, he had seemed so collected and capable, so eager not to make trouble, and she had been so anxious about James and distressed by the difficulty of the situation that she hadn't quite taken in his absolute helplessness. It came to her in a sudden flash of realisation. She felt guilty and ashamed. Her eyes filled with tears.

"Now I am much more comfortable," he said, making matters worse than ever.

"But how on earth have you managed?" she whispered. "Your poor arm. . . . I've neglected you shockingly."

All at once she became maternal and practical. It was not very difficult for her. For the greater part of her life she had been looking after helpless male creatures: first her old father and then James. Now she would not be denied.

"Where is the arm broken?" she asked.

It was nothing, he said, only a smashed collar-bone. It had been broken before. "Only, you see, I must keep the upper arm close to the side. It acts as a sort

55

of splint. In a fortnight it will be sound. I know all about this sort of thing. I have to."

"I'm going to wash you, anyway," she said.

I do not suppose such a thing as this had ever happened to Hare in all his life; but now he was too helpless and the idea too reasonable for him to protest. To Eva the business came quite naturally. Very tenderly she disentangled the dirty shirt of khaki drill from his left shoulder, slipping the sleeve over the poor pointed stump of what had once been one of the wiriest arms in Africa. It was a painful process to her; all the time she felt that she was hurting him; but he smiled up at her with a look of confidence and shyness which one might more easily have seen on the face of a child than of this old hunter.

The shirt was dirty . . . horribly dirty; but he made no apologies which might have embarrassed them both. The injured shoulder was more difficult. Pain twisted his lips into a sort of smile. "Easy . . . if you don't mind," he said.

"If you wouldn't mind my slitting up the sleeve," she suggested.

"No . . . that wouldn't do. It's my only shirt. It's only dirty because of this accident. I generally wash it every few days."

At last it was over. Now she could see the angle of the broken collar-bone, and from it a great bruise, purple and yellow, tracking down into the axilla. She washed him, passing gently over the bruised area. When she had finished he thanked her. "This is not a woman's work," he said.

"Oh, but it is," she smiled.

"Perhaps I am wrong. It is many years since I have spoken to a woman. I live a very solitary life. Even before I had the misfortune to lose my arm." It was funny to see how his little self-consciousness showed itself.

Now she was anxious to rescue his very awful shirt; for she had decided that it would be easy to fit him out in one of James's until it was clean. He was almost as anxious about that as he had been about the rifle. He didn't want to offend her; but for all his gentleness he was determined to get it back.

"But we must wash it," she said. "What is the matter with you?"

"You can have it, but . . . did you notice that there's a big pocket in the left breast? Yes . . . that's it. Will you be kind enough to look in it. There's a wee packet of papers in a waterproof cover. That's what I want. It's very near the only thing in my gear that I've saved. It has only a personal value." He paused and then modestly added: "It's the fruits of several adventurous years. It's a book—"

He looked at her very narrowly. She could see now that his eyes were of a very clear blue-grey. In the lamplight they sparkled like the eyes of a bird. Then he smiled.

"I may tell you," he said, "that you are the first human being I have ever told that to . . . and there aren't many . . . who would not have thought it rather a joke."

"But that would be ridiculous," she said. "For I don't know you. When I come to think of it, I don't even know your name."

"I'm called Hare," he said, "Charles Hare. It's possible you've heard the name. Not probable you've heard any good of it." It sounded as if he were trying to make the best of it himself.

She repeated: "Charles Hare." But when he heard the words in her voice his incorrigible romanticism wouldn't permit him to let them pass. It was like Hare to abandon in one moment an alias that he had carried for a quarter of a century. I suppose it was just the directness and simplicity of Eva that worked the miracle: it suddenly occurred to him that it would be a shame to deceive her in the least particular. He said:

"You can forget that name. It's none the better for my having carried it. I don't know"—there was a bright challenge in his eyes—"that it's really much worse. But it isn't mine. My name is M'Crae. Hector M'Crae."

She was bewildered. "But why—" she began.

"I had sufficient reasons for losing it," he said. "I've found it again. I've found a lot of things during the last four days. You must forgive me for having deceived you. One gets into the habit . . ."

It sounded rather a lame finish.

"Oh, it's a long story," he said, "a long story. Some day if you'll listen to me I'll tell it to you. Now, if you please, we'll leave it. I want to know about your brother. I should like to know a little about you . . ."

He began to question her narrowly on the subject of James, approving, with monosyllables, what she had done. And then he told her seriously that she was looking over-tired. "You want sleep," he said. "We mustn't talk any more to-night. Will you throw this blanket over my shoulders? Oh . . . and there's one thing more. I've been clumsy enough to break the point of your pencil. There's a knife on my belt. Will you sharpen it for me?"

III

It was four nights later that M'Crae—it is better to call him M'Crae, if it were only to dissociate this new being from the figure which so many people in Africa know—came to his story. Eva had never asked for it; and I think this delicacy on her part did something towards making him feel that it was her due. Besides this, the passage of time had made an intimacy between the two more easy. For one thing, James suffered no return of his fever: Eva was less harassed and for that reason more able to devote herself to the other invalid. She had made it clear to him, once and for all, that a man with one hand, and that in a sling, was in no position to look after himself. At first, no doubt, his native pride, of which he had more than a man's ordinary share, and which had been fostered alike by his infirmity and his solitary manner of life, made it difficult for him to accept her attentions with ease; but by degrees the naturalness and the simplicity of her outlook overcame him. Perhaps this was not so strange as one might imagine, for the man's independence was more a matter of habit than of instinct. Her deftness and her tenderness together made it impossible to resist even if he would have done so. And her beauty . . . I do not know. I don't think I want to know. Perhaps he was in love with her from the beginning. If he were, I can only believe that it was a great blessing to him: the very crown and fulfilment of a strangely romantic life.

On the fourth evening he had evidently prepared himself for his recitation. He would not talk of other things. Eva couldn't understand it at first: for he answered her questions as though he were not in the least interested, and she thought that for some queer reason of his own he was sulking, or perhaps that he was in pain. I suppose he was in pain. It was not an easy matter for a man like M'Crae to get a story off his chest. She had hung the blizzard lamp at the mouth of the banda and she was sitting in a deck-chair close to the partition, where it was so dark that neither of them could see the other's face. She was just conscious of his eyes in the darkness, and it seemed to her that they never left her face. It was a very quiet, moonless night. For some reason the sky was unusually cloudy. The noises of the dark, the zizzing of cicalas and the trilling of frogs were so regular that they became as unnoticeable as silence. In the roof little lizards were moving; but they, too, came and went as softly as shadows. No violence troubled their isolation, unless it were the impact of an occasional moth hurling out of the darkness at the lantern's flame or the very distant howling of a hyena on the edge of the forest. It was a silence that invited confidences. No two people in the world could have been more alone.

At length Eva asked: "Mr. M'Crae, what's the matter with you?"

He said: "Nothing." And there followed another long silence.

Then, without a word of introduction, he began talking to her about his childhood. A long and disordered story. He didn't seem to be considering her at all in the recitation. She might not even have been there, she thought, if it had not been that his eyes were always on her. It was a remote and savage story, which began in the island of Arran, fifty years ago: a small farm of stone in the mountain above Kilmory Water, dreaming above a waste of sea in which, at night, the lighthouse on the Isle of Pladda shows the only token of life. But by day all the mouth of the firth to Ailsa Craig would be streaked with the smoke of steamers making for the Clyde, and others reaching out from those grey waters to the ends of the earth. "If it hadn't been for the shipping," he said, "I might have lived all my life at the Clachan and never known that there was anything else in the world. I should be living there now. Let me see . . . July. . . . It'll be over-early for the heather. I can see my father there now. But he must be dead for all that. When I left him he was a strong man of sixty without a single grey hair to his head. Strong. . . . Ay, and just. But hard. Hard as granite. I don't judge him harshly. I often see, now that I'm not so young as I was, that if I had stayed in Arran, as my brothers did, I might have grown into something very like him. Sometimes I catch myself in a gesture or even a turn of speech which is him to the life. That is the outside of me. All the battering about the world I've had hasn't been enough to get rid of the externals. Inside it's very different. My father's eyes never saw farther than the firth or the sound; his life kept inside the Old Testament, while I've seen more of the world than most people, and played skittles with the Ten Commandments too. Understand that I'm not sorry for it. There aren't many regrets in my life. . . . Just a few. I've missed things that are a consolation when a man grows old . . . a home . . . children . . . but I believe the balance is on my side. They taught me the whole duty of man in a thing they call the Shorter Catechism. They would say that I've failed in it. But there's more than one way of glorifying God, and there are more gods than the God of my fathers . . ."

He was sixteen when his mother died, and her loss had desolated him. He was only a boy, but he saw already that life at the Clachan must resolve itself into a struggle between the two strongest wills within its walls, his own and his father's. If he had lived in some inland valley it is possible that he would have found no way of escape, even though the most inland Scotsmen have a way of escaping. As it was, his prison, however remote it may have seemed, overlooked one of the great highways of the world, and escape was easy. He left Lamlash one day in a ketch-rigged, round-bottomed barge that was sailing for Glasgow, and from that day forward he never saw his home again. Sometimes, he said, he had felt a sudden impulse to return. He had a little theory of his own that for a man to be completely satisfied he must see every place that he has visited at least twice; no more than twice; for the first return was an inevitable disillusionment, the only cure, in fact, for the wanderer's hunger. Once indeed, in the early years of his sea-faring, he had returned to the port of Glasgow in the stokehold of a cattle ship rolling over from Brazil. He had been talking to the third engineer, whose home was a village called Kirn, on the Holy Loch; and this man, who glowed with anticipation at the thought of nearing home, had promised to call him when they should draw abeam of the Pladda light. "A sight for sair eyes," he had called it, and M'Crae had half persuaded himself that he was going to share in this tender emotion. It was three o'clock in the morning when the good-natured engineer shouted to him as he toiled, sweating and stripped to the waist, before the fires. He had thrown a shirt over his shoulders and climbed up the iron ladder of the engine-room, where the pistons sighed and panted, to the dark deck. It was a pitchy night, the sky full of a howling wind and cold flurries of snow. In the 'tween-decks sea-sick cattle were stamping and making hideous noises. "You'll see the light of Pladda over on the port bow," the third had shouted, and the word "bow" was caught in the tail of the wind and borne away astern. M'Crae could see no light. There were no stars in the sky; only a riot of windy space in which the feeble headlight of the ship made dizzy plunges, lighting for a moment ragged flakes of snow. Flying scuds of snow, driven through the darkness, spat upon his sweating chest. Over there, in the heart of that wild darkness, Arran lay. The shoulders of Goat Fell stood up against the storm; Kilmory Water should be in a brown spate; there, in the Clachan, they would all be sound asleep, all but the two sheep-dogs lying with their noses to the hearth, where fiery patterns were stealing through white ashes of peat. M'Crae stood waiting in the cold for the expected thrill. It didn't come.... He could only think in that perverse moment of sunshine and light; of the green mountain slopes above Buenos Ayres and blue, intense shadows on the pavement of the Plaza where dark-skinned ranchers from inland estancias lounged at the scattered tables of the cafés. His utmost will was powerless to enslave his imagination. He shivered, and turned gratefully to the oily heat of the engine-room.

"Well, did ye see it?" the engineer shouted. "Yon's a fine sight!"

"Ay, I saw it," M'Crae lied, and his reply was accepted for the proper Scots enthusiasm. He was not sorry when the ship sailed south again. All the time that she stayed in the port of Glasgow was marred by snow and sleet and rain.

For all that, in later years he had thought of returning more than once. One day, at Simonstown, he had watched a Highland regiment sailing for home at the end of the Boer War. Someone had started to sing The Flowers of the Forest in a high tenor voice. Tears had come into his eyes, and, having a heap of gold sewn in his waistcoat, he had almost decided to book his passage on a mail-boat, until, loitering down Adderley Street on his way to the shipping offices, he had fallen in with a man who had found copper in Katanga, near the shores of Tanganyika, and in half-an-hour they had decided to set out together by the next northward train. And it had always been like that. Some chance had invariably stood between him and his old home. "Now I shall never see it again," he said.

"I wonder," said Eva softly.

"You needn't wonder," he replied. "It's one of the things of which I feel certain. I shall never leave Africa now. Even in Africa I've come across things that made me think of Arran. I remember.... There's a place up above the Rift Valley, eight thousand feet of altitude. It's called Kijabe. One of these Germans built a hotel there. N'gijabi had the meaning of wind in Masai. And it can blow there. Long before the German came near the place I was there ... before the railway ran to Naivasha. I camped there for a week, and all the week I never so much as saw the valley or the lake. Nothing but thin white mist, mist as white as milk, just like the stuff that comes dripping off Goat Fell. I remembered.... But it's a long digression."

He laughed softly. And then he told her of many voyages at sea in which he had come upon strange things that are no longer to be seen. Once in a sailing ship he had doubled the icy Horn; and later, sailing out of 'Frisco, had been wrecked on Kiu-Siu, the southern island of Japan, being cast up on a beach of yellow sand where the slow Pacific swell was spilling in creamy ripples. A woman found him there, an ugly, flat-faced woman, who carried a baby on her back. It was a little bay with a pointed volcanic hill at either horn all covered in climbing pine-trees. At the back of it stood the reed huts of fishermen and on the level plats of sand brown nets were spread to dry. "A beautiful and simple people," he said. "In these days, they tell me, they have been spoiled." For a month he lived there, lived upon dried fish and rice, wandering over the red paths which climbed between the pines on those pointed hillocks. It was February, and peerless weather. By the wayside violets were hiding, and in the air flapped the lazy wings of the meadow browns that he had known in Arran. "I have seen those butterflies in Africa too. It's strange how a thing like that will piece together one's life. I could tell you things of that kind for ever, if it weren't that they would tire you. And they don't really matter."

"And then I killed a man."

He paused, and she felt that his eyes were on her more than ever.

"That's how I lost my name. The one that I found again the other night. At the time it seemed to me a terrible thing. I'm not so sure that I think it terrible now. If I hadn't killed him he would have killed me; but for all that the quarrel was of my making. It was in Singapore . . . in Malay Street, Singapore. A street with a bad name. He was a Russian sailor, and he was treating a woman in the way that no woman, whatever her trade might be, should be treated. I didn't know the woman. I shot him. In a second the place was swarming like an ant's nest. I had my clothes torn from me, but I got away. I was three weeks hiding in an opium shop in Singapore. The Chinese will do anything for you for money. I didn't want to be hanged, for in those days I put a higher value on life than I do now . . . a funny thing to say of a man who had just killed another. I hid among the long bunks where Chinese sailors were lying. The place was dark, with a low roof, and full of the heavy smoke of opium. I was used to that; for one of our quartermasters was an opium smoker and the fo'c'sle of the Mary Deans always smelt of it. I spent three weeks thinking of my past sins and watching a pattern of golden dragons on the roof; and I did more thinking there than I had ever done in my life.

"At the end of those three weeks Ah Qui—that was the Chinaman's name—got me away. I remember the night. We pulled out in a sampan from Tanjong Pagar under the lee of a little island. Pulo . . . Pulo something or other. There was an oily sea lapping round the piles on which the Malays had built their huts and one of those heavy skies that you get in the Straits washed all over with summer lightning. But the taste of clean air after three weeks of opium fumes! They got me on to a junk that was sailing for Batavia, in Java. Old Ah Qui had stripped me of every dollar I possessed. He wouldn't do it for a cent less. When I found myself on the deck of that junk, breathing free air under the flapping sails, the want of money didn't trouble me. I stretched out my arms. I filled my lungs. I could have sung for joy . . .

"At Batavia I shipped under the Dutch flag under the name of Charles Hare. It wasn't a bad name. It came to me in a flash. We landed at Capetown in the year eighteen eighty-five. It was the year after the discovery of gold at De Kaap; Moodie's farm had just been opened. Everybody was talking of gold. While we lay in Table Bay waiting for cargo they found the Sheba reef. We heard of it, myself and another man named Miles, in a dope shop down by the harbour. We didn't think twice about it. That very night we set off for the Transvaal on foot.

"I was one of the lucky ones. We had a fair start of the others who came flocking out from Europe. And it wasn't only luck. I kept my head. That is part of the virtue of being a Scotsman. I kept my head where poor Miles didn't. I had had my lesson: those three weeks of hard thinking in Ah Qui's opium shop. And Miles went under. Twice I put him on his feet again, but he didn't pay for helping. He was never the man that I should have chosen. He just happened to be the only white man aboard that Dutch ship. I couldn't make a new man of him. I suppose he was a born waster. There were plenty like that on the Rand in eighty-six. I saw scores of them go under. And as for murder . . . that was common enough to make me wonder what all the fuss had been about in Singapore.

"I was lucky, as I told you. I left the Rand in eighty-seven. During the last year, when I had parted with Miles and was working for myself, I had experienced a big reaction. It seemed to me that the adventurous way in which I had been living wasn't worth while. I'd seen the example of Miles . . . poor fellow . . . and remembered Singapore. Besides, I had a good bit of money banked with the Jews—enough to live on for the rest of my life—and the mere fact of possessing money makes you look at the world in a different way. It's a bad thing for a young man . . . I'm sure of that. But I was a lot older than my years.

"At any rate, when I left the place where Jo'burg is now I swore that I'd keep what I'd got. I came down to the Cape again, and built a little house out Muizenburg way . . . up above the winter pool they call Zand Vlei . . . a fine little wooden house; and I planted peaches there, and a plumbago hedge round my mealies. It was all my idea of a home. And then, just as the house was beginning to be all that I expected it, I came across a woman. I had never known what it was to be in love before. I was a simple enough lad, for all my money and my pretty house. She was an assistant in one of the stores that stood where Adderley Street is now. An English-woman. She had come out there as 'mother's help,' or whatever they call it, to some Government people; and when they were recalled Mr. Jenkins had asked her if she would come into his store. I fancy they came from the same part of the country. Her home was in Herefordshire. She stayed at Jenkins', and it was there I found her.

"A beautiful woman . . . beautiful, I mean in every way. But it was for so little, so very little . . .

"I can tell you . . . I feel I can tell you because—if you'll allow me to be personal—she had much the same colouring as you; the same eyes, the same straight eyebrows, the same sort of hair. I almost fancy her speech was like yours too. But one forgets. It was thirty years ago . . .

"I can't say much about it. The whole of that experience was like an evening in spring. As short and as beautiful. And we felt . . . we felt that this was only the beginning. One feels that on an early spring evening there is so much in reserve; first the season when the may comes; and then full summer—long summer evenings with bees in the heather; and, afterwards, autumn with the rowan berries. It was like that. We were waiting on an evening of that kind with just the confidence that young people have in all the beautiful things which will happen in the ordinary passage of time.

"And that was all. She died. Cruelly . . . cruelly. Without any warning. She was only ill three days. That is the kind of thing that makes a man despise life. I had lost everything . . . everything . . . utterly lost everything . . ."

He paused. Eva had drawn back her chair a little from the light. She was crying. It was impossible for her to speak. She wondered if she should have spoken. Out of the darkness they heard a deep and throaty rumble.

"Lion," said M'Crae.

After that there followed a silence.

At last he spoke.

"And then my life began . . .

"A blow of that kind knocks a man silly for a time. When he opens his eyes after it nothing looks the same. I was restless. I wanted to find something new to fill the gap in my mind. I hated that little house at Muizenberg in which I had promised myself to end my days. The only thing that did me any good was walking, the lonelier the better. I used to walk over the neck of the peninsula and climb Table Mountain, up above the Twelve Apostles. I'd walk there for hours in the white mist that lies on the top—they call it the tablecloth. I've slept there more than once when the fog has caught me. And though I've never been back there since those days I was just sane enough to remember that it's a wonderful place for flowers. There's many very pretty things there.

"One evening when I came down from the mountain I saw a youngish man looking at my plumbago hedge. 'Pretty place you've got here,' he said. 'Kind of place that would just suit me.' 'What do you want it for?' says I. He blushed . . . he was a nice young fellow. . . . 'Getting married,' said he. That nearly did me. I could have burst out crying on the spot. But I got him in for a sundowner all the same. He started telling me all about the young lady. 'If you don't mind,' I said, 'I'd rather not hear. Don't think that I want to offend you. But if you want the house you can have it. You can have it for two-thirds what it cost me.' I'd almost have given it him.

"In a week we had the thing settled. That year they found gold in the Zoutspanberg district. It was new country, very mountainous and wild. I didn't mind where I went as long as I could forget the other thing. I went there by easy stages, seeing a goodish bit of country. I sunk my money there . . . there and in

63

Zululand. And I lost it—every penny of it but the little bit which was coming in to me, with a scrap of interest, for the Muizenburg farm. I lost my money . . . but I think I found myself.

"It was a great game country, that. I don't suppose there's much game left there now, but in those days it was swarming, all the way from the mountains to the Limpopo. It was a big, lonely country. Those were the two things that got hold of me. I used to ride out there on hunting expeditions with no more company than one boy. I remember sitting there one night after supper with a pipe of Boer tobacco, and then the thought came to me: 'Good God! as I sit here now there's probably not another white man within fifty miles.'

"That was the beginning of it. I began to follow out the idea, and I soon realised that my fifty miles was nothing to speak of. North of me it would easily run into thousands . . . thousands of miles of country that no living man knew anything about; where, for all we knew, there might be rivers and lakes and cities even that had never been seen, all waiting for a man who would set out to find them for the love of the thing. It was a big idea, almost too big for one man's life. But it was the very thing for which my loneliness had been waiting. Africa. . . . Years afterwards—I think it was after the war—I came across a poem by Kipling: a man, one of your amateur settlers, showed it me in the Kenya province. It was about Africa. He called Africa 'the woman wonderful.' Yes . . . 'lived a woman wonderful,' it began. I'd lost one wonderful woman. Now I found another. I've lived with her for thirty years and I have never come anywhere near the end of her wonder, though I know more of her than most men. Why, there is no end. There is always something new. Even in the last week I have stumbled on something new and wonderful. Tonight . . .

"I had three years of it south of the Limpopo. In eighteen ninety I heard that Rhodes was sending an expedition into Mashonaland. There were only five hundred of us in 'ninety; but I always want to shake a man by the hand if he was with us in those days. The men who rode up to Salisbury . . . men that I'd still give my life for: men like Selous. A great hunter, and a good man!

"From that day to this my life has been much the same. There have been one or two diversions. In ninety-five the Jameson raid, and a few years later the Boer War. Wasted years . . . but I didn't fully realise the value of time in those days. I was a wild fellow too. God knows how much I drank. A young man thinks that he is going to live for ever. Still, I suppose there was a mess to be cleared up and it had to be done, and after the war I had my own way. I never slept where I couldn't see the Southern Cross.

"I could tell you a good deal about Africa, all Africa from the Orange River to Lake Chad and the Blue Nile, and the Lorian Swamp. I've hunted everywhere—not for the love of hunting, but because a man must live. I've not been one of those that make hunting pay. I've shot elephants because ivory would keep me in food and porters and ammunition. I've poached ivory with a clear conscience for the same reason. I've found gold, gold and copper: and I've let other men scramble for the fortunes. I didn't want their fortunes. I wanted to know Africa. And always . . . for my own sake, not for the sake of other people, I have made notes of the things that I saw, of kindly peoples, of good water, and things like that. Some day I might make a book about them; but it would be a big book, and I haven't any skill in writing. If I could write of all the beauty and strangeness that I've seen as I saw them a man would never put down the book that I wrote. That's the meaning of the notebooks that I carried in my shirt pockets. There are a lot more stored with the Standard Bank. You see, I've been at it for thirty years.

"Now it's not so easy as it used to be. The zest is there. I'm as eager, you might almost say, as a child; but the power isn't the same. I can't starve in the same way as I used to. In the old days I could live on a little biltong and coffee and the mealie flour I got from the natives. And I'm handicapped in other ways. Five years ago I lost my left arm. I was lucky not to lose my life, for a wounded elephant charged and got me. I'm glad he didn't kill me, for in spite of it all I've had a good time since. I can shoot straight, thank God, if I have something on which to rest my rifle. German East has always been an unlucky country for me. It was near Meru that the elephant got me. One of the Dutchmen in the Arusha settlement had a down on me, and there's been a warrant out for my arrest. The other day, if it hadn't been for you, they would have had me. It's a good thing they didn't, for I want to see this country. I've heard funny things about the Waluguru. They're worth more to me than ivory. When this shoulder's better perhaps I shall find out if the things I've heard are true . . . and I've never been to Kissaki or the Rufiji Delta . . . .

"I think that is all. It's strange how little a man can really tell of his life. The things that matter, the wonderful moments, can't be told at all. What I've been able to tell you sounds like . . . like nothing more than what might have happened to any hard case who's knocked about Africa for thirty years. But for all that life has been precious to me. Perhaps you will think it the kind of life that wasn't worth saving. You mustn't think that. Because I'm grateful. I'm grateful even for these last hours. I'm grateful that you've allowed me to make this sort of confession. It worried me that I should have started off with a lie to a woman like you. It hadn't struck me that way ever before. I dare say it was foolish of me; but when one is weak one gets those twinges of . . . of conscience.

"I'm hoping that you'll forgive me . . ."

CHAPTER VIII
I
I suppose that their talk that night made a good deal of difference to the intimacy of their relation. No doubt it cost M'Crae a considerable effort to speak of things which had been locked in his heart for years. As he himself said, "he was no great hand at talking." With Eva it was different. The small things of which her life had been composed came to him easily, in the ordinary way of talking. Among them there were no passages of which it was difficult to speak; nothing in the very least exciting had ever happened to her before she had set foot in Africa, so few months before.

Since then, indeed, there was a great deal that was both difficult and puzzling. It was so great a relief to her to be able to speak of them that she told him everything, freely, withholding nothing. She told him how, at first, she had mistrusted the man Bullace: of the equivocal way in which he had spoken of Godovius.

"Bullace?" said M'Crae, thinking, "Bullace. . . . I'm afraid I can't help you. Although I know the name. It's possible, even probable, that he drank; though I must tell you that he is the first missionary I've ever heard of who did. People at home talk more nonsense, I should imagine, about missionaries than about any other body of men. On the one side of their sacrifices. They do make sacrifices. We know that. But you must remember that a man who has once lived in the wilds of Africa doesn't take kindly to life at home. They have their wives. They have children. That, I think, is a mistake. But there's the other side; the people who laugh at all missionary work and talk about the folly of ramming Christianity down the throats of people who have good working religions of their own. They are just as wide of the mark as the others. I've known a good many missionaries; and for the most part I believe they're neither worse nor better than their fellows. They're just men. And men are mostly good . . . even the worst of them. If this poor fellow Bullace drank there's a good deal to be said for him. Most Europeans who live in the tropics, particularly if they live alone in a place like Luguru, do drink. At one time—about the time of the Boer War—I drank about as much as any man could do and live. Loneliness—loneliness will drive a man to drink, if he hasn't some strong interest to keep him going. I had Africa. Probably Bullace had nothing. I told you that I've heard strange things about the Waluguru. I daresay Bullace found that he was a failure . . . a hopeless failure, without any chance of getting away from the scene of his failure. And so he drank to kill time. I don't altogether blame him . . ."

He talked to her also a good deal about James, and the particular side of the missionary problem which he had the misfortune to illustrate. It was a great relief to Eva that they were able to do this. In those earlier days when Godovius had appeared to her in the rôle of a helper and adviser, they had often spoken of James and his troubles; but in this matter Godovius had been obviously unsympathetic: he hadn't thought that James was worth Eva's troubling about, and had therefore decided that the topic should be discreetly and swiftly shelved. M'Crae was very different. He listened to Eva's troubles without a hint of impatience, realising just how important they were to her. It flattered her to find herself taken seriously in little frailties of which she herself was not sure that she oughtn't to be ashamed.

One evening, when confidences seemed to come most easily, she told him the whole story of her relations with Godovius: the first impressions of distrust which his kindness had removed, his bewildering outbursts of passion and at last the whole story of her visit to the House of the Moon. She told him, half smiling, of the frightening atmosphere of her journey, of Godovius's amazing room, of the shock which his photograph had given her. It astonished her to find how easy it was to confide in this man.

He listened attentively, and at last pressed her to tell him again of the terraces on the side of the hill; and the abandoned building of stone from which the doves had fluttered out.

She told him all that she remembered. "But why do you want to know?" she said.

"It is very curious," he replied, "very curious. When we rode up into Rhodesia in we came across the same sort of thing. But on a bigger scale. It's likely you'll not have heard of it, but there are great ruins there that they call the Zimbabwes, about which the learned people have been quarrelling ever since. They're near the site of the Phoenician gold workings—King Solomon's Mines—and they're supposed to be connected with the worship of the Syrian goddess, Astarte, of whom your brother could tell you more than I can. But I take it she was a moon goddess by her symbols. And it's curious because of the way in which it fits in here. Kilima ja Mweze. . . . The mountain of the moon. Godovius's home, too. And the strange thing is that it tallies with the stories which I heard from the Masai about the Waluguru; the stories that brought me over into this country."

"It was the night of the new moon when I went there," she said. "And Onyango was afraid to go to the Waluguru for the same reason."

He said: "Yes . . . it's a matter that needs thinking over." And then, after a long pause: "But I'm thankful that I came here."

"For my sake," she said softly. He only smiled.

After that they did not speak of Godovius for a long time. I think those evenings must have been very wonderful for both of them; for it is doubtful if either M'Crae or Eva had ever shared an intimacy of this kind. In it there was no hint of love-making. The extraordinary candour of their relation made impossible the bashfulness and misunderstanding out of which love-making so often springs. The difference of age between them made it unlikely that Eva should think of M'Crae as a lover; and he was not a young man in whom the mere physical presence of a woman would awaken passion. Many years ago he had outgrown that sort of thing; so that the result of their intimacy was a wholly delightful relation, which resembled, in its frankness and freedom from the subconscious posings of sex, the friendship of two men or of a man and a woman happily married who have rid themselves of the first restlessness of passion. To Eva it seemed that this state of innocence might last for ever. To M'Crae, who knew the workings of the human heart more widely, it seemed very beautiful, and very like her, that she should think so.

But if Eva realised no threat to their peace of mind in the shape of passion, she was certainly conscious of other dangers to their secret happiness. She knew that the day must come when the presence of M'Crae would be revealed to James, who seemed, for the time, to have got the better of the fever in his blood. She dreaded this because she knew that when it came to that she must almost certainly lose M'Crae; and the presence of M'Crae had made her happier than she had ever been before at Luguru. James wouldn't understand their position. She could be sure of that in advance. To say that James wasn't capable of relieving her of the attentions of Godovius would not help matters much, for James had a good opinion of himself in the rôle of the protecting male. The idea that his place should be taken by a one-armed elephant-hunter of the most doubtful antecedents, who had stolen into his house in the night while he lay sick with fever, would not appeal to him. Indeed, there was bound to be trouble with James.

I do not suppose that the question of what James' attitude would be gave much worry to M'Crae; but there was another threat to their peace of mind, of which they both were conscious and which could not be regarded so lightly. Godovius.... All the time Eva was conscious of him in the back of her mind, and particularly at night when she and M'Crae sat in the banda talking. Then, from time to time, she would find herself overwhelmed with very much the same sort of feeling as that which she had experienced on the way down from Njumba ja Mweze, just before she had met M'Crae. Now, as ever, the nights were full of restless sound; and every sound that invaded their privacy began to be associated with the idea of Godovius; so that when a branch rustled or a twig snapped at night she would never have been surprised to have seen Godovius standing over them. He had always had the way of appearing suddenly. She grew very nervous and jerky and, in the end, possessed by the idea that all their careful concealment was an elaborate waste of time; that Godovius knew perfectly well all that had happened from that night to this; that her precious secret wasn't really a secret at all.

It would almost have been a relief to her if he had appeared, not only to save her from the anxiety of M'Crae's concealment, but because no material manifestation of his presence or his power could be half so wearing as the imponderable threat of his absence. For she knew that it had got to come. The story of his strange passion could not conceivably be ended by her flight from Njumba ja Mweze. She knew that he would not have let her go so lightly if he had not been confident that she couldn't really escape from the sphere of his influence. It was as though he had said: "Flutter away, tire yourself out with flutterings. I'm quite prepared to wait for you. The end will be the same." She could almost have wished that he had followed her in more passionate pursuit instead of nursing this leisurely appetite of a fat man who sits down in a restaurant waiting complacently for a meal which he has ordered with care.

II

In this way the weeks passed by. At last James was so far recovered that he was able to sit out on a long basket-chair upon the stoep, surveying the field of his labours. Every evening he would sit there until the sun set and the frogs began their chorus. His last experience of fever had made him a little fussy about himself; not so much for his own sake as because he knew that a few more attacks of this kind would make life impossible for him in that country. He might even be forced to leave it, a failure; and this humiliating prospect made him unusually careful. When he had sat on the stoep for a few evenings he began to try his legs. He walked, leaning upon Eva's arm, the length of the garden beneath the avenue of the acacias.

In those days he seemed to Eva increasingly human. Indeed, this was the nearest she ever came to loving him. "I'd no idea," he said, "what miracles you had been performing in this garden. I've been too absorbed in my work—selfishly, perhaps—to notice them before." He showed a childish interest in fruits and flowers which he had never taken the trouble to observe before. "When you have been ill indoors," he said, "everything that grows seems somehow . . . I can't get the right word—the fever has done that for me . . . somehow fresh. Almost hopeful."

They were standing together at the far end of the garden, so near to the banda that Eva knew that M'Crae must hear everything that was said. Indeed, M'Crae was listening. "Do you know, Eva," he heard James say, "I've never been inside your summer-house. It must be cool—beautifully cool on these hot afternoons. Better than the house. Do you remember the summer-house at the bottom of the garden at Far Forest? You'd never let anyone use that." M'Crae heard Eva laugh softly. "And this one's the same," she said. "You mustn't be jealous, for you've got our best room for your study." Her voice trembled a little at the end of the sentence. M'Crae realised that she was frightened for him. It disturbed him to think that a creature so beautifully innocent as Eva should be forced into dissimulation for his sake. The experience of the last few weeks seemed to have made him surprisingly sensitive on matters of honour; a curious phenomenon at his time of life. He tackled Eva the same evening.

"James would have come into the banda," she said. "You never know what might happen. Probably he would have wanted to look through into your part of it. And then . . ."

"What would you have done?"

"I should have stopped him somehow; I should have told him some story or other." She became acutely conscious of his eyes on her face and blushed. "Yes, I should have told a *lie,*" she said, "if that is what you mean."

He shook his head. "Things will get more and more difficult," he said. "For you, I mean. Now that I can look after myself, I don't think I ought to stay in your banda."

He waited a long time for her reply. She sat there with downcast eyes; and when, at last, she raised them, even though she was smiling, they were full of tears. It was a very sweet and dangerous moment. She heard the voice of James calling her from the stoep, and was glad of the excuse to leave him.

These were trying days for all of them. James didn't pick up very quickly. The weather had begun to show a variation from a type that is not altogether uncommon in the neighbourhood of isolated mountain patches such as the Luguru Hills. The time about dawn was as fresh and lovely as ever, but as the day wore on the heavy mood with which noon burdened the countryside increased. Upon the wide horizon companies of cloud massed and assembled, enormous clouds, as black and ponderable as the mountains themselves. By the hour of sunset they would threaten

69

the whole sky and ring it round as though they were laying particular siege to the Mission Station itself and must shortly overwhelm it in thunder and violent rain. Beneath this menace the sunsets were unusually savage and fantastic, lighting such lurid skies as are to be found in mediæval pictures of great battle-fields or of hell itself. These days were all amazingly quiet: as though the wild things in the bush were conscious of the threatening sky, and only waited for it to be broken with thunder or ripped with lightning flashes. With the descent of darkness this sense of anticipation grew heavier still. It was difficult to sleep for the heat and for the feeling of intolerable pressure. But when morning came not one shred of cloud would mar the sky.

As I have said, it was trying weather for all of them. For James, who read in the sunset apocalyptic terrors; for M'Crae, sweating in the confined space of Bullace's banda; for Eva, who found in the skies a reinforcement of that sense of dread and apprehension with which the menace of Godovius oppressed her. Still it would not rain and still Godovius did not come . . .

One evening M'Crae said to her suddenly:

"I never hear your Waluguru boys working near the banda now. I suppose you'll have kept them at the other end of the garden for my sake?"

She told him that she was always frightened when anyone came near him.

"You mustn't be frightened," he said. "At the worst, nothing very serious could happen. But I want you to keep them working near me. I think this sisal hedge at the back of the banda is badly in need of thinning. You can put them to weed it if you like. Any job that you like to give them, as long as they are working near me. I want to listen to them."

"They will find out that you are here," she said in a voice that was rather pitiable.

"I expect they know it already, but they probably don't know that I can understand what they say when they are talking together. I am curious, as I told you, about the Waluguru. And I'm curious about Godovius too."

Next day she put the boys to work upon a patch of sweet potatoes under the sisal hedge. In the evening when she came to M'Crae she could see that he had heard something. For all his hard experience of life he was a very simple soul. Once or twice when she spoke to him he had to wait a second to remember the echo of her question, and she quickly saw that his mind would really rather have been thinking of something else. This was the only sign of his preoccupation. In every other way he was his solemn self, taking everything that she said with a seriousness which was sometimes embarrassing. She didn't want always to be taken in such deadly earnest, and now it seemed to her almost as if he were taking advantage of this peculiarity to evade her. She wasn't going to have that.

"You might just as well tell me first as last," she said.

At this he was honestly surprised. "But how do you know I have anything to tell you?"

"You are so easy to understand," she said.

He smiled and looked at her, wondering. It had never exactly struck him that a woman could understand him so completely. Of course he knew nothing about women, but for all that he had always been completely satisfied that there wasn't much to know.

"You want me to tell you things that I'm not even sure of myself," he said.

"All the more reason . . . for I might help you."

He shook his head. "No. . . . I have to think it out myself, to piece a lot of things together: what I heard from the Masai: what I hear from you, the things I've heard the Waluguru talking about to-day. I can't tell you until I'm satisfied myself . . ."

She said: "You think I'm simply curious . . ." and blushed.

"No," he said, "you mustn't think that. You're so straight. You need never think that for one moment. Even if it were difficult I should be perfectly straight with you. We began that way. We mustn't ever be anything else. Or else . . . or else there'd be an end of . . . of what makes our friendship unlike any other that I have known. I shall never hide anything from you. Do you understand? Is that quite clear?"

She said: "Yes, I understand. I feel like that too . . ."

"Oh, but you . . ." he said. And he couldn't say any more. It was not seldom that he found himself at a loss for words in his dealings with Eva.

For two or three days M'Crae lay close to the grass wall of his banda, listening to the talk of the boys. For the most part it was a thankless and a straining task; for they talked nearly always of things which had no part in his problem: of their own life under the leaves, of James, whom they had christened N'gombe, or Ox, for the obvious reason that he was a vegetarian. Only here and there could he pick out a sentence that referred to Sakharani—it was certain that the Waluguru were afraid to speak of him—but in the end he learned enough to confirm the story of the Masai: that the Waluguru were a people among whom an old religion, connected in some way with the procreative powers of nature and the symbol of the waxing moon, survived; that this faith and its rites were associated by tradition with the hill named Kilima ja Mweze, on which the house of Godovius was built, and that a white man, now identified with Sakharani, was in some way connected with its ritual. How this might be, M'Crae could not imagine; for the thing seemed to him contrary to all nature. There was no reason for it that he could see, and the mind of M'Crae worked within strictly logical boundaries. He hadn't any conception of the kind of brain which filled Godovius's head. He simply knew that to the Waluguru he was the power they feared most on earth, as a savage people fears its gods. He was anxious to know more; this was exactly the sort of adventure for which he had lived for thirty years.

One other thing troubled him. He was certain that at some time or other he had heard a story about Godovius which now he couldn't remember; he could not even remember when or where he had heard it. But one morning, when the light which penetrated the grass walls of his banda wakened him, it suddenly returned to him; suddenly and so clearly that he wondered how he could ever have forgotten it. It concerned a woman: in all probability the woman in the photograph which Eva had seen. Of her origin he knew nothing, nor even how she had come to live with Godovius. In those days there had been another man at Njumba ja Mweze, a planter, expert in coffee, who had ordered the cultivation of Godovius's terraced fields. His name was Hirsch. He had rather fancied himself as an artist in the violent Bavarian way, and it was probable that the pictures of native women on Godovius's walls were his work. One day while the Waluguru were clearing the bush from a new patch of coffee-ground near the house they had disturbed and killed a big black mamba, one of the most deadly of African snakes. He had brought it into the house to show Godovius, who straightway discovered in it the making of an excellent practical joke. For the woman who shared their house had always lived in dread of snakes, and the dead monster coiled in her bed might very well give her a pretty fright. The joke was carefully arranged, the woman sent to bed by candlelight and the door of her room locked by Godovius as soon as she had entered. They had waited outside to listen to her shrieks of terror and she had shrieked even louder and longer than they had expected. An altogether admirable entertainment. At last she stopped her shrieking. They supposed that she had suddenly appreciated the humour of the situation. They thought that she would come out and tell them so; but she didn't—and Godovius, supposing that she was sulking, unlocked the door and went in to console her. She was lying on the bed, very white, beside the dead snake; and there was a living snake there too, which slid away through the window when Godovius entered the room. It was the mate of the dead mamba which had followed the scent of its comrade into the room and attacked the woman as soon as she appeared. She died the same evening. No one that has been bitten by a black mamba lives. It was an unpleasant story and probably would never have been known if Godovius had not quarrelled with Hirsch a few months later. Hirsch had told it to a couple of men who had come through on a shooting trip at Neu Langenburg, in the hotel where he eventually drank himself to death; for he never returned to Munich, being barely able to keep himself in liquor with the money which he earned by painting indecent pictures for the smoking-rooms of farmers on remote shambas. M'Crae had heard the yarn in Katanga. A horrible business, but one hears many strange things, and stranger, between the Congo and German East. Now, remembering it, he thought of the pathetic figure in the photograph which had shocked Eva. And this time the thing seemed more real to him, even if it had little bearing on the dangers of their present situation. He realised that he was beginning to be sentimental to a degree on the subject of women. And when he thought of women in the abstract it was easy to find a concrete and adorable example in the shape of Eva herself. He smiled at himself rather seriously, remembering his age, his vagrant way of life, his tough, battered body, the disfigurement of his lopped arm.

III

On an evening of unparalleled heaviness Godovius came at last to Luguru. He rode down in the stifling cooler air which passed for evening, tied his pony to the post of the gate and, crossing the front of the stoep on which James languished without notice, made straight for the sand-paved avenue of flamboyant trees where he knew that Eva would be found. This time there was no question of her running away from him. He came upon her midway between the house and M'Crae's banda, and she would have done anything in the world to prevent him approaching nearer to this danger-point. She stood still in the path waiting for him. It was a moment when the light of the sun was hidden by monstrous tatters of black cloud, and this suppression of the violence of white light intensified for a while a great deal of rich colour which might never have been seen in the glare of day; the tawny sand with which the avenue was floored, the rich green of the acacia leaves, the inky hue of those imminent masses of cloud . . . even the warm swarthiness of Godovius's face: the whole effect being highly coloured and fantastic as befitted this scene of melodrama. There is no doubt but that it showed Eva herself to advantage. Godovius paused to admire.

"The light of storms becomes you, Miss Eva," he said, smiling. "Nature conspires to show you at advantage . . . to advantage . . ."

It seemed to her strangely unsubtle that he should talk to her in this way; for she was sure that he knew perfectly well what she was feeling. Why should they trouble themselves with such elaborate pretence? She said:

"Why have you come here?"

"You mean: 'Why didn't you come before?' You expected me?"

"Yes, I expected you. But I didn't want you to come."

He laughed. "Very well," he said. "We won't pretend that you did; but for all that I think you used me roughly the other night. Your departure was . . . shall we say . . . lacking in ceremony. Unreasonably so, I think. For what had I done? What confidence had I abused?"

She shook her head. "You must not ask me to explain," she said. "You won't press me to do so. I wish you hadn't come now. It will be a good deal better if you will leave us alone. I think we should go our own ways. It will be better like that. I wish you would go now . . ."

"But that is ridiculous," he said. "In as desolate place like this you can't quarrel about nothing with your only neighbour. In the middle of a black population it is necessary that the whites should keep together. Your brother would understand. I don't think you realise what it means. I'll tell you what it means. . . . And yet I don't think there is anything to be gained by that. It is you who must tell me what is the matter with you. Tell me why you were frightened where there was nothing to fear. What were you frightened of?"

She would not answer him. He became agitated and spoke faster.

"I suppose you were frightened of me. Oh, you were very clever. . . . But why should you have been frightened? Because of the name of Sakharani, the ridiculous name that I told you. Because you thought I was drunk? I told you, long ago, that there was more than one way of drunkenness. Ah well, to-night it is a drunken man that you face. Listen to me, how I stammer. How the words will not come. You see, I am drunk . . . burning drunk. You who stand there like a statue, a beautiful statue of snow, can't the tropics melt you? . . . How long have I waited for this day!"

There came to her a sudden glow of thankfulness that this had not happened on that terrible night and in that strange house. Here, in the homeliness of her own garden, the situation seemed to have lost some of its terror.

And all the time, in the back of her mind, she was wanting to keep him away from the banda in which M'Crae was lying. She said: "My brother is in the house. If you want him, I will show you the way."

He would not let her pass.

"I don't want to see your brother," he said. "It is you that I want. That is why I came here. Why can't you trust me? Why? You are not like your brother. . . . Your brother will be all right. You are meant for me. That is why you came here to Luguru; that was what brought you to me the other night. You don't realise your beautiful youth . . . the use of life. You are like a cold, northern meadow in a dream of winter. You lie waiting for the sun. And I am like the sun. It is for you to awaken into spring. You don't know the beauty of which you are capable. And you'll never know it. You'll never blossom in loveliness. You'll waste your youth and your strength on your damned brother, and then you'll marry, when there is no more hope, some bloodless swine of a clergyman like him. So to your death. You will have no life. Death is all they think of. And here is life waiting for you—life bursting, overflowing, like the life of the forest. You won't have it. You will fly in the face of nature, you'll fight forces stronger than yourself . . ."

His enthusiasm spent itself. He fell to tenderness. She was like a flower, he said, a fragile, temperate flower that he had tried to pluck as if it had been a great bloom of the forest. It had not been fair to her. So rein, und schön und hold. So like Eva. She must forget all his drunkenness. It was not thus that the spring sun beat upon the northern fields. More gently, more gently, and he was capable of gentleness too. No people were more gentle than the Germans, even as no people could be more magnificently passionate. "We feel more deeply than other races," he said. "It is a fault, sometimes, but a magnificent fault." He seemed to think that by this sudden change of tactics she must inevitably be softened.

She stood with face turned away, conscious of his outstretched hands.

She said: "When you have finished . . ."

"Ah . . . you think you have beaten me," he said. "But what if I don't let you go?"

"You will let me go," she said. "You can't frighten me as you did Hamisi. And you can't keep me here. You know you can't. It wouldn't be decent or honourable."

"There is no honour here," he said. "You're in the middle of Africa. No one can judge between us. . . . That is why you're mad," he added, with a gesture of impatience, "to waste your beauty, your life. Oh, mad . . ."

She would not reply to him.

"And there is another thing which you don't remember. You don't realise my power. Power is a good thing. I am fond of it. I possess it. In this place I am as reverenced as God. In another way I am as powerful as the Deity; there is nothing that is hidden from me. Now do you see, now do you see how you stand? Think. . . . You love your brother? So . . . your brother is in my hands. This mission is only here because I allow it. If I will that it succeed, it will succeed. If I decide that it shall fail, it will fail. I can break your brother. If you love him it will be better for us to be friends. And that is not all . . ."

He waited and she knew what was coming. She felt that she was going to cry out in spite of herself. She heard herself swallow.

"I know other things. I happen to know exactly how much your pretence of immaculate virtue is worth. We have always known that the first characteristic of the English is hypocrisy. Do you think I don't know all about the guest in your banda? No doubt the news would entertain your brother, who is already shocked by the morals of the Waluguru. A very pretty little romance, which has no doubt been more amusing to you than it would have been to him. I believe your missionaries are very particular on the point of personal example, and it is possible that he would . . . shall we say? . . . disapprove. Oh, but you need not be frightened. I shall not tell him, unless it happens to suit me. As a nation we are very broad-minded. We do not preach. And I do not condemn you. That is the most orthodox Christianity. It is natural that a young and beautiful woman should have a lover. It is natural that she should have more than one lover. I am gentleman enough not to grudge you your romance, even if I don't altogether approve your taste. So, now that your pretence of indignant virtue is disposed of, there is a possibility that you will be natural. I am not unreasonable. I merely ask that I may share these distinguished privileges. Obviously no harm can be done. I am content to be one of . . . as many as you wish. Women have found me a lover not wholly undesirable. I am not old, or unappreciative of your beauty. Now you will understand."

She understood.

"You have nothing to say? I have sprung a little surprise on you? Very well. I am sufficiently gallant not to hurry you. You shall think it over. A week will give you time to think. It is always a shock for a virtuous woman to realise.... But we will leave it at that. You will see that I am neither jealous nor ungenerous. You have an opportunity of doing a good turn to your brother and to the man in whom, to my mind, you are so unreasonably interested. One may be magnanimous. You call it 'playing the game.' You shall think it over, and then we shall come to an agreement—but you wouldn't be so foolish as not to do so—certain unavoidable things will happen; as unavoidable as if they were acts of God. I am God here. And you will have yourself to thank. So, for the present, we'll say 'Auf Wiedersehn.' Perhaps you would like to return to your friend in the banda. He will help you to make up your mind. You can tell him that this is a bad place for ivory. The elephants played the devil with my plantations and were all killed years ago. When he wants to go back he had better apply to me for his porters. As to whether he'll have any further need for porters . . . well, that's for you to decide. His fate is in your very beautiful hands."

With this he left her.

CHAPTER IX
He left her standing alone under the avenue of acacia. A variety of projects swiftly filled her mind. She must go to M'Crae, and tell him everything. It was strange that M'Crae came first. She must find James without further delay and explain to him the difficulty in which she was placed. But it wouldn't be easy to explain; the process involved the whole story of the fugitive, and she wasn't sure that this was hers to tell. And in any case, James would be sure to misunderstand. She realised, for the first time, that her relation with M'Crae actually might be misunderstood; and this filled her, more than ever, with a sort of blind anger which wouldn't let her see things clearly. It overwhelmed her with shame to think that M'Crae, too, must look at the matter in the odious light which Godovius had suggested. It seemed to her that the lovely innocence of their relation had been smirched for ever. She must have time to think. Now she couldn't think at all. If she were to creep quietly into the house and shut herself up in her bedroom she would be able to cry; and then, perhaps, it would be easier. Beneath this awful heavy stillness of the charged sky she could do nothing. It seemed to her in the silence that all the enormous, unfriendly waste of country was just waiting quietly to see what she would do. Yes, she had better go to her room and cry. And then, before she knew what was happening, a demon of wind swept down from the sky and filled the branches of the avenue above her with rushing sound. A scurry of red sand came whirling along the path, and above her the black sky burst into a torrent of rain; rain so violent that in a moment her flimsy dress was saturated. Beneath this radical and alarming remedy for mental anguish she abandoned any attempt at

making up her mind. She simply ran for shelter to the nearest that offered itself, and this was naturally the banda of M'Crae.

She arrived, breathless, and beautifully flushed. M'Crae was lying at the end of the banda next the path. She could see that he had been watching them all the time, even though he could not have heard them. Through the flimsy wall of grass he had pushed the muzzle of his rifle.

He smiled up at her. "You see, I had him covered," he said. "Now you'd better tell me all about it."

Then, quite against her will, she began to cry, making queer little noises of which she would have been ashamed if she had been able to think about them. It had to come . . .

To M'Crae the position, in its sudden intimacy, was infinitely embarrassing. At any time it would have been painful for him to have seen a woman cry; but Eva was no ordinary woman in his eyes. She had brought, in a little time, a tender and very beautiful ideal into his life. He had thought of her as the incarnation of all the lovely and desirable things which had passed for ever out of his grasp, and chiefly of youth, which carries an atmosphere of beauty in itself. But even more than this, he had worshipped her naturalness and bravery, so that it was a terrible thing for him to see her in tears. He knew that no everyday trouble could have broken her simple and confident courage, and the consciousness of this adorable weakness overwhelmed him even more than his admiration of her strength. He saw in a moment what a child she was, and longed to protect her, as a young man and a lover might have done. He realised suddenly that the right to do this had passed from him, years ago . . . years ago. His eyes filled with tears, and he could do nothing; for the only things which he might naturally have done were obviously included in the prerogative of that parental interest which is the name under which the middle-aged man most often hides a furtive sensuality. Altogether, the matter was too harrowing in its complications for an honest man to deal with, and M'Crae, as we have said, found himself in these days a mass of the most sensitive scruples. For all this he felt that he couldn't merely sit there with tears in his eyes and do nothing. It was natural for him to put out his hand and take hold of her arm. Though she had often enough been nearer to him than this in her ministrations, he had never actually touched her before. Through the sodden muslin of her sleeve his fingers became conscious of her arm's softness.

He felt the piteous impulse of her sobbing. Perhaps it was because of the coldness of the wet sleeve which he pressed against her arm that Eva shivered, and M'Crae felt that he had been surprised in an indelicacy. Yet he had only done the thing which seemed most natural to him. All the time that she was sobbing, and he so desperately embarrassed by her tears, the rain was beating on the roof of the banda, so that if they had spoken they could scarcely have heard each other; and in a little time its violence penetrated the slanting reeds of the roof, and water dripped upon them; splashing into pits of the sandy floor. This rain did not fall as if it were harried by wind, but with a steady violence, increased from time to time to an intolerable pitch, as though the sky were indeed possessed by some brooding intelligence determined to lash the land without pity. Eva had never heard such rain. For an hour, maybe, they crouched together without speaking, and at the end of it, when the wildness of the storm had abated a little, she had managed to pull together her broken thoughts and make some decision as to what she would do.

In the beginning she had imagined that she must tell M'Crae everything, but when the first moment at which this might have happened had passed, and her fit of crying had overtaken her, she began to count the consequences. She knew that he would not stay at Luguru for a moment if his presence endangered her peace. She knew that he would do anything in the world to save her; and it suddenly struck her that this involved an obligation on her side. She must not throw him into Godovius's hands. Even if she had not realised this duty, there was always in the back of her mind the conviction that M'Crae was, in fact, the only man on whom she could rely. She had felt the pressure of his fingers on her arm, and even though she had shivered she had been touched by this rather pathetic attempt at sympathy. In that moment he became no longer a man to be relied on, but one to be protected. In an ardent vision she saw herself saving the two of them. Him and James. How? . . . Godovius had offered her terms. From this alone she knew that she had power to deal with him, to make some sort of bargain, if only she had time. Time was the thing for which she must fight. Given time, some happy chance might move them from Luguru altogether. It seemed that it might even be necessary for her to receive Godovius's addresses. Even if it came to that, she was determined to see the matter through. As the minutes passed, and the strain of the sobs which she could not control abated, she began to see the whole matter more clearly. The rainfall, too, was becoming less intense, and the evenness of her mood was increased by the peculiar atmosphere of relief which descends on all living creatures when a tropical sky has been washed with heavy rain. So strangely was her state of mind modified by the downpour, that she was almost happy. Now that the storm was lighter she would be able to run into the house without getting much more wet, and above all things she was anxious to escape any ordeal of questions.

"You're like to get very damp," said M'Crae. She knew that this was his last way of asking her to tell him what had happened; and if he had pressed her, as he might easily have done, it is probable that her resolutions would have vanished and she would have told him. She smiled and shook her head. In that dim light, under the dripping banda roof, he looked very pathetic. It occurred to her that she had better hurry up. Outside it was still raining, as it might rain in the height of a thunderstorm at home. The eastern sky was ringed with masses of lurid yellow cloud. In the garden the hot earth steamed already, and the rain had washed away the sandy path, which it had been her pleasant labour to construct. Between her and the house a tawny torrent ran. She made a rush for the stoep, and while she ran, with her skirts picked up, she laughed as she would have done when she was a child running in from the rain.

The person who felt the strain of this enforced imprisonment between four walls most deeply was James. Every day of late he had been gaining strength and looking forward more than ever to the renewal of his work. He had even been less concerned with his minor prophets and had picked up from among a heap of Mr. Bullace's books an account of the life and labours of his great forerunner, Mackay of Uganda. This book, the work of the missionary's sister, had impressed him enormously. It was strange that he had never come across it before; for the early field of Mackay's splendid failures had lain upon the edge of the Masai steep, only a few hundred miles to the northward of Luguru. There, in his collapsible boat, Mackay had explored the waters of the Lukigura and the greater Wami; there he had first striven with the coastal Arabs, by whose whips chained gangs of slaves were driven from the Great Lakes to Bagamoyo and Zanzibar. He read how Mackay's comrades had died of fever, one by one: how the missionary himself had been beaten from time to time by that most cruel land, how he had overcome at last, by virtue of hardihood and enthusiasm, obstacles far greater than any which had stood in the steps of the most famous African explorers. It filled him with a flaming hope to realise that the caravans of shackled slaves moved no more along the trade routes through M'papwa on their way to the coastal markets; but he knew that a slavery as degrading was still the lot of peoples such as the Waluguru, among whom his business lay.

He was very excited about it all, and wanted Eva to read the book. "You'll see," he said, "that we have no cause to grumble. A glorious life: a wonderful death. And yet one can't help feeling that small isolated peoples like the Waluguru have been left behind. Missionaries have been eager to get at the intelligent races, such as the Baganda, and left the more primitive for poor people such as us. I almost think that our task is more difficult. There are things I can't understand about them. It is a privilege to be dealing with virgin soil . . . and yet . . ."

Always when he spoke of virgin soil the old hunter's warning as to the deadly humours which its disturbance released returned to him.

"When the rain stops," he said, "I shall be able to start work again. Mackay's story has taught me a lot. I sha'n't expect quite so much. I hope this weather will be over by Sunday. It may change by then, for on that day there's a new moon. We always used to say at home that the weather took a turn for the better or worse when the new moon came."

She listened to him, but only heard the words that he said without entering into his thoughts. Her own mind was too full of wondering what she was going to do, always obstinately hoping that time would show her a way out of her difficulties. Only occasionally a word would detach itself from James' conversation and startle her by its peculiar suggestions. Such was his conventional mention of the new moon. The two words had suddenly thrust his presence into the full current of her subconscious mind. And the strangeness of this frightened her. It made her suddenly want to tell James everything; but when she turned, almost resolved upon the spur of the moment to do so, she found that the gleam of intimacy had faded and that she couldn't possibly do anything of the sort: that James was as distant and precise as ever, an absolute stranger whom she could never hope to understand, far more of a stranger even than M'Crae.

During the rainy days she saw as much as she dared of M'Crae; but it was hard to find an excuse for going to her banda in the wet. He suffered there a good deal of discomfort, which struck her as intolerable, but which he almost seemed to enjoy. "A wonderful thing, rain," he said. "In a dry land like this. When you've lived longer in Africa you'll know how precious it is."

She tried to make him as dry and comfortable as she could. She knew that he was watching her narrowly, felt that he was waiting for her to tell him all that had happened with Godovius, but though she knew well enough that she couldn't keep it up for ever, she didn't see how matters would be bettered by her telling. In a way it was almost as well that he shouldn't know how she stood between him and disaster. If he had asked her. . . . But he didn't. He had seen on the first night that for some reason or other she didn't want to take him into her confidence, and had decided, in pursuance of the peculiarly delicate code of behaviour which his idealism had invented for their relation, that it was not for him to press her. Everything that she did, every one of the little tendernesses by which she ravished his soul, must be of her own sweet giving. He had an infinite and touching faith in her simple wisdom. And it is difficult to say what would have happened, how this story might have ended, if she had told him. From the beginning it had been certain that it must come to an end of violence. It is possible that M'Crae would have killed Godovius. For the sake of Eva he would certainly have doubled the offence for which he had lost his name and suffered for so many years. His own life would have been the last thing which he would have considered. In the end it was the last thing.

CHAPTER X

I

For three days the rain fell so heavily that the mission lay isolated on its hillside, as surely as if the country had been submerged by floods. And yet no waterways appeared. That dry land drank the water as it fell to reach the hidden channels by which it had drained for centuries into the central ooze of the M'ssente Swamp. On Sunday, the fourth day, the rain ceased about the time of a sullen and misty dawn, and by ten o'clock in the morning the sun had triumphed. No one would have believed that any rain had lately fallen; for the bush was full of dry and brittle sound; the leaves of the undergrowth were of the same ashen hue; the straggling candelabra cactus stood as withered as if they were dying of drought; the hornbills were calling on every side. Only on the higher mountain slopes, where the grassland had been burnt to a shade of pale amber, a sudden and surprising flush of the most tender green appeared, as transitory, alas! as it was beautiful.

There could have been no more lovely or affecting augury for James' return to work. He was up early, walking to and fro upon the stoep, watching a flight of starlings, whose glossy plumes shone in flight with the blue of the kingfisher. The night before he had struggled through a long conversation with the headman of the nearest Waluguru village, that circle of squat bandas from which their own servant, Hamisi, came. He had made it the occasion of an experiment upon the new lines which his reading of the life of Mackay had suggested. He had found the man more curious about the use of the steel carpentering tools with which the mission was well supplied than any questions of morality or faith, and when he had gone James had also missed a chisel. But that didn't matter. It was the price of an interest which he hadn't imagined to be possible in the apathetic mind of the Waluguru. He was beginning to see his way. Even if it meant the sacrifice of some sabbatarian scruples, he was prepared to go through with it. "To-morrow, M'zinga," he said at parting, "I will show you other things. To-morrow, after the service at the church. All these things and many more wonderful you can learn from books. In a little while we will have a school, and I will teach your totos to read Swahili." And M'zinga had smiled with that soft, sly smile of Africa . . .

On Sunday mornings, at half-past nine, it had been the privilege of the boy Hamisi to go down to the chapel and ring the little bell. It pleased him, for it was a work that needed little effort; the toy produced an unusual noise and the performance exalted him above his fellows. At the best it was a small and pathetic sound in the midst of so great a wilderness, but very pleasing to the ears of James. This Sunday morning he was a little restless. As he paced the stoep, with his Bible in his hands behind his back, the time seemed to pass more slowly than usual. He looked at his watch. It was already half-past nine. He called to Eva in the kitchen to see if his watch was fast. "Five and twenty to ten," she called. He was annoyed. The Africans, no doubt, were sleeping. They would sleep for ever unless they were disturbed. But Hamisi had never failed him before. He hurried across the compound to the hut in which they slept. They were neither of them there. For a moment he was angry, but then remembered that forbearance was the better part; that even the best of Africans were unreliable. Some day a time would come when things would be different. Until then he must work for himself.

He set off, almost cheerfully, down the sandy path toward the chapel. The rain had scoured its surface clean of the red sand and disclosed beneath a mosaic of quartz, pure white and yellow and stained with garnet-red. The fine crystals sparkled in the sun. "So many hidden wonders," he thought. It came into his mind that there might even be precious stones among them. He picked up a little fragment of pure silicon and held it up to the sun. "So many hidden wonders . . ." He put it in his pocket.

In the middle of the path, in a pocket of sand round which the storm water had swirled, one of the lily-like flowers of Africa had thrust its spiky leaves. The rain and sun had nursed it into sudden bloom, and the pale cups drooped at his feet. "In this way," he thought, "the whole world praises God. Behold the lilies of the field . . ."

His first instinct was to pick the flower; but on second thoughts he had left it, hoping that Eva would see it also on her way down. He passed for a little while between close walls of tall grasses on the edge of the bush. Through this channel a clean wind moved with a silky sound, and its movement gave to the air, newly washed by rain, a feeling of buoyancy and freedom, a quality which was almost hopeful. It was a wonderful thing, he thought, to be alive and well. His soul was full of thankfulness.

He came at last to the church. Hamisi was not there, and so he settled down comfortably to toll the bell himself. The incident would be an amusing one to write home about. There were many little things like that in Mackay's letters. From that high slope the note of the bell would penetrate the edge of the forest, and soon his congregation would appear, the men in their decent gowns of white, the women in their shawls of amerikani print, the bright-eyed, pot-bellied children. And this was a new beginning . . .

He tolled the bell until his watch showed the time to be five minutes short of the hour, but up to this time none of his congregation had appeared. He began to feel a little nervous and puzzled. It couldn't be that he had mistaken the hour, for the Waluguru took their time from his chapel bell. He wondered if, by some ridiculous miscalculation, he had mistaken the day. The idea was grotesque. And yet when he was ill he had missed two whole days as completely as if he had been lying dead. No . . . it couldn't be that. Only the day before he had verified it. It was Sunday. He remembered the text on the German calendar, which he had struggled to translate, and above the number of the day the little concave shape of the new moon. He remembered telling Eva that the weather would be likely to change.

At ten o'clock exactly he entered the church. Eva was sitting there in her usual place; otherwise the building was empty. It smelt stale and slightly musty with the odour of black flesh. He remembered suddenly that once before he had entered an empty church that smelt like that. Where or when, he couldn't imagine . . . either in some other life or in a dream. The coincidence made him shiver.

And Eva was sitting there, very pale. When he stalked past her her lips moved in a piteous shape, as if she wanted to speak or to cry. But he would not stay for her to speak. He went straight to his desk and began to read the form of worship which their own Church prescribed, just as if he might have been conducting a service in the small stone chapel at Far Forest. For Eva this was a very terrible experience. It seemed to her somehow unreasonable to prolong what she could only think of as an elaborate and insane pantomime. She felt that, after all, it would have been so much simpler for her to explain, to take him aside and tell him that this was nothing but a freakish demonstration of the power of Godovius, a hint to her of the kind of torture which it would be easy for him to employ. But James spared her nothing. Instead of the familiar Swahili words, they sang together a hymn of Moody and Sankey, which had been a favourite of her father's, a wearisome business of six long verses. The performance nearly did for her. All the time she was ridiculously conscious of the feebleness of their two voices in that empty, echoing church. She was almost driven to distraction by the impersonality of James. "Afterwards I will tell him," she thought. She wanted to tell him there and then, but the immense force of tradition restrained her. It wouldn't have been any use for her to tell him: for the time he was no longer her brother—only a ministering priest rapt in the service of his Deity. Never in her life had she felt more irreligious. No vestige of the illusion of religion could overcome the excitement of her own fear. Reading alternate verses they recited a psalm of David, a passionate song against idolaters; and a little of the passion came through into the voice of James, so that he spoke less precisely than usual, like a peasant of Far Forest, forgetting the accent which the training college had taught him. His voice rose and fell and echoed in the little church:

"Insomuch that they worshipped their idols, which turned to their own decay; yea, they offered their sons and their daughters unto devils."

And she heard herself reply:

"And shed innocent blood, even the blood of their sons and their daughters; whom they offered unto the idols of Canaan; and the land was defiled with blood."

—heard her own voice, lowered and reverentially unreal. She supposed that women always spoke like that in church; as if they were afraid of hurting the words they spoke. She was thankful when the psalm was over.

And then James prayed. In their denomination the long extempore prayer was an important part of the service, and ministers were apt to acquire a rather dangerous fluency. But that morning James was inspired, if ever a man was inspired, with religious ecstasy. He wrestled with God. In his words, in the commonplaces of religious phrase, glowed a passion to which she could not be wholly insensible. She pitied him . . . pitied him. It seemed to her that God must surely pity a man whose soul was so abased and in such agony. At times he rose to something that was very like eloquence. One phrase she always remembered. He had been speaking of Africa—that sombre and mighty continent and its vast recesses of gloom—and then he burst into a sudden and fervent appeal for light, for a cleansing light which might penetrate not only Africa but "these dark continents of my heart . . ." The dark continents of my heart. Those were the words which she remembered in after days.

For a little while he knelt in silence, praying, and then, hurriedly, he left the church before she knew what he was doing. She put out her hand to detain him, but he shook his head and said: "Not now, Eva, not now . . ."

She was left standing alone at the door of the church. No other soul was near. In the mid-day quiet of the bush she heard a small bird singing. It was a rain-bird, and its simple song of three descending notes subtly wooed her dazed mind to a remembrance of the bells of the little church at Mamble, whose homely music floats above the wooded valleys to the green beyond Far Forest. And in a moment of vision she was assailed by the tender, wistful atmosphere of a Sunday in the March of Wales, where simple people and children were perhaps at that moment moving to church between the apple orchards, and men were standing in their shirt-sleeves at their garden gates. A gust of warm wind swept through the bush, carrying with it the odour of aromatic brushwood. It was this scent that broke and dispelled her dream.

II
Above all other things James wanted to be alone, not in his church nor in the horror of the forest, but in his own room at the mission. He passed swiftly over the

path which he had followed that morning so happily; he entered the empty mission-house and locked himself in his bedroom. The sudden disillusionment which had come to him in the empty church had overwhelmed him; but when the first shock of the incident had passed and he lay upon his bed, with his hands pressed to his eyes, conscious only of the extreme heat and of his throbbing pulse, he suddenly found himself able to think more clearly. In spite of his passion he was almost calm. He realised, in the hardest terms, that he was facing a power which might be the ruin of his mission; that he wasn't merely opposed by the vast apathy of Africa, but by something definite and appallingly strong. He saw that his real troubles were beginning; that, even if he failed, he had got to fight. It was the first time in his life that he had been forced to stand with his back to the wall.

Already he had a suspicion of the cause of the trouble. The problem towards which M'Crae had been attracted in his amateur studies of ethnology by the stories of the Masai was presented to James for solution, with no evidence beyond the few dark hints which he had gathered in his work among the Waluguru and the collateral testimony, the significance of which he had hardly realised before, present in the only book with which he was intimately acquainted: his Bible. But already he had picked up the scent. A lucky mischance, the purest accident in the world, had arranged that the psalm which he had chosen for the day's service had been the hundred and sixth. In the idolatry of the children of Israel, which the Psalmist so passionately lamented, he found a significant parallel. In a little while his imagination was at work. He sat at the table, turning over the worn pages of his Bible, finding everywhere in the songs of the prophets words which strengthened his incredible surmise.

The new moon. . . . That was the key to his suspicions. A number of sinister remembrances came to reinforce the idea. He remembered the young girl in the Waluguru village who had disappeared about the time of the new moon. He remembered the story of the boy Onyango, who had said that on the night of the new moon the Waluguru would kill him if he were found in the forest. He remembered, astonished that he should not have noticed it before, the name of that smooth mountain and of the house of Godovius itself. The moon. . . . He wondered how he could have been so blind. And the heathen inhabitants of Canaan worshipped the moon in abominable rites. Ashtoreth, the Goddess of Groves, was a moon deity. And Moloch. . . . Who was Moloch? The Bible would tell him; and most of all his own passionate prophets. He opened Isaiah.

"Bring no more vain oblations: incense is an abomination unto me; the new moons and sabbaths, the calling of assemblies I cannot away with; it is iniquity, even the solemn meeting.

"Your new moons and your appointed feasts my soul hateth; they are a trouble to me; I am weary to bear them . . ."

Someone was knocking at the door. He supposed it was Eva. Well, Eva must wait. He was sorry for her; he would explain later. He came to the door and spoke.

He was astonished at the steadiness of his own voice. He said: "Don't be frightened and please don't disturb me. I must be alone to-day."

"But your door was locked. I wanted to see you if I could. I want to speak to you," she said.

"Later, later.... Not now."

She told him that his dinner was nearly ready.

"I don't want food," he said. "Don't think I'm doing anything desperate. I'm not. I only want to think. Now be a good girl..."

Baal and Ashtoreth and Moloch.... He wished that he could go into the library at college and look the business up. In those days he had never taken that sort of thing seriously. It had seemed to him so utterly divorced from the spiritual needs of the present day.

A strange people, the Waluguru. He remembered that once Godovius had told him that they were of Semitic blood, a remnant of those Sabæans whose queen had corrupted the court of Solomon, a fair-skinned people who had sailed to Africa for gold. And Godovius was a Jew.... It was plausible, plausible. And yet, in these days...

For all that, the Jews had never failed to be attracted by the worship of lascivious Syrian deities. Ahaz, he remembered, who "burnt incense in the valley of Hinnom and burnt his children in the fire after the abominations of the heathen.... He sacrificed also and burnt incense in the high places and on the hills and under every green tree."

"The high places and on the hills..." Kilima ja Mweze: the hill of the moon.

He remembered the denunciations of the prophet Ezekiel: "For when I brought them into the land for the which I lifted up my hand to give it to them, then they saw every high hill and all the thick trees, and they offered there their sacrifices.... Thou hast built thy high place at the head of every way and hast made thy beauty to be abhorred, and hast opened thy feet to every one that passed by, and multiplied thy whoredom."

And then, with a chilly heart, he passed from these prophecies to the awful legends of Tophet and the sacrifice of children in the fires of Moloch. These passages, in their mystery, had always seemed to him among the most terrible in the Old Testament. He seemed to remember a lecture in which he had been told that Moloch was the male counterpart of Ashtoreth or Astarte, the great goddess of fertility; that the worship of both, and the licentious rites with which their mysteries were celebrated on Syrian hill-tops, were really ceremonies of homoeopathic magic by the practice of which the fertility of fields and cattle might be increased.

So far, at any rate, the planter, Godovius, if he believed in any such superstitions, had an object. But there must be more in it than this. It was possible that in his rôle of hierophant he might be able to exert a more terrible power over his slaves, the Waluguru. A man will do almost anything for the lust of power; and one presupposed that Godovius was in some way a psychopathic and a megalomaniac. Those were the two types of mind in which the moral decadence of modern Germany had been most productive. Was this the ecstasy which had won him the name of Sakharani? Or was it a simpler, more crudely carnal passion, for which this worship gave him an excuse, a celebration of those phallic rites with which the Cilician high places had been defiled?

"Soon, at any rate, I shall know," he thought. Perhaps the Waluguru, whom the boy Onyango had feared, would kill him, before he had surprised their secret. For a long time he lay on his bed contemplating the dangers of his new duty. And then, for a long time, he prayed.

III

Now, at any cost, he was determined to see for himself. Nothing must stand between him and his duty. This was a man's work. He decided that Eva must have no part in it; and so, a little later in the afternoon, when the fiercer heat of the day was waning, he left his locked room by way of the folding windows and took his way towards the forest. This time he went there with none of the vague terrors which had troubled him before: apart from a suspicion of shame in his deliberate secrecy, he had no misgivings. He was happy to find himself so firm in his purpose, thankful that the fever had left him free to meet this ordeal.

By the time of sunset he had reached the edge of the forest, in the very hour at which its life awakened. As he passed into its shadow he was conscious of this, as of a faint stirring in many millions of awakened leaves suddenly aware of his presence. In this he found nothing sinister. He was only filled with a wonder which had never come to him in moments less intense at the existence of these countless multitudes of green living creatures to whom the power of motion was denied. He was impressed with the patience and helplessness of vegetable life, seeing an aged and enormous tree strangled where it grew by the writhing coils of some green parasite. And yet it seemed to him that life must be far easier for a tree than for a man. A light breeze, herald of the evening, threw the plumes of the forest edge into tossing confusion. The ways of the wood were full of gentle sound.

And suddenly it was dark. He was on the edge of the nearest Waluguru village, the home of the mission boy, Hamisi. He did not want all the people of the forest to know of his errand; but blundering in the dark he found himself under the shadow of their bandas, and seeing that concealment was useless, he entered the circle of the village. The sound of his step set up a small commotion among their goats, who were folded within a boma of thorns, but no human shape came to welcome him in the village. He went to the door of the headman's hut, expecting to find the man M'zinga, who had stolen his chisel. But M'zinga was not there, nor any of the wives of M'zinga. And this struck him as strange; for only a little time before the youngest of these women had given birth to a baby, whom it was his ambition to baptize. He tried another hut. All were empty. The village was empty and stank more foully than if it had been crammed with Waluguru. It was as if some plague had stricken its people, leaving nothing behind but the stench of corruption.

He pushed on. In a little while he came to the M'ssente river, whose crossings he now knew so well. By this time his eyes were becoming accustomed to the gloom of the forest, so that when he came to the felled tree which served him for a bridge he was astonished at the amount of light which still lingered in the sky and its faint reflections cast upwards from that swift, dark water. Lingering here a moment, entranced by the sound of the stream and the glimpse of open sky, his eye was surprised by a sudden gleam of silver. It was the broken image of the new moon's silver sickle. He raised his eyes to the sky in which that pale and lovely shape was rising. He watched her sailing upwards through the indigo air. And while he watched, it seemed to him that other eyes must have seen her. In the distance, over towards Kilima ja Mweze, he heard the throbbing of a drum.

At length he came to the village at which he had first surprised the devil dance. This, too, was empty, empty and stinking. He wondered why it was that Waluguru villages smelt so horrible at night. Where had the people of all these villages assembled? The words of Isaiah returned to him: "The new moons and sabbaths, the calling of assemblies I cannot away with. Your new moons and your appointed feasts my soul hateth." And the baffling sound of drums drew nearer. On every side he heard the throbbing of drums. It was as though all the drums of Africa had been gathered together for this assembly. Every moment it seemed to him that the night grew more suffocating. He felt afraid of the darkness, as children are afraid. . . .

He had come to that thinner zone of the forest in which the terraced walks which had puzzled Eva began. And now it seemed to him that the wood was full of more than shadows. On every side of him, in the darkness, he heard the rustle of bodies moving through the leaves. He was conscious of the smell of the castor oil with which the Waluguru smear their limbs. Sometimes he heard the sound of heavy breathing and once or twice a laugh or a stifled cry. A terrible and bewildering experience. He could see nothing; and yet he knew that the darkness was crowded with men and women hurrying to and fro, who heeded him no more than if he had been a shadow, and were as intangible as shadows themselves.

Nor was this all; for it seemed to him that this atmosphere of hidden evil—for assuredly it was a devilish thing—aroused in him a curious excitement. It was as though there were in his composition nerve-endings of which his senses had never been cognisant, and his mind never master, which were responding against his will to these ancient and most subtle stimuli. He didn't feel sure of the self of which he thought he had explored the utmost hidden recesses. Perhaps it was the hypnotic influence of the drums' monotonous rhythm; perhaps some special enchantment hidden in this darkness full of whispers and breathings and stifled cries. He understood now what the old writers had experienced when they invented a devil, an incarnation of the spirit of evil. He wanted to turn his back and run away from the whole adventure. He lay in the grass and prayed.

Thus fortified, he struggled on, climbing the zigzag path which skirted the Sabæan terraces. In the act of climbing he was happily less conscious of that populous darkness. In front of him many lights flickered through the trees. The noise of the drums grew very near. Suddenly, rounding a corner in the twisting way, he found himself on the edge of an open expanse, a wide shoulder of the hill, from which the light had come. For fear of being discovered he dropped down on his stomach in the grass. He slipped, and the blades at which he clutched cut his hands. In the middle of that shoulder of the hill stood the circular building of undressed stone which had astonished Eva on the night of her visit to the House of the Moon; but here there was no longer mystery or desertion; the open ground was crowded with black men and women. From his place of concealment in the spear-grass he could look straight through the gateway in the outer wall to the circular kiln which rose in the centre of the building. Here a fierce fire of wood was burning, the core, indeed, of all that buzzing activity. Towards it the men and women of the Waluguru, whom he had heard moving and panting in the darkness, were carrying bundles of dry fuel. They ran to and fro like the black ants, which the Swahili call maji ya moto (boiling water), from the seething noise which they make when they are disturbed. Even so this welter of the Waluguru boiled and sweated; and to add to the fantastic horror of the scene, which resembled some ancient picture of a corner in hell, the flames in the central kiln crackled and flared, casting immense shadows from the black forms which leapt around them, flinging tongues of light to search the dark sky and lighten the swaying crowns of the forest trees. Sometimes, in this upper darkness, the vagrant lights would pick out the wings of pale birds that fluttered there. These were the doves which had nested within crevices of the walls.

But what most deeply filled the heart of James with dread was the expression of the faces of the naked men and women who danced about the flame. They were not the faces, the pitiable human masks of the Waluguru, but the faces of devils. He saw the transformed features of men whom he knew well: the mouth of the mission boy Hamisi, opened wide in horrible laughter, the red eyes of the headman, M'zinga. M'zinga was carrying the stolen chisel, waving it as his muscles twitched to the rhythm of the drums. He danced right up to the mouth of the kiln, then suddenly collapsed before it, hacking at himself with the sharpened edge till his legs streamed with blood. James could not see the end of this horror, for a company of sweating fuel-bearers from the depths of the forest swarmed before him, pushing the crowd to right and left. They threw the branches which they had carried on the fire. There followed a hissing of sap, for the boughs were green, and a cloud of smoke spouted from the chimney of the kiln. At the crackling of the furnace the fuel-bearers shouted for joy, scattering in the crowd of women, some of whom they dragged away into the edge of the forest. The acrid wood-smoke made the eyes of James smart.

And now the furnace was so heated that the stones which lined it shone with a white heat. No more loads of fuel were brought to it from the outer woods, and though the drumming never ceased, it seemed as though the wilder ecstasy of the dancers had worn itself out. They lay stretched out, many of them, on the sandy ground in attitudes of abandonment and fatigue, their sweaty bodies shining like wet ebony. James noticed a thing which he had not seen before: a group of women, swathed in the black cloth, which the Waluguru affect, who had been sitting patiently on the right hand of the opening in the temple wall. The nearest of them he recognised as that slim girl the wife of the headman M'zinga; in her arms, held tightly to her breast, she carried her baby. From time to time she covered it with her black cotton cloth to shield its face from the scorching fire.

Already James had guessed what was coming. Standing at the side of the furnace door, he saw a tall man in white. He heard a whisper of the word Sakharani . . . Sakharani. In a moment another figure had leapt out into the light. It was the headman, M'zinga, still dripping blood from his most terrible mutilation. He pulled his baby from the arms of its mother. She clung to it, but the other women tore at her arms, and the rest of the Waluguru snarled. He held the child high above his head in the face of the furnace. The Waluguru shouted. For the moment the sacrifice of Ashtoreth was forgotten. And the white figure of Godovius was Moloch, the king.

CHAPTER XI

I

When Eva, resolved on confession, had come to the door of her brother's room and knocked, she had not been altogether surprised at his anxiety to be left alone. James had always been like that, and she knew that there was nothing to be gained by disturbing him. Through the heat of that peerless afternoon she waited. But when the evening came and he had not yet emerged from his chosen solitude, she began to be more anxious. Even if he were in a state of extreme spiritual depression, starvation wouldn't improve matters. It had always been a great part of her function in life to see that he was properly supplied with food and raiment and all the physical comforts which his spirit so heartily despised, and even in this extremity her thoughts moved in the accustomed channel. Seeing herself, as from a distance, pursuing these eminently practical affairs, she was even faintly thankful that she had still the distraction of her habitual activities. She went into the garden to find the boys. Onyango was there alone, sleeping in the sun. She woke him, and in a little while he returned, bringing with him a yellow gourd full of the thin milk of the country. She boiled a little of this over her fire of sticks, and took it to the door of James' room. This time there was no answer. Perhaps, she thought, he was asleep. A blessed relief from all his troubles.

Two hours later she knocked again, and when, again, she received no reply, she suddenly took fright. She wasn't afraid that he had done anything very desperate: she knew that his religious sense was too strong for this: but she knew that he was the lightest of sleepers, and his silence suggested to her a return of the illness which had robbed him of consciousness before. She remembered so well the ghastly sight which he had presented to her on that day, when he had laid on his back with his eyes staring at the ceiling, breathing stertorously. She listened carefully at the door, trying to hear if he were breathing like that now. She remembered her despair on that terrible night and the callous unconcern of Godovius, and her thoughts turned gratefully to M'Crae. Now, thank heaven, she was not quite alone. She tried the door and found that it was bolted. The window.... It opened on to the stoep at the place where the great bougainvillea hung in thick festoons, mitigating kindly the whiteness of the light. At her passage a flight of nectarinidæ passed with whirring wings. The window stood open. The room was empty ... that little room of James', pathetic in its bareness, with no ornamentation but a cabinet photograph of old Aaron Burwarton and the coloured texts which James himself had achieved in his schooldays. On the table lay the open Bible and a sheet of paper on which James had scribbled texts. If she had looked up the references she might have discovered a series of obvious clues to the mystery of his new adventure. But she didn't. She folded the paper and closed the Bible. She saw that he had lain on the bed, and even while she wondered what could have happened to him, she was smoothing the sheets and putting the creased bedclothes in order. She was only thankful that he was not ill. It didn't so much concern her where he had gone; for it was a very rare thing for James to invite her confidence in his plans. Even at Far Forest he would often annoy her by an air of secrecy which emphasised his importance. So when she had put his room, that scene of so recent a spiritual anguish, in order, she sighed, and returned to the kitchen with her cup of milk.

All that afternoon she did not go to M'Crae. Since the day on which Godovius had threatened her she had never been quite comfortable with him. She had felt an awkwardness which it was hard to explain: almost as if M'Crae were aware of the character which Godovius had given to their relation. In some subtle way it seemed that the frankness of their first friendship had been spoiled. That was how she put it to herself; but the more probable reason for their awkwardness was the fact that he knew that she was excluding him from her confidence and would not say so. She would not admit to herself that she, more directly than Godovius, was responsible for the strained atmosphere.

In a very little while night fell. Still James did not come; and this seemed to her unusual, for the thorn bush about Luguru is no place for a man to wander in at night. From her chair in front of their living-room window on the stoep she watched the rising of the moon. At that very moment James was crossing the M'ssente River. A beautiful slip of a thing she seemed to Eva, and of an amazing brilliance. Even before her shining sickle had floated above Kilima ja Mweze the sky was flooded with a pale radiance, and the outlines of the trees which climbed the sky-line and had already been merged in the soft darkness of the mountain's bulk grew suddenly distinct.... Then the restless noises of the night began. Eva felt suddenly and rather hopelessly alone. She was not very happy in the dark.

Now she would not have to wait very long for James. No doubt, too, he would be hungry. She went into the house and laid the table for supper. After all, one must eat. On the table she placed a single lighted candle. Then she pulled on a pair of leather mosquito boots to protect her ankles, and sat there, waiting, and listening to the night. Far away in the forest she heard the sound of drumming. It did not bring to her mind the sinister suggestions with which it troubled that of James. But she felt unhappy, and, somehow, a little cold. She found herself shivering. And just as she had begun to wonder if she, like James, were on the edge of the inevitable fever, a strong-winged moth, hurling out of the darkness at her candle, put out the flame, with a noise of singeing wings, and left her in darkness.

It was a small thing, but it frightened her. She relighted the candle and settled down again to waiting for James; but now she found it more difficult than before to be self-contained. Indeed this culmination to her long day's anxiety had been rather too much for her; she had tried too daringly to walk alone. The incident of the empty church, which at first had seemed to her no more than a set-back to be encountered, now returned to her with a more sinister suggestion. All atmospheres of that kind are more formidable by night: and this night of Africa, with its high and velvety sky in which the crescent moon was still ascending, seemed peculiarly vast, and alien in its vastness. All the time, from the recesses of the forest, she heard the beating of drums.

The little clock on the mantelpiece struck eight. The candle on the supper-table was burning down with a steady flame. James had never in all their life at Luguru been as late as this. It occurred to her that perhaps she was feeling nervous just for want of food. She decided that at the very worst she would not have to wait much longer, and that in any case it would be foolish to give way to her fancies. And then, at a moment when she was really feeling more secure, fear came to her, as swiftly and blindly as the moth which had blundered in out of the night, and all her bravery was extinguished. She left the light burning in the room and ran along the garden path to M'Crae's banda.

"I was frightened," she told him, quite simply. And then she told him of the surprise at the church that morning; of how James had left her and locked himself in his room; how he had left the mission and had not yet returned. And when once she had begun to tell him these things, and had heard his grave replies in a voice that was steady and devoid of fear, she began to feel lighter and happier. When once she had managed to talk like this she found it wonderfully easy to go on, and in a little while she had unbosomed herself of the whole story of her meeting with Godovius, his entreaties and his threats. Until she had ended he did not speak; but she knew that it was with difficulty that he heard her through. At the end he said:

"You should have told me. It would have been more like you."

"I don't know . . ." she said. "Perhaps I was ashamed. I think I was ashamed. At the suggestion . . . you know . . . that we were anything but friends."

He gave a short laugh. "I'm not laughing at you," he said quickly.

"I know you're not. It was silly of me. I ought to have trusted you. I wanted to. But I was shy, I suppose. And shocked by the mistake that he'd made. I was afraid that you might suffer because of his mistaken idea. And I was selfish. I couldn't bear the thought of your not being here: and I thought that I could somehow wait until things cleared up. I thought I could just keep it to myself and hold on."

"You were wrong. It never pays to put things off. No doubt it was a shock for you to have it taken for granted that I had made love to you. I wouldn't have you worried by that. I suppose I am old enough to be your father. You mustn't think any more of that."

Quite candidly she said: "I won't." It was no more than he expected.

She sighed. "I am happier now," she said. "I can't tell you how much I have gone through in these days." And then her thoughts returned suddenly to her fears for James.

"You must tell me what to do. I don't feel as if I can do any more thinking. I've been such a failure when I tried to do it. I can't think. I don't believe I can feel. I'm not like a woman at all. I'm callous. No . . . I'm not really callous, but awfully tired. Oh, what can we do?"

"There's nothing to be done in the night," he said. "You don't know where he went. In the night we are quite helpless. On the night when you found me it was just a matter of luck . . . a matter of Providence. When you get to my age you begin to believe in Providence. If you are lonely or frightened you had better stay here with me."

"I'm not frightened now," she said. "But . . . but I think I'll stay here."

M'Crae made room for her on the heap of sisal beside him. They sat there for a long time without speaking amid the restless sounds which passed for silence in that night. In the remotest distance they heard the drums at Kilima ja Mweze. They were like the beating of a savage heart.

"I shouldn't have kept it all to myself," she said at last. "Are you very angry with me?"

He was a long time answering her childishness. "I couldn't be angry with you. You should have known that. But if I had heard what he said to you I should have killed him. I couldn't have missed him."

"Then I'm thankful you didn't."

In the long silence which followed her tiredness gradually overcame her. It was no great wonder that in a little while she fell asleep. M'Crae, lying beside her, felt her tired limbs twitch from time to time, as the muscles, conscious of the brain's waning control, tried to keep awake. These feeble movements aroused in M'Crae's mind an emotion which was nearer to pity than to anything else. They reminded him of the helpless incoordinate movements which he had often seen in the limbs of young animals. He pitied her childishness, and loved it; for he had come to an age in which youth seems the most pathetic and beautiful of all things. Gradually this restlessness ceased. Eva sighed in her sleep, and the hand which lay nearest to him slipped down until it touched his bare arm. In its unconsciousness the action was as tender as a caress. He permitted himself to be conscious of the hand's slenderness; but it seemed to him very cold. Gently, without disturbing her slumber, he lifted with his foot the blanket which she had lent him and pushed it over her. Then, lying still in the same cramped position, he settled down to think.

II

It was plain to M'Crae from the noise of drumming which had filled the forest all that evening that some great festival was in progress at the Hill of the Moon. Lying awake in his banda, he listened to the sound. It accompanied, with its bourdon of menace, all the deliberations of that night. It was now evident to him that if a way were to be found out of Eva's difficulties he must find it himself; and though he had fought his way often enough out of a tight corner, he had never been faced with a problem of equal delicacy. On the face of it, the matter seemed insoluble. In the first place, he could not count on James for any behaviour that was not admirably perverse. In any project of escape James counted for so much dead weight. Again, even if James should not return from his adventure on this night—and there was no reason to suppose that he would not do so—M'Crae's peculiar position as a man "wanted" by the German Colonial Government made it impossible for him to be a free agent. Here, as in most things, Godovius had the whip-hand, and however gallantly M'Crae might have desired to play the knight-errant in the case of Eva, it would always be doubtful if her association with him could be of any use. It might even be better for her if he were to disappear, as a man with his knowledge of bushcraft might conceivably do, and leave her unhampered by his unfortunate association. But he couldn't do that. For if he left her, only James would remain, and of what use in the world was James?

Thinking the matter over coldly and with deliberation, he regretted that he had not been able to hear the shameful suggestions of Godovius on the evening of the rains; for if he had heard him he would assuredly have shot him where he stood, and the world would have been rid of another wild animal, as savage as any beast in the bush but without any redeeming dower of beauty. He would have shot him. There would have been another murder to his account. But this time he would not have needed to change his name, to lie hidden in an opium house or ship furtively under a strange flag. No . . . the matter would have been far simpler. He would have stepped out into the bush a free man, and then the vastness of Central Africa would have swallowed him up, him and his name. He would have trekked to recesses where no European could have found him. He would simply have disappeared. Perhaps he would have lived for many years: the M'Craes were a long-lived race. Perhaps he would have died soon and in violence: it would have made no difference. The life which he would have led would not have been very much more solitary than his life had been for the last thirty years, except for one thing—the fact that he would be condemned to it for ever. And here, even though his love for Africa was so vast and varied, he found that there was more to renounce than he would have believed. For many years, as he had told Eva, the memory of his early life in Arran had been nothing more to him than a memory: he had never really hoped to return to her misty beauty. But now, when he found himself faced by an absolute renunciation of the possibility of returning, he couldn't quite face it. The sacrifice would be as final as death. For a short moment he was troubled by a vision of his ancient home: a day, as chance would have it, of lashing rain without and the smell of peat within. And he knew that if he did return he would have no more part or lot in the life of that remote island than a ghost revisiting the haunt of vanished love. For a little while the picture held his fancy: and then, imperceptibly, faded. The huge insistence of the tropical night, the high note of the cicalas, the whistling of the frogs rejoicing in the vanishing moisture of the rains, recalled him to the life which he had chosen, and he realised how imponderable was his dream. If he had killed Godovius that dream must have been surrendered. Very well . . . let it go. Even now it might be that he would have to kill Godovius . . .

He wished that he could smoke. Such meditations as these were less easy without tobacco. His tobacco hung in a yellow canvas bag at his belt, but his pipe was in his pocket, and in any case his hand was not free, for Eva's fingers lay upon his arm, and she, poor child, must sleep. By this time his eyes were so accustomed to the dim light of the banda, now faintly illumined by starlight and the beams of the rising moon, that he could see every feature of her pale face and the gloom of her hair. He had never before been able really to see Eva's face. In the daylight the candour of her eyes would have abashed him; he would not have dared to look at her eyes. Now he saw how much her beauty meant to him. If he should kill Godovius he would never see her again . . .

Against this final cruelty his spirit rebelled. It was not for nothing that he had been brought up in the hard creed of Calvinism. Here, even in spite of the new beliefs which life had taught him so bitterly, he found himself instinctively remembering the words of the Old Testament, and the brand of the murderer Cain, whose fate it had been to wander to and fro upon the face of the earth. So deeply ingrained in his mind were the teachings of his childhood that he was almost ready to accept this cruelty as justice: a kind of religious justice which decreed that if he were to save her loveliness from the defilement of Godovius he must relinquish for ever the one surpassing revelation of beauty which had crowned his wanderings.

Even so it seemed probable that he would have to kill Godovius. There was no other way out of it. At his side lay his rifle. The chambers were loaded with soft-nosed four-fifty bullets. He remembered the scandals which centred in the soft-nosed bullet in the Boer War. A bullet of that kind inflicted terrible wounds. That wouldn't matter if only he shot straight: and there was no fear of his missing, for his rifle was almost part of his maimed body.

Eva stirred very gently in her sleep. She made a strange choking noise that was like a sob. M'Crae's fingers grasped her hand. He had never done anything like that before: but it seemed natural to take hold of the hand of a child who was frightened in the dark.

III
It was past midnight when the stillness of the night was broken by the sound of Africans grunting beneath a burden and the clatter of many tongues. In the front of the mission there was a great commotion and M'Crae roused Eva from her sleep. Now that the game of secrecy was over there seemed to be no point in concealment;

and Eva was far too sleepy to question what he did. They stepped out together into the pale night. The sky was very high and clear, but immense billows of milky cloud were ranged along the hill horizons, which in their huge whiteness overpowered the little earth. Beneath the stoep a crowd of Waluguru were setting up a kelele. Most of them were naked and their polished skins shone in the moonlight. They swarmed like black ants about a piece of carrion, and the body which they had dragged from the forest to the mission was that of James, bleeding and torn by the thorns of the bush and smothered in red dust. Hamisi, who appeared to be in charge of the expedition, was loud and anxious in explanation.

"Hapana kufa. . . . He isn't dead," he hastened to tell them. Sakharani, he said, had sent him home. He had been found unconscious in the forest: even now he was unconscious, but breathing, and alive.

Now, at any rate, he had little chance of air, so completely was he surrounded by the sweating Waluguru. M'Crae told them to go back to the forest. Already Eva was kneeling at her brother's side, while the boy Hamisi, pleased with the importance of his mission, grinned and repeated the words: "Hapana kufa. . . . Hapana kufa. . . . He isn't dead."

He wasn't dead, but, for all that, a very ghastly sight. His face was deadly pale and smeared with the blood that had trickled from a split in the skin above his right eyebrow. His right eye was full of blood. The blow must have stunned him fairly effectually, or else the rough journey would have awakened him.

"We must get him into the house," said M'Crae. He saw Eva help Hamisi to lift him and cursed his own maimed strength. It was beautiful of her, he thought, that she should consent to do such things. They lifted him and dragged him to his own room, and laid him on the bed. Eva brought a bowl of water from the kitchen and bathed his head. M'Crae, miserably helpless, questioned Hamisi.

Bwana N'gombe (James), he said, had been found in the forest near Kilima ja Mweze. The cut on the head was nothing. Perhaps he had fallen against a tree. Perhaps a leopard had torn him. They had found him lying in the grass. Lying asleep. Even now he was asleep. Hamisi relapsed again into his monotonous "Hapana kufa. . . . Hapana kufa." Perhaps he had gone to sleep for want of blood. Perhaps a devil had done it. He knew nothing whatever about it. He only knew that the man had been picked up asleep in the grass and that Sakharani had told them to carry him home. And here he was. Hamisi grinned, being satisfied that he had taken part in an excellent piece of work.

All the time that M'Crae was questioning the Waluguru he had his eye on Eva. He watched the splendid way (as he thought) in which she suddenly adapted herself to the demands of the moment. Once again, as on the night when he had staggered out to waylay her, she was showing him her deft, practical side; the aspect which appeals most strongly to a man who has made a woman the vehicle of a tender ideal. It reminded him of that first night. It pleased him that it should do so, and so he kept Hamisi talking, and tried lovingly to recover the atmosphere of their first meeting, thinking: "You wonderful woman . . ."

He packed Hamisi off to bed in his smoky hole. He and Eva together stripped James of his torn and muddy clothes.

"You see he has been through the swamp," he said.

It pleased him to find that he could use his arm with very little discomfort now, and the sense of helplessness which had lain upon him so heavily in the banda disappeared. It was difficult to realise that he had led the life of a prisoner in a dungeon for a month. And Eva, too, was amazed at the help which he gave her, for she had grown to think of him as a helpless and pitiable creature. When she had started to undress James she had not imagined that the task would be so difficult. The weight of his unconscious body surprised her. A poor, thin creature, wasted by fever . . . he looked as though she could easily pick him up in her arms. But she couldn't. Even with the help of M'Crae it was a struggle.

"It's no good wasting your strength," he said. "You'd better slit up the sleeve." So she went to her room and fetched a pair of scissors, and then M'Crae found himself watching her slim, capable fingers again.

"I won't leave you now," he said, and was rewarded by her smile.

They sat there for a long time together, speaking in whispers, as if they were afraid of waking James, although, in fact, they were most anxious that he should wake. It was a very strange night for M'Crae. Removed at last from the gloom of the banda, it seemed to him that he had never really seen Eva before. In this light and spacious room she was quite a different creature from the gentle presence which had haunted his prison; endowed, in some way, with a more beautiful freedom of movement . . . more alive. More hopelessly unattainable. But it was ridiculous on the face of it that she should occur to him in these terms. He thrust the fancy aside obstinately, only to find it obstinately return. For why in the world should he not enjoy this brief interlude of beauty and light, seeing that in a very little time, a few days . . . perhaps a few hours, he himself must vanish altogether into a darkness from which he would never emerge? For, without any doubt, he must kill Godovius. There was no way out of that.

At length, a little time before the dawn, when the night was at its coldest, James stirred in his bed. His hand uncertainly sought his bandaged head, and Eva very tenderly guided it downwards and laid it beneath the blanket. The movement was an immense relief to both of them. Neither of them spoke; and yet M'Crae could see that a shadow had been lifted from her face.

And now James became increasingly restless. Once or twice he gave a groan of pain, and then a deep sigh, almost a sigh of content. He tried to lift himself up in the bed, though Eva gently restrained him. At last he spoke.

"I must have left it behind . . . in the church . . . it is so light."

He tried to open his eyes. M'Crae could see his brows wrinkling beneath the bandage. "Too light . . ." he said.

M'Crae moved the lamp further away from the bed. His footsteps disturbed James.

"Who's that? . . . There's somebody there," he said. "Oh, my poor head . . . my poor head."

Eva laid her hand lightly upon his forehead. "It's all right, dear, don't worry," she said.

For a little while he was contented; but then he said again: "There's someone else in the room. . . . Who is it? He isn't here, is he?"

Even in this dazed condition he was typically persistent.

"There's somebody there . . . who is it? You're keeping it from me. It isn't fair. Who is it?"

Eva's voice trembled as she answered. She was listening to her own voice.

"It's only a friend," she said.

"A friend? . . . We have no friends."

"A stranger. A Mr. M'Crae. A hunter who was lost near here and came to the mission."

There followed a long silence. She was dreading what would come next. To her relief she found that he was treating it as a matter of course.

He said: "Oh . . . all right. My head does ache so."

For the first time Eva breathed freely. No doubt it was strange that she should be so relieved; but the difficulty which she had dreaded most in James' awakening had been his discovery of M'Crae's presence. From the very first she had wondered how he would take it. She had feared that his peculiarly jealous regard for all strangers, a thing which he had overcome with difficulty in his youth, would be too much for him. The anticipation of this had been bad enough; but after her interview with Godovius, and his most hateful insinuations, she had felt that James would be almost justified in thinking the worst of her, and that she could have no defence to offer which wouldn't sound like the flimsiest excuse. But the pain in James' head asserted itself too cruelly for him to think of anything else for the moment. He accepted the presence of M'Crae as nothing more than a curiosity, and the little that she told him seemed to satisfy him. A little later, when his enhavocked brain began to clear a little, the horror of the night before, which had been mercifully forgotten, stole back again. Suddenly, as he lay there, with his hand in Eva's, he was shaken by a fit of sobbing. At the best of times the sight of a grown man so tortured is terrible. And he was Eva's brother. The one emotion with which she had habitually regarded him was that of pity. Now her compassion was overwhelming. She would have given anything in the world to be able to soothe him. He was clutching so hard at the hand in which his own had lain that he actually hurt her. M'Crae saw her bending over James. He stepped through the open window out on the clammy stoep.

"You poor, poor dear," he heard her say. "Is your head so bad?"

James spoke chokingly through his sobs.

"The pain's nothing . . . nothing. I've only just awakened . . . remembered. Eva, I've been in hell. There can't be anything worse in hell. I'd forgotten. Oh, my God, my God. I shall never forget again. My God. . . . My God . . ." And he started crying again.

She could do nothing with him. Her own helplessness amazed her. At times the storm of sobs would cease; but even then the light of his reason shone balefully. The words which he spoke were disconnected, and all were madly tinged with the remembrance of horror. Again and again he would say that he had been in hell, in the uttermost hell. And then his fancy would suddenly be taken with the idea of fire. "Look," he cried, "look, they're bringing dry wood to the fire. The heat . . . think of the heat. . . . Seven times heated. Nothing could live. The stones are white-hot. Oh, God . . . God . . . can you see it?" Then he would scream: "They're coming . . . they're coming . . ." and clutch at his head and grip Eva's hand; and she would grip his in her turn, as though the consciousness of her nearness and her strength might help his lonely spirit. Once, indeed, she found that he was stroking her hand. He had never done such a thing before, and the action brought tears to her eyes. But it was not Eva, of whom he was thinking. He said: "Mother . . . dear mother." In a little while the violence and frequency of his fits of sobbing abated. He babbled less wildly, and fell at last, as she thought, into a state that resembled sleep. Indeed, she would have left him if his fingers had not been still clutching her hand. Thus they waited, until in the hour before their sudden dawn a rain-bird sang. The sound was doubly sweet to Eva, for she knew that the daylight was at hand, and in daylight she need not be so frightened. But with the dawn she heard another sound. And the sleeper heard it in his dreams, for he surprised her by leaping up in bed, with terror in his grey face. "The drums . . ." he said. "Do you hear them? The drums of hell."

CHAPTER XII
I

M'Crae, walking up and down the stoep, and meditating on the strangeness of life, was aware of the drumming which ushered in the dawn. In the ears of James it awakened only memories of a recent terror; but M'Crae, more deeply learned in the ways of Africa, knew that it portended something more than an echo of the night's frenzy. The sound no longer centred in the villages about the foot of Kilima ja Mweze. It came to him from every point of the compass and from places where he had no idea that there were villages at all. The rhythm of the music, again, no longer followed the headlong triple time which had been beaten out by the drums of the N'goma. He noticed that the rhythms were broken and very varied: almost as if the hidden drummers were tapping a message in Morse or some other recognised code. The change filled him with a subtle anxiety: and in a little while he realised that he was not the only person whom the sound had disturbed. On the edge of the compound he heard African voices. Hamisi and Onyango and another M'luguru, a ragged savage whose business it was to herd the mission goats, were talking together in high-pitched voices. Determined, if he could, to find the cause of this excitement, he slipped across the compound under the cover of a hedge of young sisal, and saw that they were sitting in front of their shanty. The boy Hamisi was engaged in polishing the long blade of a Masai spear: and the word which emerged most clearly from their talk was the Swahili, "Vita," which by an inversion of sense peculiar to Western ears has the meaning of "War."

M'Crae was troubled by this word, and, with it, the somewhat sinister occupation which Hamisi was enjoying. He knew all about war: the assegais of the Zulu, the Mauser bullets of the Boer snipers. Africa is a land in which that fire has never ceased to smoulder: he had always accepted it as part of the continent's life. No more than that. He had never dreaded it; but now it seemed to him that in some way his attitude had been subtly changed. When he thought of war he began to think also of Eva, and to realise that for a woman native warfare includes terrible possibilities. Now, more than ever, it occurred to him that Destiny had brought him famished to Luguru to fulfil the part of a protector, for which she had already, brutally, almost disqualified him.

He wished that he could read the message of these disquieting drum-taps. Most probably, he thought, they announced some forlorn hope of a native rising already destined to wither before the German machine guns in the slaughter of black hosts. He knew the history of German South-West and the end of the Hereros. And he wondered—for he had lived so long in Africa that he knew the humble ideals of its millions—why these people should suffer our civilisation in the hail of Maxim fire. Yet, even while he indulged this vein of wonder and pity, he realised that a European community so small and so isolated as their little company at Luguru might very well be exterminated in the first outburst. In his years of wandering he had learnt that the best way of dealing with the African is to be direct and truthful. He stepped out into the path, and Hamisi, hearing his approach, pushed his spear into the hut and greeted him with a very charming smile.

"I have heard you talking of the war," said M'Crae. "And I have heard the drums say the same thing. What is this war?"

Hamisi smiled languidly, scratching his legs. "There is no war," said he.

"But I have heard all that you said. And you were making ready a spear. You were not going to spear lions like the Masai. The Waluguru are not brave enough for that. You had better tell me."

The idea that his lie had been taken for what it was worth seemed to please Hamisi. This time he laughed outright. If the bwana knew that there was a war, he said, why need he ask questions? The Wasungu (Europeans) knew more about everything than the Waluguru. They only knew that there was a war, and that they were going to fight.

"And who are you going to fight?" asked M'Crae.

Hamisi smiled, but said he did not know; and when M'Crae had questioned him a little longer he became convinced that in this, at least, Hamisi was speaking the truth. Somewhere in the world, somewhere in Africa—perhaps no nearer than the northern fringe of the Sahara—the smouldering flame of violence had flickered out. He did not know then any more than did Hamisi, sharpening his spear, that these angry drum-throbs were no more than the diminished echoes of the guns that were battering Liège.

He went into the house to find Eva. James, it seemed, had fallen once more into an uneasy and exhausted sleep. Even now his poor brain was haunted by the memory of the night's horrors; but the watching had told so heavily on Eva that she thought she had better leave him for a little. M'Crae found her in the kitchen making coffee for breakfast. She spoke in a whisper, as though she feared that her voice might be heard above the clamour in James' brain. "He's sleeping, or at any rate he's stopped talking," she said. She smiled quite bravely, but saw in a moment that some new thing was troubling M'Crae. "What's the matter now?" she said.

"I had wanted to keep it to myself," said he. "I don't think we need worry about it."

"Nothing much worse could happen," she said. "I think I could face anything now. What is he going to do?"

"It has nothing to do with Godovius this time . . ."

"Then why did you frighten me?" she said.

"It's war . . . there's a war somewhere. I don't know where. In Tripoli, perhaps. The Waluguru know something about it; but I don't suppose they know more than I do. I don't suppose Godovius knows."

When he first spoke she had gone very pale; now her colour returned.

"It was too bad of you to frighten me like that," she said. "I thought you had heard something terrible about . . . him . . ."

They took breakfast together in the little room, and the atmosphere of that meal had a peculiar quality of lightness; as though, indeed, they had just weathered a violent thunderstorm, and were talking together in a silence which made their voices sound small and unreal. By the time they had finished their breakfast the sun had risen and filled the air with golden light. They stood on the stoep together gazing out over the newly awakened lands. Beneath the sun these lay in a vast and smiling lethargy. Thus would they awake to-morrow and for many weeks to come. Thus had they awakened for countless centuries before the ships of Sheba came to seek their gold. M'Crae gazed fondly: there was no wonder that he loved Africa: but Eva was far less conscious of this revelation of beauty than of the presence of the man at her side. Neither of them broke the silence: but from within they heard the wailing sound of James' voice, raised in complaint:

"A voice was heard upon the high places . . . weeping and supplication . . . weeping and supplication . . ."

Eva turned and left the side of M'Crae. As she passed him she laid her hand gently on his arm.

II

Into the heat of the day the rumble of war-drums never ceased. Their sound contributed an uneasy background to the wanderings of James. It was no matter for surprise that his night of exposure in the forest had awakened the activities of the hosts of fever which slept in his veins. Perhaps this was a blessing; for now his body was so shaken with ague or burned with the alternate fire that the hot reality of his last horror no longer filled his brain. Eva sat beside him. In the rare intervals of lucid thought his mood was merely childish and querulous. M'Crae, seeing that there remained for him no sphere of usefulness in the house, retired, as if by habit, to the shade of his banda, and began to busy himself with the notes of his book.

He wrote in a cramped and undeveloped hand, but very seriously. Even in the banda he felt the heat of that pale sky. He wrote slowly, as one would expect of a man for whom life was infinitely spacious and leisurely, with long pauses between the sentences, in which, perhaps, he was choosing the unwilling words, or even thinking of very different things. At times, again, he would stop in the middle of a sentence, remaining painfully still, as if he were listening. He listened, but heard no sound beyond the thin, clear note of a grass country under a tropical noon. Nothing more . . . and yet a curious instinct prompted him to put out his hand for his Mannlicher, and lay it gently at his side. He went on writing again. Again stopped and listened. He was not happy. He wished now that he had kept to his post on the stoep within call of Eva in James' room. He gave the matter a moment of serious thinking. It was a pity, he thought, that he had come into the banda, where he could see nothing: for now there was no need of concealment, and a man was a poor creature without the use of his eyes. His ears, indeed, had been so long attuned to the condition of silence that they were quick to notice the least sound of moving beast or bird and to distinguish these from the noises which are made by men. Now he instinctively felt that men were near. In this there was nothing essentially dangerous, for Hamisi and the other boys might well be in the garden. But he knew that Eva was tied to the bedside of James, and that no African, unless he were going to steal, would enter the garden of a European, or work without being told to do so. And so he wondered, feeling curiously insecure.

He decided that it would be best for him to see for himself. He raised his body, very quietly, from the heap of sisal, and stole to the door of the banda. By the time that he reached it he knew that he had made a mistake in leaving his rifle behind. But then it was too late. A group of armed Waluguru threw themselves upon him. They were so many that he had no chance. In a moment he was thrown to the ground with a gag in his mouth, while his arm and his legs were bound with a rope of sisal fibre. He knew that it was no use struggling. And, after all, this was neither more nor less than he had expected. The only thing which struck him as strange was the costume of these Waluguru and the arms which they carried. He couldn't imagine that the Germans had trained such savages for police, armed them with rifles, and put them into shorts and jerseys. They dragged him along the avenue under the flamboyant trees, and in his hurried passage the events of the morning suggested to him an incredible solution. War . . . there was war. Not merely one of the black wars of Africa, but a war of white men in which his own people were engaged. The magnitude of the business, its possibilities in the wilds of Africa, overwhelmed him. He thought of Eva. . . . If he had only guessed that morning when they first heard the drums . . . if he had not been so ridiculously unimaginative. . . . But now he could do nothing.

In front of the house Godovius was awaiting him. Behind him, in orderly silence, stood another dozen of armed askaris. As the others, grunting, dragged in the body of M'Crae, the noise of this commotion reached Eva, and she ran out on to the stoep. At first she didn't see the bound figure of M'Crae. She saw only Godovius—Godovius in the white uniform of the German colonial army: and the sight disturbed her, strangely enough, not so much because he was the enemy whom she dreaded most, but because he happened to be wearing the uniform which she had seen in the picture which had first frightened her in his house. "That was all I saw," she said. "He was holding himself in the same military way, and looking so important."

He lost no time in coming to business. He clicked his heels and saluted. "This is a serious matter, Miss Eva," he said. "I am no longer here as your friend and neighbour, but as a soldier of Germany. The Fatherland imposes hard tasks upon us, but we have no alternative but obedience. It is only this morning that the message has reached me. Our countries are at war. This is the work of Russia and France. England, their dupe, has had the insolence to join them. It is a bad day for England in Africa. It is the end of England in Africa. Your brother and you and the man Hare are my prisoners. You will appreciate the fact that I have nothing to do with this personally. I only do my duty."

Through this piece of deadly serious bombast Eva had stood bewildered. When he mentioned the name of Hare she came suddenly, as it were, to herself. She saw the body of M'Crae lying bound in the dust. She saw nothing else. She wanted to see that he wasn't hurt. She hadn't nursed him so tenderly all those weeks for this. She saw the veins of his bound arm standing out as thick as the cords which bound them. His face was turned away from her. She hurried to his side. The askaris stood between them with their bayonets. Godovius shook his head.

"Even now I see that you do not understand. This man is a prisoner of war. However dear he may be to you, this is the fortune of war. I could not help you to your desires if I would. You will see no more of him. But even in war Germany is generous. The Germans do not make war on women or on priests. You will stay here, for the present at any rate, under my supervision. What the Government may do with you and your brother later I do not know. The man Hare will be shot. That I do know. But even so I shall not shoot him. I shall not shoot him unless you misbehave. He is your hostage with me. But you will stay here. You will give me your word that neither you nor your brother will leave the mission nor attempt to communicate with others of our enemies. I must see your brother about this. You will be good enough to lead the way."

"You cannot see him," she said. "He is ill, oh! very ill. He would not be able to understand you. Even I don't understand. I can't understand . . ."

He bowed gravely. "I am sorry to hear of your brother's ill health. It is the night air. The night air of the swamp is very poisonous to a missionary. It was imprudent. I have noticed it before. But I will take your word."

He bowed again, and turned to his askaris. "Chekua," he said. "Lift . . ." They raised the lean body of M'Crae, and set off down the hill-side. Godovius came very near to Eva, so near that she shuddered. Again the nightmare of the picture. . . . "Miss Eva," he said, "between us there should not be war. You see the man Hare goes to my house. He may escape. . . . It is possible that he will escape . . . possible, but not probable. If he should escape, what will you give me?"

III
The next few days were very terrible for Eva. Perhaps it was fortunate for her that her brother needed so much attention and that his state harrowed her sufficiently to keep her mind from the greater tragedy. James made a very slow recovery, and she could not feel that she was justified in telling him of a climax in their affairs which might fall with devastating effect on a mind already torn by his adventure. Little by little he began to talk more freely of this, and always with a communicated awe. At first it seemed that he could never recover his hopes, or his faith in himself. He was far too weak to feel that he could ever return to the struggle; but in a little while he began to realise that he must make a new beginning. Then, as the fever left his body, and his mind became less perilously clear, the old impulse gradually returned, and he began to make plans for the new campaign. "This time," he said, "I shall not be fighting in the dark. I think I know the worst. Nothing could be worse . . . nothing. If only God will give me strength. I must not be beaten. I'm only dealing with the same thing as the prophets and the early Christians. If I were not quite so utterly alone . . . And yet, if the trial is greater, so will be the triumph."

In the end she found he could speak to her almost dispassionately of his adventure, although he never told her any details of the affair, and she knew better than to ask him. Indeed she knew very well that when he spoke to her it was really no more than a little attempt to share his trouble with another creature, to evade the utter loneliness of which he had complained, and that it didn't matter to him whether she understood him or no. All the time it was clear that he found the whole business in retrospect rather thrilling, and even though he never once mentioned the crowning horror of the night, he talked quite frankly of small things which he remembered: of his passage of the M'ssente River under the rising moon; of the coarse grasses which had cut his fingers. Indeed he might well remember those, for his hands were still bandaged so that he could not hold a book. The ragged wound on his forehead worried him: for he could not be certain how he had come by it. "I remember nothing after a certain point," he said. "I know it seemed to me that they were all rushing towards me. Perhaps I cried out, and they hadn't seen me before. And yet they must have known that I was there. The hill was full of them. I just remember them all rushing towards me in the firelight. I remember how white their eyes and their teeth were. And that's all. Yes . . . I think I must have cried out in spite of myself."

And all the time that he spoke of these things she was thinking of M'Crae, wondering what enormities he might be suffering in the house of Godovius. She did not realise herself how much she missed him, what a stable and reassuring element in her life he had been. She supposed that she would never see him again; and though this seemed no stranger to her than the fact that they had ever met, she found it difficult to reconcile herself to the prospect; for she had begun to think that nobody else in the world could possibly look after him, remembering, with the greatest tenderness, the time when he had been so dependent on her care. She had never in her life known a man so intimately as M'Crae. She didn't suppose that another man like him existed. The impression which she recalled most fondly was that of his absolute frankness: the desperate care which he had taken to make their relation free once and for all from anything that was not strictly true. She was thankful that it had been so. Musing on the strange story of his life, she was grateful to him for having told her so much without extenuation or pleading. She would have felt less happy if he had not cleared the way for their friendship by abandoning the name which he had worn as a disguise.

From time to time, thinking of his captivity and of what she owed him, the last words of Godovius would return to her: "If he should escape, what would you give me?" She knew exactly what that meant: and when she thought of it, even though the idea were so unspeakably horrible, she couldn't help fancying that after all she might trick Godovius, that she might keep him to his side of the bargain and escape the fulfilment of her own, very much as she had planned to do when first he had threatened them. It seemed to her that this would be a natural thing to do: that if she could screw up her courage to a certain point she might manage to keep Godovius going and give M'Crae at least the chance of escape. After all, it was the sort of thing that a woman could easily do. It might even be done without any too terrible risk. But always when she allowed her thoughts to turn in this direction she would find herself peculiarly conscious of the absent M'Crae's disapproval. She remembered how gravely he had spoken to her when she had made her last confession. "It never pays to put things off," he had said, and even though she couldn't persuade herself that in this case it might not pay after all, she felt that in taking so great a risk of failure and its consequences she would not be as loyal to his ideals as he would have expected her to be. And so, even though the project pestered her mind, she felt that she was bound in honour to abandon it. He wouldn't like it, she thought, and that was enough. "I am not as good naturally as he thinks me," she said to herself. "Not nearly as good as he is."

Once when she was sitting beside James' bed and thinking as usual of M'Crae, the voice of her brother invaded her thoughts so suddenly that she found herself blushing. He said: "I've just remembered.... On the night when they brought me back there was somebody here. I asked you who it was.... I remember asking. And you said it was a hunter, a stranger who had turned up. You told me the name. Mac... Mac... Mackay.... No, it wasn't Mackay. I get things mixed up. Who was it?"

"M'Crae," she said. "That was the name."

"But what happened to him? I don't remember. I'm sorry I didn't see him. Where did he go?"

"He went away next day," she said.

"I hope you made him comfortable. It's the least one can do. Where did he go when he left us?"

"He went to Mr. Godovius's house," she said. It amazed her to find that it was easy to speak the truth. M'Crae would have approved of that, she thought.

"I would have done anything to prevent him going to that house," said James.

"Yes," she said. "It was a pity, but it couldn't be helped. I shouldn't think any more about it. You were so very ill. And you couldn't help him going there."

"I wonder if he is staying there still," said James.

The irony of this conversation troubled her. She felt that if she spoke another word about M'Crae she must either go mad or tell James outright the whole story of the fugitive. "But if I did," she thought, "he wouldn't understand. He can't do anything. It would only be a waste of breath." She felt that she would like to cry.

She was so lonely and bewildered. It seemed in these days as if she couldn't take things in. The imprisonment of M'Crae meant so much more to her than its cause, the European War which Godovius had so impressively announced. She knew that England was at war with Germany: that she and her brother, still happily ignorant of the whole trouble, were in reality prisoners on parole: but for all that it didn't seem to her possible that this state could alter their position in any way. Already, ever since they had been at Luguru they had been prisoners serving an indefinite term of solitary confinement. She could not realise what war meant to the rest of the world any more than to themselves. Eventually, and bitterly, she knew. Nothing could be very much more terrible to a woman than the prisons of Taborah; but at this time the war didn't seem to her a thing of pressing importance: it was no more than a minor complication which might upset James if he knew of it and make his recovery slower, and the excuse—that was the way in which she regarded it—for M'Crae's imprisonment.

Yet, all the time, in the back of her brain, another indefinite plan was maturing. If the liberty of M'Crae might not be purchased by the offer of a bribe which she could never bring herself to pay, there remained at least a chance—how near or how remote she was quite unable to guess—of rescuing him herself. If once she could manage to seek out the place in which he was confined, it might be possible for her to help him to escape. She remembered a few stories of this kind which she had read. Women had done such things before. They might be done again. A knife, a rifle and food, that was all that he would need. A knife was an easy thing to find; and on the very day of his capture she had taken M'Crae's Mannlicher from the banda and hidden it beneath her bed.

As the days passed, and the sinister figure of Godovius failed to reappear, this plan began to take a more definite shape. She determined to make the most careful preparations for M'Crae's provision, and then, when everything was ready, to go herself in search of the captive's prison. And now it seemed less necessary for her to be secret in her planning; for James was still in his bedroom, while Hamisi and Onyango, who had disappeared together with their subordinate Waluguru on the day of M'Crae's arrest, had never since returned. Indeed she had been happy to find that they stayed away, for now there was no doubt in her mind but that they were in the hands of Sakharani as much as the forest people. At length, having planned the matter in detail, she decided upon a day for her adventure. It surprised her to find how little she found herself dreading the event: it seemed as if, in this particular, she had almost outgrown the possibility of fear. Her violent memory of the House of the Moon no longer disturbed her. She was even prepared to meet Godovius. Nothing mattered if only she might free M'Crae.

The day which she chose for her attempt was the fourth after M'Crae's arrest. During the interval she had never left the mission compound. Now, leaving James in what seemed like a natural sleep, she left the garden in the first cool of the evening at the back of the sisal hedge by Mr. Bullace's banda. The bush was very quiet in this hour. The silence seemed to argue well for her success. She herself would be as quiet as the evening.

She had chosen this unusual way of leaving the mission so that she might not be seen by any lurking natives on the forest road. The smooth peak of Kilima ja Mweze still served her for a guide, and feeling that she could rely a little on her sense of direction, she had expected to enter the forest at an unusual angle and make straight for the hill itself and the house of Godovius without ever touching the zigzag path which climbed the terraces. She stepped very quietly into the bush, and soon struck one of those tenuous paths which the goats of the Waluguru make on the hillsides where they are pastured. A matter of great luck this seemed to her: for she knew that it must surely lead directly to some village in the forest. She began to hurry, so that she might advance some way into the forest before the light failed. She ran till she lost her breath, and when she stopped and heard the beating of her own heart, she was thrilled with a delicious anticipation of success. It was all very adventurous, and her progress, so far, had seemed so secret that she couldn't help feeling that luck was with her.

It was not long before she was disillusioned. Emerging from the path in the bush into a wider sandy lacuna, she found herself suddenly faced by Hamisi, a transfigured Hamisi, clothed in the German colonial uniform, and armed with a Mauser rifle. With him stood a second askari, one of the Waluguru whom she did not know. Both of them smiled as though they had been expecting her, showing the gap in the lower incisor teeth which the Waluguru knock out in imitation of the Masai. Hamisi saluted her, and she began to talk to him, much as a woman who talks in an ingratiating way to a dog of which she is afraid. But from the first she realised that it was no good talking. She guessed that these two men were only part of a cordon of sentries drawn about the mission, and that Godovius was relying on other things than the parole which she had broken so lightly. It hadn't struck her until that moment that she had actually broken it. In a flash she began to wonder if M'Crae would approve. It was strange how this dour new morality of his impressed her even in this emergency.

From the first she realised that her game was up. She saw how simple she had been in underrating the carefulness of her enemy. "How he would laugh at me," she thought. "He" was M'Crae. She knew very well that Hamisi, for all his smiles, had orders not to let her pass. Indeed she was rather frightened of this new and militant Hamisi. She made the best of a bad job, and rated him soundly in kitchen Swahili for having left her in the lurch when the bwana was ill. . . . Hamisi scratched his back under the new jersey and smiled. He was evidently very proud of his cartridge belt and rifle and the big aluminium water-bottle which he wore slung over his shoulder.

In the failing light Eva made her way back to the mission. Rather a pathetic return after her plans and hopes. In the dim kitchen at the mission she saw the packet of food which she had prepared for M'Crae. She had put the strips of biltong and the biscuits with a tin of sardines and a single cake of chocolate into a little linen bag. In spite of her disappointment she could almost have smiled at her own simplicity.

For all that, the failure of this enterprise opened her eyes to a great many things which she had stupidly missed. Hamisi in a burst of confidence and pride in his equipment had told her that he was no longer a house-boy but a soldier, a soldier of Sakharani; that Sakharani was going to give him not five rupees a month but twenty; that he, being a soldier, could have as many women as he liked wherever he went, with more tembo than he could drink, and minge nyama . . . plenty of meat.

It became clear to Eva that Godovius was busy raising an armed levy of the Waluguru. That was the meaning of many strange sounds which she had heard in the forest but hardly noticed before: the blowing of a bugle, and the angry stutter of rifle fire. She began remotely to appreciate what war meant: how this wretched, down-trodden people had suddenly begun to enjoy the privileges and licence of useful cannon-fodder. After that evening she was conscious all the time of this warlike activity. All day Godovius was drilling them hard, and at night she heard the rolling of the drums, and sometimes saw reflected in the sky the lights of great fires which they lighted in their camps. In the presence of this armed force she wondered however she could have been so foolish as to think that it was possible to rescue M'Crae. She knew once and for all that the idea of succeeding in this was ridiculous. The knowledge that she and James were really prisoners began to get on her nerves. She could not imagine what would be the end of all this. She almost wished, whatever it might be, that the end would come soon. It came, indeed, sooner than she had expected.

CHAPTER XIII
I
For two days the forest below Luguru echoed the German bugle calls and the sound of rifle fire. At night the throbbing of drums never ceased, and the reflection of great fires lit along the edge of the bush reddened the sky. During this time the prisoners at Luguru heard nothing of Godovius. James, who was still keeping to his room, had not been able to notice the absence of the mission boys. Now he was quickly regaining strength and confidence. It was strange how brightly the flame of enthusiasm burned in his poor body. As soon as the cuts on his hands were healed he began to consort once more with his friends the prophets, and Eva was almost thankful for this, for it kept him employed as no other recreation could have done. Indeed, beneath this shadow of which she alone was conscious, their solitary life became extraordinarily tranquil. The atmosphere impressed Eva in its deceptiveness. All the time she was waiting for the next move of Godovius, almost wishing that the period of suspense might end, and something, however desperate, happen. One supposes that Godovius was busy with the training of his levies, instructing them in the science of slaughter, flattering them in their new vocation of askaris with the utmost licence in the way of food and drink and lust, as became good soldiers of Germany. That was the meaning of those constant marchings and counter-marchings by day, and the fires which lit the sky at night above their camps upon the edge of the forest.

The failure of her feeble attempt at an escape had shown Eva that it was impossible for her to help M'Crae in the way which she had planned. Again and again the idea of bargaining with Godovius returned to her. It came into her head so often, and was so often rejected beneath the imagined censure of the prisoner that, in the end, her sense of bewilderment and hopelessness was too much for her. She could not sleep at night, even when the drums, at last, were quiet. The strain was too acute for any woman to have borne.

In the end even James, who never noticed anything, became aware of her pale face and haggard eyes. Anybody but James would have seen them long before. He said:

"You're not looking well, Eva. . . . You don't look at all well. I hope you're not going to be ill. You've taken your quinine? What's the matter with you?"

Rather wearily she laughed him off; but James was a persistent creature. He wouldn't let her excuses stand: and since it didn't seem to her worth while sticking to them, she thought she might as well tell him everything and be done with it. Not quite everything. . . . She didn't tell him about M'Crae, for she felt that his clumsiness would be certain to irritate her. She told him, as simply as she could, that they were both prisoners; that England was at war with Germany, and how she had promised Godovius that they wouldn't try to escape. "I don't suppose it will make any difference to us out here, so far away from everywhere," she said. "That's why I didn't tell you before. And of course you were too ill to be bothered."

At first he was only annoyed that she had kept him in the dark. Then his imagination began to play with the idea. He began to walk up and down the room, rather unsteadily, and talk to her as his thoughts formed themselves. Eva was too miserable to listen.

"This is terrible," he said. "A monstrous thing. Here it may be nothing, but in Europe it will be terrible beyond description. This is the awful result of the world's sin. Europe is like the cities of the plain. All the evil of her cities will be washed out in blood. It is an awful awakening for those places of pleasure. London and Berlin. Sodom and Gomorrah. This is the vengeance of God. It has been foretold. No war will ever be like this war. If the peoples had hearkened to the word of God. . . . For He is slow to anger."

Eva had never imagined that he would take it so hardly. She hadn't for a moment envisaged the awfulness of the catastrophe. All the time she had been thinking not of the agony of Europe nor of the possible consequences to themselves, but only of M'Crae, whom the accident had thrown into Godovius's hands. Even when she had listened to James' very eloquent oration she found herself thinking of the helpless figure which the Waluguru askaris had carried into the bush, of the knotted veins on his arm beneath the bonds.

That evening the fires in the askaris camp shone brighter than ever, the throbbing of the drums more passionate. James, realising now the meaning of all that distant noise and light, became restless and excited. He would not be content to go to bed early, as Eva had intended. He said that he would be happier sitting out on the stoep in a long chair, listening to all that was going on below. After their evening meal they sat out there together, and while Eva nearly fell asleep from sheer tiredness, he talked as much to himself as to her. It was a night of the most exquisite calm. Beneath them the thorn bush lay soft and silvered in the light of the moon. The upper sky was so bright that they could even see beyond the forest the outlines of the hills. In all that vast expanse of quiet land only one spot of violent colour appeared, in a single patch of red sky above the German camps.

"You see it burning there," said James. "That is War. That is what War means. A harsh and brutal thing in the middle of the quietness of life. A fierce, unholy, unnatural thing."

She said "Yes," but that was because she did not want him to ask her any questions.

A strange night. From time to time the lightened circle of sky would glow more brightly, the drums throb as wildly as if all the drummers had gone mad together. Sometimes the unheeding distance muffled their sound, so that only a puff of wind brought it to their ears, waxing and waning like the pulsations of a savage heart. Once, in the nearer bush, they heard the voice of a man crying out like an animal. Eva begged James to go to bed. The nearness of the sound frightened her.

"You can't stay here all night," she said. "Soon you will be cold, and that means fever."

He was almost rough with her. "Leave me alone . . . please leave me alone. I want to think. I couldn't think indoors."

Suddenly they were startled by the sound of rifle fire. All over the bush people were firing guns. They couldn't understand it. At first it came from very near, but gradually the firing died away in the direction of the forest.

"It must sound like that," said James, "in a moving battle: a running fight that is passing out of hearing."

At nine o'clock the drums and the firing ceased. Even the fires in the camp must have been allowed to die down, for the silver of the moon washed all the sky. The bush stretched as grey and silent as if no living creature moved in it; and with the silence returned a sense of the definite vastness of that moonlit land, the immemorial impassivity of the great continent. It was a beautiful and melancholy sight.

"In Europe millions of men are slaughtering each other," James whispered.

"Now you will go to bed?" she pleaded.

He took her arm, as though he were really unconscious of it, and allowed her to help him to his feet. They stood there still for a moment, and while they watched, both of them became suddenly aware of the small figure of a man running towards the bungalow from the edge of the bush. His clothes and his face were of the pale colour of the moonlight, so that he might have been a ghost, and when he caught sight of their two figures on the stoep he waved his hand. It was his right hand that he waved. The other arm was missing. While James stood wondering what had happened, Eva was running down the garden path to meet him. Half-way they met. M'Crae could see the tears Eva's eyes shining in the moonlight. He had never seen her face so pale and beautiful.

II

M'Crae came to the point quickly, too quickly, indeed, for James, whom the sight of this passionate meeting had bewildered.

"We have no time to lose," he said. "My rifle is in the banda. I suppose Mr. Warburton has a rifle of some sort?" Of course James hadn't.

"And food. . . . It may take us nearly a week. Three of us. But we mustn't be overburdened."

James waved his arms. One can imagine the gesture of this lanky figure in the long black coat with his head in a bandage.

"I don't understand you, Mr. M'Crae. . . I hope I have the name right. . . . I don't understand the meaning of this. Will you be good enough to explain?"

"There's no time for explanation," said M'Crae. "I'm saying that we have to leave here, all three of us, as quickly as we can. It'll be a hard journey in front of us, but I'm thinking it's better to be driven than to be dead. That's what it comes to. . . . There's no time for talking."

He told them swiftly and dryly what had happened to him after his arrest. How the askaris had dragged him to the House of the Moon and left him, with hands and feet bound, in a shanty at the back of the long white building; how the old woman whose tongue had been cut out had brought him porridge of mealie meal in a bowl, and how he had been forced to lap it like a dog. Once Godovius had been to see him, bringing the pleasant announcement that he was soon to be shot: soon, but not yet; that England was already paying for her infamy in the sack of London and the destruction of her fleet. "In a year's time," he had said, "no swine of an Englishman will be able to show his face in Africa. The black men will laugh at you. You have already lost South Africa. The German flag is flying in Pretoria and Capetown. It is probable that you will live to hear worse things than this, even though you do not see the end."

M'Crae did not tell them what Godovius had said of Eva, nor of the anger which had nearly driven him mad in his bonds.

"And then," he said, "he came again to-night. I never saw a man so changed. He was pretty near the colour of his uniform. 'If I cut the ropes,' he said, 'will you promise that you will not attack me?' A ludicrous question to a one-armed man, cramped with captivity and weaponless!"

M'Crae had given his word, and Godovius had released him. "Now listen," he said. "You are an Englishman and I am a German. That is one thing. For others we have good cause to hate each other. War is war, and it is our duty to hate. But besides this we are both white men. At Luguru there is a white woman. I will be frank with you. For the moment our hatred must go, for we are all in the same danger. Where the danger has come from I cannot tell you. Probably it is part of your damned English scheming. The English have always paid other races to fight their battles. You know that this colony is now one armed camp. In every tribe we have raised levies and armed them. My black swine, the Waluguru, are getting out of hand. To-day I have shot seven of them; but things are still dangerous. It may spread. All the armed natives of Africa may rise against us, German and English alike. They hate us . . . we know that . . . and in an isolated place like this we shall stand no chance. To-night, on my way home, I have been fired at by my own people. They may try to burn the house over me. That will not be so easy, for I have a machine gun. But the mission they will strip and burn without trouble. You can think of the fate of your two English. And I cannot save them; perhaps I cannot save myself. Somehow they must get to M'papwa, where there are plenty of white men to protect them. I am a German soldier. My post is here; and in any case I must stay and teach these black devils what the German rule means in their own blood. You are an enemy and a prisoner. See, I give you your liberty, and in exchange you give me your word that you will return here when you have saved them. I am taking the risk of letting you go. If we meet again I shall know that you too are a soldier and worthy of my nobility. Miss Eva is in your hands. You had better go quickly."

He had asked for arms, and Godovius, after a moment of hesitation and distrust, had given him a Mauser pistol. "You will put it in your belt," he said. "I shall watch you go. You will hold your hand above your head. Remember, I have a rifle, and you will be covered until you are out of range."

M'Crae had laughed. "I hate all you damned Englanders," said Godovius. "You have no sense of seriousness. I do not do this of my own will. But I love that woman. I would rather she were killed by my hand than given to the Waluguru. And I wish her to live. You understand?"

M'Crae understood. His journey to the mission had not been easy: for his body was still cramped by his long confinement and the woods were full of watching Waluguru whom it had been difficult to evade. "At the present moment," he said, "they are all about the bush round the house. As I said, there'll be no time. Miss Eva will put together some food, and I will slip out again to see where the way is open."

In Eva's mind there was no questioning. In whatever other way she may have regarded M'Crae, she trusted him without reservation. She had reason to trust him. As soon as he gave the word she was ready to obey. She remembered the parcel of food which she had made ready for M'Crae on the evening of her hopeless expedition, and turned to go. The voice of James recalled her.

"Eva... where are you going? You had better stay here for a moment."

"There is no time for waiting," said M'Crae. "I've told you..."

James waved his arms. "That is for me to decide," he said. "The matter must be considered. It is possible, sir, that your story is true..."

"James!" she cried.

"Eva, I must ask you to hear me.... I say that this man's story may be true. But how can we know? We have no particular reason to believe him. Think a moment. How do we know that this is not some new deviltry of that dreadful man? After all, it is not unreasonable to suspect a messenger who comes from that house. We know nothing of him... nothing at all."

"Oh, but we do..." she said.

"Nothing. This isn't a matter in which a woman is competent to judge. It's a matter for a man. I'm your brother. There's no one else to stand between you and the world. You know nothing of the world's wickedness. No doubt, in your inexperience, you would trust the first man you met with your honour. Thank God I am here, and ready to do my duty."

"It's your duty that I am showing to you," said M'Crae. "Evidently you haven't taken in what I've been telling you. Godovius's natives have got out of hand. They're armed. If you stay here we shall all be butchered, all three of us. Of course I should stay with you. And I should rather kill your sister with my own hands than let her be taken by the Waluguru. We have to try and get away in five minutes at the most, and make for the Central Railway, where we shall be taken prisoners by the Germans. Perhaps we will not get there. That is in God's hands. But we must have a try. 'God helps them that help themselves' may not be Scripture, but it's common-sense. You'll admit that I'm reasonable."

"You may be reasonable, sir," said James, "but I'm not going to be ordered about in my own house."

"The alternative is being killed in it. For God's sake, man, don't trifle."

James passed his hand over his forehead.

"Perhaps I am wrong... I don't know. My head's in a muddle after the other night. I can't think."

"Miss Eva," said M'Crae, "get everything ready quickly. Five minutes..."

She said "Yes."

M'Crae turned to James. "Man," he said, "do you realise the awful responsibility that you're taking upon yourself in the sin of your pride? Would you see what you saw the other night, and your sister in it?"

For the moment he was very Scotch, and the actual intensity of his words made them impressive.... Some peculiar quality in this appeal made James crumple up.

"God forgive me," he sobbed. "God forgive me.... You had better take her. If it is to be, the sooner the better..."

"Very well then," said M'Crae. "Hurry up and get some clothes on. You can't set out in pyjama legs and a black coat. Let me help you if you are weak."

By this time the pitiful figure had got over his sobs. Once more he was formal and precise. He spoke very much as if he were conducting a Pleasant Sunday Afternoon at home.

"You have mistaken me, Mr. M'Crae," he said. "I have given you my authority to take my sister. You realise, no doubt, the trust which that implies, and that we are quite in your hands. But my own position is quite different. Perhaps you do not know what religion means to a man, or how a man in my position regards his mission. I was sent to Africa to devote myself to these unfortunate people. I have a responsibility. If the devil has entered into their hearts this is the occasion in which they need me most. You spoke just now a little contemptuously of Scripture... I am a minister, and perhaps it means more to me. At any rate these words, if you'll have the patience to hear me, mean a great deal: 'He that is an hireling, and not the shepherd, whose own the sheep are not, seeth the wolf coming and leaveth the sheep and fleeth.' You know who spoke those words. Mine must be the part of the good shepherd. If I behaved as a hireling I could not bear to live."

"There is such a thing as reason," said M'Crae; "I beseech you to listen to it. A dead shepherd is of very little use to his flock."

James glowed. It was extraordinary to see the pale creature expand.

"Ah," he cried, "Mr. M'Crae, that is where you make the greatest of mistakes. It was a dead Shepherd who redeemed the world. If you are a Christian you cannot suggest that that sacrifice was of no use."

"It is not a matter for argument," said M'Crae. "I recognise your point of view. Against my will I respect it. I think you are an honest man and that's the best title I can give you." They shook hands. It is an amazing commentary on the naturalness of theatrical conventions that common men, in moments of the greatest stress, tend to the most obvious gestures. M'Crae, gripping the hand of James, noticed that it was as cold as if the man were already dead.

They spoke no more, for Eva entered the room, carrying the linen satchel full of food and a couple of water-bottles. She saw the two men standing in silence. "You are ready?" she said. "You've settled everything?"

"Yes, we've settled it," said M'Crae. "But your brother will not come. He says that his duty lies here."

"Oh, James, but you can't!" she cried. "You poor dear, of course you can't!"

James shook his head. "We can't argue," he said. "Mr. M'Crae says there's no time."

"Then we will all stay together," she said.

She laid her hands on James' shoulders and looked up at him. He smiled.

"No, Eva.... It is as much your duty to go as mine to stay. You ... you must fall in with my wishes ... you must be reasonable ... you must be a good girl ..." He stroked her cheek, and the unfamiliar tenderness of the action made her burst into tears. She sobbed quietly on the breast of his black coat. Quite gently he disengaged her hands.

"Now you must go, dear. I am trusting you to Mr. M'Crae. God keep you."

They kissed. They had never kissed each other since they were children.

"Oh, James ..." she said.

"I am very happy ... I am perfectly happy ..."

"Come along," said M'Crae in a peculiarly harsh voice which he did not know himself.

She slipped the band of the Mannlicher over his shoulder and they left the house. Left alone, James sighed and straightened his hair. He went on to the stoep and looked out over the silent lands. The growing moon now sailed so splendidly up the sky that he became conscious of the earth's impetuous spin; he saw the outstretched continent as part of its vast convexity and himself, in this moment of extreme exaltation, an infinitesimal speck in the midst of it. Even in the face of this appalling lesson in proportion his soul was confident and deliciously thrilled with expectation of some imminent miracle. His lips moved:

"And fear not them which kill the body, but are not able to kill the soul; but rather fear him which is able to destroy both soul and body in hell. Are not five sparrows ..." He moistened his lips "... five sparrows sold for a farthing? and not one of them is forgotten before God."

III

M'Crae and Eva moved quietly through the garden. The shadow of the avenue of flamboyant trees shielded them from the moonlight, their steps could scarcely be heard upon the sandy floor, and she could only see M'Crae, moving swiftly in front of her, where the blotches of silver falling from the interstices of woven boughs flaked his ghostly figure, the hump of the knapsack slung across his shoulders, or sometimes the blue barrel of the Mannlicher which he trailed. She followed without question, pausing when he halted, creeping forward when he moved: and, deeply though she trusted him, she found herself wondering at the strangeness of the whole proceeding, at its fantastic unreality, at the incredible perversity of a chance which had sent them out into the darkness together on this debatable quest. Her reason told her that the two of them were in stark reality running for their lives: that in all probability she had said good-bye to James for the last time: that there was nothing else to be done. She couldn't believe this. It was no good, she told herself, trying to believe it. It was simply a monstrous fact which must be accepted without questioning. It was no good trying to think about the business which must simply be accepted. She sighed to herself and followed M'Crae.

At the corner of the banda he halted. "Wait here till I come back," he whispered. "Stand in the shadow and wait."

He disappeared. He seemed to her to be making a great deal of noise. She couldn't understand it, for it seemed to her that he ought really to be making no noise at all. She wanted to tell him to go more quietly. She felt inclined to follow him and explain this to him. For quite a long time she heard his movements, and then, in a little interval of silence, the sound of another body which had lain concealed behind the banda, following him. Then she wanted to cry out and warn him, or even to run after him. She wished that wherever he was going he would have taken her with him. She remembered his last whisper, "Wait here till I come back," and waited . . . endlessly waited. It was not easy. It would have been easier, she thought, if she had not been left so near home. There, in the shadow of the acacias, she had not yet taken the final, irrevocable step. There still remained for her an avenue of retreat.

Here, only a few feet away from her, was the opening of Mr. Bullace's banda. The moonlight showed her, through the doorway, the table on which her work-basket lay and beside it an open book, which she had been reading only a few hours . . . or was it centuries? . . . before. At the other end of her dark tunnel she could see the angle of the house, with its festoons of bougainvillea; and all this looked so homely and safe, so utterly removed from the nightmare atmosphere of danger and flight. These things, it seemed to her, were solid and permanent, the others no more than a mad, confusing dream. And there, in his little room, was James. The whole business could be nothing but a dream which had ridiculously invaded her consciousness. She felt that if she were to go back to the silent house and find James, and slip once more into the pleasant order which she had created, she might wake and find herself happy again. And yet, all the while, she was remembering the whisper of M'Crae, "Stand here in the shadow. . . . Wait till I come back again," and found herself obeying. Not without revolt. It was too bad of him, she thought, to try her in this way, to leave her there in the threatening shadow. Too bad of him...

In the darkness she heard a shot fired. Again silence. Perhaps that was the end of it. But though the idea tortured her, the sound of that report did actually bring her to herself again. It showed her that the danger was real after all. She pulled herself together. "I must wait here until he comes," she thought. "Even if it's for hours and hours I must wait here . . ."

It was not for very long. Suddenly she became conscious of a shadow behind her, and before she had time to cry out she saw that it was M'Crae, who beckoned her from the end of the avenue nearest to the house. . . . He stood waiting for her, and though no word passed between them, she followed.

Their way led at right angles to the one which he had taken at first, close under the shadow of the house. On the edge of the compound he dropped down and wriggled between two clusters of spiked sisal leaves. She bent down and did the same. In a little while they were threading their way between the twisted thorns of the bush. A branch, back-springing, tore Eva's cheek. They must have moved more quickly than she had imagined, for her heart was fluttering violently, but M'Crae never hesitated, and still she followed after.

She wondered often how in the world he knew which way he was taking her, for all the trees in this wilderness seemed to her alike, and she had no knowledge of the stars. Somewhere on the right of them she heard shots, and when the firing started he stopped to listen. A ridiculous thing, that any man who was running for his life should waste time in that way. The first shots sounded a long way from them, in the direction which he had taken when he first left her; but while they stood listening a group of four followed, and these were of a terrifying loudness, beating on their ears as if, indeed, the rifles were levelled at their heads. Eva had often heard the echoes of Godovius's rifle in the bush; but it was quite a different thing to feel that she was being fired at. She shivered and touched M'Crae's arm.

"Where are they?" she whispered. "Can you see them?"

"No. . . . You mustn't be frightened," he said. "The bush magnifies the sound. They are quite a long way away."

But with the next shot something droned with the flight of a beetle above them, and a severed twig dropped on Eva's hair.

"It's all right," said M'Crae; "they're firing on chance, and they're firing high. They always fire high. Are you rested now? Come along."

Strangely enough, she found herself no longer tired. Her heart ceased its feeble flutterings. She had reached her "second wind." Now they moved faster than ever. Even though the bush never thinned, M'Crae seemed able to find a twisting way between the thorns; almost as if he had planned the route exactly, yard for yard, and were following it exactly, never changing pace nor breaking stride.

Suddenly, in front of them, the bush grew thinner, and Eva was thankful, for it seemed to her that now they were no longer shut in a cage of thorns. A moment later they emerged upon the edge of a wide slade of grasses, very beautiful and silvery in the moon. For a full mile or more it stretched before them, unmoved by any breath of wind, and the night so softened the contours of the black bush which lay about it that a strange magic might have transported them without warning to some homely English meadow, set about with hedges of hawthorn and dreaming beneath the moon. No scene could have been further removed from her idea of Africa and its violence.

"We must keep to the thorn," whispered M'Crae.

She obeyed. But here, on the edge of the bush, where the lower branches of the thorn-trees had pushed out into sunlight and more luxuriantly thriven, it was not easy going. They moved slowly, and in a little while Eva's dress was torn in many places. Thorns from the low branches tore at her back and remained embedded in her flesh. She was very miserable, but never, never tired. In the bush on their left they heard a melancholy, drooping note. It was the cry of a bird with which Eva had grown very familiar at Luguru, and she scarcely noticed it until M'Crae stopped dead.

"It was a hornbill," she said.

"Yes. . . . But a hornbill never calls at night."

While he spoke the call was echoed from the woody edge beyond their slade of grasses. Again on their left: and this time very near.

"An escort," said M'Crae. "We must get closer in."

"Towards the sound?"

"Yes . . . Come along."

He led the way into a denser thicket of thorn. "We can never force our way through this," she thought. Upright they could not have penetrated this spinous screen. Crouching low, they managed to pass beneath its lower branches where they drooped to the level of many fleshy spears of the wild sisal. At last Eva found that they had reached a little clear space about the root of a gigantic acacia.

"Now lie down," said M'Crae. She lay down in the dark and the shed spines of other years drove into her limbs till she could have cried. In this secret lair they waited silently for a long while. They heard no longer the mocking hornbill call, nor any sound at all until their silence was suddenly shattered by a burst of firing over the grass-land on their right. "They think that they have seen something," said M'Crae. "Don't be frightened. You are quite safe here. Quite safe."

And so this firing ceased, or rather bore away to the south-east across the line which they were following, and then again to the full south, in distant bush, where it muttered and died away. All this time Eva was lying with her arms between the thorny ground and her head, gazing up at the flat, horizontal tapestries of the acacia and beyond to a clear sky in which the moon sailed lightly as though it were rejoicing in the freedom of the heaven from any wisp of cloud to mar its brightness; for all the cloudy content of the sky lay piled upon the hills beyond which she had risen, in monstrous gleaming billows that dwarfed the dark hill-chains, but stood up so far away that Eva had no notion of their presence. A little wind passed in the night, and she grew aware of many dead or dry leaves shivering all around.

"Come along," said M'Crae, helping her gently to her feet. She was horribly stiff, but still not in the least tired.

Now it was not easy to escape from their hiding-place, so thick-set were the trees and so tangled about their roots with an undergrowth as wiry in the stem as heather but fledged with softer leaves. Eva's hands clutched at these as they passed, and she became aware of a pungent and aromatic odour.

"Don't do that, please," said M'Crae. "On a windless night that will smell for hours."

She felt like a naughty child at this reproof. She found herself rubbing her hands on her skirt, almost expected to be scolded again for ruining her clothes. That skirt, at any rate, was past ruination. She felt inclined to laugh at her own feeling of guilt as much as at his seriousness; for she couldn't get over the idea that even if they were going to die it would be just as well to make a little joke about it. M'Crae's intense monosyllables worried her and, thinking of this, she came to see that in reality it was the man, and not she, who was childish. "If I laugh," she thought, "he will think I am mad. But if I don't laugh soon I shall simply have to cry or something." She learnt a great deal about M'Crae in those early hours of their flight, realising that he was as blind to the essential humour of nearly every catastrophe as all the other men she had met would have been: as James, as her father, the minister at Far Forest who drove out on Sundays from Bewdley; as every one of them, in fact, but the second mate who had tried to make love to her on the mail-boat. "And he wasn't really a nice man," she thought.

In a little while they had pushed their way through several miles of this kind of bush. For a long time now they had heard no noise of firing, nor indeed any other sound; but at length there came to their ears a shrill, trilling note of a curiously liquid quality, and Eva knew that they must be approaching water of some kind, for she had often heard the same music on the edge of the swamp or near their own mission after rain. M'Crae was still walking a little in front of her—never during all this chase had she seen his face—and suddenly she saw his shoulders dip as he disappeared over a grassy edge into a deep channel sunk in the ground. She followed him cautiously, for she did not know how steep the bank might be or what depth of water might be lying at the bottom. Her feet landed on a bank of soft sand.

"No luck," said M'Crae. In the dry watercourse no drop of moisture remained. "But I think we are near water for all that," he said.

She could not think why he should be worrying his mind about water when the bottles which they carried were full. Already she was uncomfortably conscious of the weight of her own. They crossed a second narrow donga, and then another: both dry. At a third, sheltered by a graceful screen of taller acacias, they found a bottom on which there was room for both of them to turn. The whistling of the frogs grew so shrill that it hurt their ears. In the middle of the donga no stream flowed; but caught in a series of shelving rock-pools a little of the water of the last rains had lodged. It smelt stale and was cloudy with the larvæ of mosquitoes.

"Now we had better drink," he said.

"This?"

"Yes. It is not bad water."

"But I'm not thirsty. And even if I were . . ."

"You must drink it all the same. We must keep the water in our bottles. We shall want that later. Drink as much as you can . . ."

He himself began to drink, ladling the stuff to his mouth with the curved palm of his hand. She had never seen anyone drink like that, and when she tried to imitate him she found that she spilt more than she drank. Nevertheless she managed to obey him, and now knew, for the first time, how parched her mouth was.

"Now we must get away from this," he said. "This place must be alive with mosquitoes."

Her wrists and ankles knew that already; but the tangle of swamps into which they had wandered was not so easily left. It must have taken them an hour or more to free themselves from its convolutions. When they merged at last into the open air and could see the moonlit sky, they settled down in the hollow of a dry river bed upon the edge of which the grass grew high and rank. The bank of this stream was strewn with fine sand and made a comfortable shelf on which to lie.

"I'm afraid you are tired," he said. "You must be tired to death."

She denied him; and indeed, strangely enough, until that moment she had not been conscious of fatigue. She even felt a mild exhilaration: a feeling that it wasn't easy to describe: and then, of a sudden, very, very sleepy.

"You are wonderful . . . wonderful . . ." he said.

He told her that if she were to be fit to march next day it was essential that she should get some sleep. "We are all alone," he said, "and you must realise that we can't be . . . be quite the same as if we were living in a civilised place. You mustn't mind what I do for you. If you trust me . . . if you realise that I reverence you . . . that . . ."

"You should know that without asking me," she said.

"It is going to be a cold night," he said. "You're warm now. But it's nearly two o'clock and the cold of the ground will strike through your clothes. I want you to share my warmth. If you aren't warm you won't sleep. And it's important you should sleep. You mustn't take any notice of it. You mustn't mind."

She made no reply. It seemed very strange to her, even though she told herself that there was no real reason why it should seem strange. And so they settled down for the night, lying very close together, with M'Crae's body pressed to hers; and when, a little later, she began to shiver, as he had told her, and found that she had huddled instinctively closer to his warmth, she felt him respond to her presence, placing his arm about her for protection. Even in her state between sleep and waking she felt her sense of modesty weakly rebel against the idea that she should be lying under the moon with the arm of a stranger about her. But when she reflected on the matter it seemed to her that in fact she knew M'Crae more intimately than any other man in the world, and smiling to herself at the strangeness of the whole business, she fell asleep again.

M'Crae did not sleep. . . . He had many matters for thinking, and even though they had made good travelling from Luguru, having left the mission twelve or fourteen miles behind, he felt that it was still his duty to watch. At this distance from Luguru it was more than probable that their pursuers would leave them alone, and particularly in the night season, which the Waluguru fear; but even if he were free from the menace of the armed savages, no sleeping man could be wholly safe from lions in a country so full of game. He wanted, too, in his own methodical way, to make his plans for the next day's journey, to calculate how far their resources of food and water would carry them, to set his course by that pale starlight for the journey towards the Central Railway with its relative civilisation.

He calculated that from the nullah in which they now lay to their object must be close on eighty miles. Of the lie of the land he knew next to nothing, for he had entered the German province from the north; but he knew enough of the general nature of Africa to guess that the country would lie higher towards the east, and that the rivers, draining to the Wami, as did the M'ssente, would be spread out like the fingers of a hand from the north to the south-west, and farther south in the line of the Equator. It seemed to him, therefore, that they could hardly ever be wholly lacking in water. But he didn't know. There was no way in which he could know. He reckoned that if he were travelling alone he could make almost certain of doing his twenty miles a day; but this time he was not travelling alone, and he had no knowledge of the strength or endurance of a woman, or how her delicate feet would stand the strain of walking day after day. That night he had made her loosen her shoes. He could see them now, ridiculously slender things, lying beside her. It was not the fact that they were unpractical which impressed him so much as that they were small. Seeing this token of Eva's fragility, he was overwhelmed with a kind of pity for her littleness. He supposed that for all her high and splendid spirit she was really no more than a child; and feeling thus incalculably tender toward her, he found that, in the most unconscious way in the world, the arm which he had placed about her to keep her warm when she had shivered would have tightened in a caress.

That wouldn't do. He knew it wouldn't do. He knew that it would have been the easiest thing to have bent a little nearer and kissed her cool, pale cheek: so easy, and so natural for a man who loved her. But he had settled it long ago in his mind that for a man of his kind to permit himself the least indulgence of tenderness would not be strictly fair to her. He knew that if he were once to admit the possibility of love-making between them there must be an end once for all of his attempts to do what he had conceived to be his duty. It would not be fair: and there was an end of it. It wouldn't be fair . . .

And so, lying alone with this woman so intensely loved, in his embrace, he resigned himself to the contemplation of the vast sky which stretched above them. God knows, it wasn't easy. All the time there was a danger—and no one could have appreciated it better than he did—of his allowing himself to be persuaded that she was really a child and that he was justified in his sense of protection: so that it was not surprising that he found himself turning for an escape towards the infinite remoteness of stellar space. It was an old trick of his. Time after time, in the past, he had used this expedient in hours of distress and disappointment. He knew nothing of astronomy, and yet he had lived under the stars. He saw now the great cloudy nebulæ of the southern sky, and that principal glory of the south, Orion, mightily dominating the whole vault. He had always cherished an idea these remote, compassionate spheres looked down with pity on the small troubles of the human race and the little, spinning world. What, after all, did it matter whether one man were lord of his desires or no? In heaven, he remembered, there was no marrying or giving in marriage. It were better so. While he watched, the great sky gradually clouded over. No driving clouds were hurried past the moon: only an immense curtain of white vapour condensed in the upper sky, and in a few moments the moon was hidden. It grew almost dark.

Next morning Eva wakened to a sound that was peculiar in its blending of the strange and the familiar. The sky hung grey above them, but the air was full of innumerable bird-song, so clear and thrilling in its slenderness that she could almost have imagined that she was waking to a morning in the first ecstasy of spring in her own home on the edge of the Forest of Wyre. She had never heard anything like that at Luguru. In the garden at the mission she had grown accustomed to the harsh note of the pied shrikes, a numerous and truculent tribe which makes its living on the smaller birds. This first and ravishing impression was a small thing: but somehow it coloured all that day. A wonderful day. The sun rose swiftly on those highlands, and in a little while her limbs lost their chill and stiffness. As soon as she had rubbed her eyes and put on her shoes they ate a little breakfast together. M'Crae allowed her a little water . . . so very little, she thought, and then they set off walking in the cool morning.

No man who has not travelled in the early morning of the African highlands could tell you of the beauty of that day. Their way led them over a wide country of waving grasses where trees were few: a high plateau, so washed with golden light, so bathed in golden air, so kindly and so free that it would have been difficult for any soul to have felt unhappy there. To the west and to the south of them stretched these endless yellow plains. In the north they could still see the bosky forms of the Luguru hills, where all their troubles lay: but even these seemed now too beautiful to have sheltered any violence or pain. Once or twice in the midst of this atmosphere of freedom and of relief from the intangible threats of Luguru Eva remembered James. She recognised, I suppose, that he was in some danger: she was grieved, no doubt, by the obstinacy which had made him stay behind, and realised that it was very courageous of him and very like him to have seen the business through: but her own relief and bewilderment were so intense that she was never vexed with the dreadful imaginations which came to the mind of M'Crae, and made him remote and preoccupied all through that golden morning.

Little by little his sombre mood was beguiled by her childish pleasure in new things, her young and healthy life. I suppose that a man can know no greater happiness than walking alone in the open air at the side of the woman he loves. In these hours the whole living world ministers to his passion, revealing countless and incredible beauties to eyes that are already drunk with joy. So it was with M'Crae. In the loveliness of Eva's gait, of her eyes, of her voice, he was lost. The way was scattered with familiar beauties which came to him invested with a strange poignancy when they were shared by Eva's eyes. Thus, in the heat of the day, they rested beneath a solitary acacia on the gravelly crown of these plains and round the dusty flowers of brushwood at their feet many butterflies hovered. M'Crae knew them all well enough, but Eva had never seen many of them before and must find a likeness for each of their silken patterns. One that she loved was blotched with peacock eyes of violet, and another wore wings of figured satin in modest browns and greys, like the sober gowns of mid-Victorian ladies: and at the sight of another Eva must hold her breath, for it floated down on great curved wings of black that were barred with the blue of a kingfisher.

All through the heat of the day they lay there listening to the sleepy calling of the hornbills until they fell asleep themselves. In the first cool of the evening they set out again, leaving the country of tall grasses as golden as ever behind them, and entering a zone of Park Steppe scattered with trees from which the nests of the bottle-bird were hanging in hundreds. Eva was beginning to be very thirsty: but M'Crae would not let her drink. Soon, he imagined, they must come to one of the greater tributaries of the Wami: there they would quench their thirst and camp for the night upon the farther side. At the time of sunset they came indeed to a sodden valley upon which the Park Steppe looked down. It promised good and plenteous water, for the bottom was hidden with tapestries of acacia slowly stirring, and a single group of taller trees with silvery trunks and great, expanded crowns stood brooding over the sources of some spring. On a slope of sand M'Crae noticed the spoor of many buck that had wandered to this oasis for water, and when he saw them his mind was clouded with a faint doubt: for the hoof-prints had set hard in moist sand and had been left there, for all he knew, as long ago as the last rains. When they came to the bottom of the valley they found that the bed of the stream was dry. M'Crae searched along its course to see if any water had been caught in the pools of rock: but whatever had lain there had long since evaporated. Somewhere indeed there must be water. So much they knew by the high crowns of that company of smooth-trunked trees and by the luxuriance of the thorned acacia. But the water was too deep for them. M'Crae spent a futile hour digging with his hand in the sandy bottom of the stream: but though the sand grew cool, no water trickled through.

"It doesn't matter," said Eva. "We have plenty of water left."

M'Crae shook his head.

That night they made their camp on a hill-side placed a mile or so above the bed of the river, at a safe distance from those sinister beauties which are known to hunters as "fever trees." Eva was very happy, even though the spear-grass had worked its way into her feet. She was healthily and pleasantly fatigued. Never in all her life had she spent a more wonderful day. She felt, too, that she was beginning to know M'Crae better and was glad of it. Time had helped her to reason herself out of a great deal of ridiculous shyness. Again they lay together under the stars, talking of trivial and intimate things. They did not speak of James or of Godovius. Their talk was as light and an inconsequent as that of two happy lovers. Indeed they were already lovers, though neither of them had ever given the other a word of love.

Eva fell asleep early, resigning herself without question to the arm of M'Crae: but M'Crae lay awake long into the night. He was thinking of water . . . always of water. Their disappointment at the river bed had made him very anxious. He had made certain of finding permanent water at this level, and the bed of the stream was sufficiently deep and wide to justify his belief. But now there was no doubt in his mind but that he had set their course too far westward for the season of the year. He had been aiming, as Godovius had told him, for M'papwa; but if he were to keep in touch with water it seemed that he must make for the line considerably farther east. The prospect which lay before him, according to his present plans, was a whole system of dry river beds which would mock their thirst at every valley and in the midst of which they must surely perish. It meant a whole revision of his plans, and, what was more, a waste of valuable time. For, even though he had undertaken to place Eva in safety on the Central Railway, the mind of M'Crae was never very remote from Luguru. He had given Godovius his word that he would return. In some small particular Godovius had shown himself to be a white man: at the last moment his regard for Eva had been sufficiently strong to place her in the protection of his only rival. M'Crae had gravely given him credit for that: and if he owed a debt of honour to Godovius, he felt himself even more deeply indebted to

James, a man of his own race, cursed with the courage and perversity of a martyr, and the only brother of the woman he loved. Yes, as soon as it were possible he must make his way back to Luguru . . . even if he were to be too late. There was so little time to spare. Once more, about midnight, the sky clouded over. On the horizon's brim he watched the flickering light of bush fires slowly burning fifty miles away.

IV

A cloudless and splendid dawn ushered in the first of the bad days. They set off early: for M'Crae was anxious to make as much progress as possible before the extreme heat of the sun developed. He had decided, in his deliberations of the night, to follow the course of the dry river valley towards the east, so that, at the worst, they might keep in touch with the possibility of water. They marched all day. From time to time M'Crae would leave Eva to rest while he reached out towards the valley of the river to see if any sign of water were there. Time after time he returned with a solemn face which told her that he had failed, and every time she was ready to meet him with a smile. It wasn't easy to smile, for though she dared not let him know, she was suffering a great deal. The little doles of water which he allowed her to take were never enough to quench her thirst. Always, in the back of her mind, whatever she might be saying or doing, thirst was the dominant idea. In all her life she had never been far away from the sweet moisture of brookland air: but the country through which they now struggled might never have known any moisture but that of the dew for all they could see of it. It was an endless, arid plain, so vast and so terribly homogeneous that their progress began to seem like a sort of nightmare in which they were compelled to trudge for ever without more achievement than prisoners treading a wheel. Always the same level skylines hemmed them in, offering, as one might think, an infinite possibility of escape, but giving none. The dry bed of the river was the same, neither wider nor narrower, and always parched with sun. The trees were the same scattered bushes of mimosa and acacia: the butterflies the same; the same hornbills called to them from melancholy distances. Once, in the appalling fatigue of the early evening, when a little coolness descended to mock their labours, Eva realised of a sudden that she was sitting under a withered candelabra cactus, a gloomy skeleton that raised withered arms into the dry air, and a haunting conviction assailed her that this was the self-same tree under which she had sat in their first halt, long ago in the dawn of the same day. The idea was almost too horrible to be true; and, when she saw M'Crae approaching, the same lean, dusty figure, his lips parched with drought, the atmosphere of a monstrous dream returned to her. Again he smiled, again he helped her to her feet. He was so kind, she thought, that she could have cried for that alone.

At sunset they lay down for the night. They spoke very little. They were too tired to speak, and the mind of M'Crae too troubled; for he knew that even if they found water next day their food was running short. For supper they chewed plugs of biltong. That night she slept very little. When she was not awake she dreamed without ceasing. She dreamed of Far Forest, and above all of a little brook which tumbles from the western margin of the watershed of Clow's Top to the valley of the Teme, and a mossy pool of icy, clear water into which the thin stream fell with a tinkling sound. When she was a child, returning on hot autumn days from the wooded valley, she had often bathed her flushed face in its basin, and let the water trickle into her mouth, and so, she dreamed, she was doing now. Then she awoke to the brilliant moonlit sky untenanted by any cloud or any dewy tenderness. In the cold, dry air she huddled closer to M'Crae. It was good, after all, not to be quite alone. She decided that she would chew no more biltong. She would rather starve than have that savour in her dry mouth. It tasted to her like the dregs of beef-tea.

A little before dawn he awakened her. Now he had determined to take the greater risk and march due south. Even without water—and the land could not be waterless for ever—it would be possible for them to cover as much as fifty miles, and he did not suppose that they could now be farther than this from the railway.

It was a bitter start. She found that her feet had become so sore that it was torture only to stand; but she supposed that when once she had got going it would be easier. He knew that she must be suffering thirst, for he himself had taken far less water than she.

"You poor child," he said. "You poor, dear child. It can't be so very long now . . ."

She knew it could not be so very long.

But that day was a repetition of the last: more terrible, perhaps, in its alternations of hope and despair; for now their way led them over a series of river valleys, every one of them full of promise, every one of them dry. She began to hate the temptations of their beckoning green. All the time he was at her side ready to cheer her, and always eager to give her rest.

"You are brave," he said, "you are splendid. You are wonderful. A little longer. Only a little longer . . ."

Towards evening she knew that she could do no more. After a longer halt than usual she made her confession.

"I'm afraid I can't. . . . No . . . I know I can't. My feet are dreadful. It's worse than being thirsty. You mustn't take any notice of me. You had better go on. You mustn't mind leaving me. I want you to do so."

"We must see what we can do," he said, "and you mustn't talk such wicked nonsense. You know that I can't leave you. Let's see what we can do to your feet."

She took off her stockings. She didn't want to do so. It was funny that in this extremity she should have been troubled by any such instinctive modesty. "I expect they look awful," she said.

Her stockings had stuck to her feet, her poor, swollen feet, with blisters, she supposed; but when, with infinite pain, she had managed to free them, she found that the skin was smothered with ghastly suppurating wounds in each of the many places where the fine spines of spear-grass had pierced it. Indeed it was a miracle of endurance that she should have held on through the day. The realisation of her suffering was altogether too much for M'Crae. He caressed the bruised feet with his trembling hand.

"What you must have suffered . . . my dear one, my dear one . . . your beautiful feet. You, a woman. You of all women in the world."

Kneeling beside her in the sand, he kissed her dusty ankles.

"I have been cruel to you. I have driven you. And just because you were so brave . . ."

"It hasn't been more for me than for you," she said. "And don't call me brave. I'm not brave. I'm only what you make me. If you call me brave I know I shall cry . . . and I don't want to do that." She raised his head and kissed his blackened lips. And then she found that she must cry after all: but while she cried to herself her hand, all of its own accord, was stroking his bowed head.

The peace of the sunset descended on the plains. The air about them was full of a tenderness which is the nearest to that of spring than any that the tropics know. A rainbird on a spray of thorn began its liquid song; but this battered and exhausted pair were too rapt in their own bewildering revelation of beauty to be aware of any other. The night fell.

They did not sleep. They lay together and talked softly of things which had not the remotest bearing on their desperate case: of the night when they had first met: the long evenings in Mr. Bullace's banda among the whisky bottles and the rest of the precious hours which now they counted as lost. For them the past and the amazing present were enough. They had no future. It did not seem to matter what the future might be now that they had reached this most glorious end. At the worst they were sure of dying together. To-morrow . . .

To-morrow came. They watched the sky grow pale over the eastern horizon. Gradually the outlines of the low trees which had lain around them in silent congregation became more distinct. The birds began to sing. Perhaps there would not be another dawn.

While they sat wondering under the paling sky a strange sound came to their ears. To Eva it sounded like the rushing of a distant river. In such a silence the least of sounds could be heard; but this sound came for a moment faintly and was gone. Indeed it was more like the sound of water than anything else: a mirage of sound that had come like that old dream to torture her thirst. It faded away, and then, very gently, it came again.

"I heard something . . . like a river. Did you hear it?" she said.

"I heard something," said M'Crae, "but I think I must have imagined it. It was like the noise that the blood makes in the vessels near your ears at night, when you are getting better from fever. I expect it's partly the quinine."

"But I heard it too.... It can't be that," she said.

"Don't think about it," said M'Crae. "We had better make a start. Now there is no reason why you shouldn't let me carry you. We will see how it works. I shall take you like they carry a wounded man. You must put your arms round my neck." Again they kissed.

He had lifted her precious weight, when she cried: "Listen.... I hear it again. It can't be imagination," and they listened together.

"My God!" said M'Crae. "My God! It's a train!"

He left her, and she watched him running into the bush, as though this were actually the last train that was ever going to grind along the length of the Central Railway, and he must stop it or die.

CHAPTER XIV
I

How many hours Eva lay alone under the thorn-tree I do not know. For a great part of the time she slept or fell into an uneasy dream that hung midway between sleep and waking. Now that her hope of water had been renewed her thirst became a torment even greater than before. Once again, in the middle of the hot noon, she thought that she heard a train moving on the line; but by this time the wind which had brought the noise to their ears had dropped, and it sounded very far away. In the intervals of waking, and even in her dreams, her mind seemed marvellously clear. She found that she wanted to talk of the ideas which whirled about it. She even wanted to laugh, although she could not imagine why. And then, in her weakness, she would topple from this pinnacle of exaltation, feeling her actual and appalling loneliness, thinking miserably of James and of any catastrophe which might have befallen him. At other times she would surprise herself, or rather one of the innumerable selves of which her personality was compact, engrossed in the contemplation of some minute part of the multitude of silent life which surrounded her. At one time, moving rapidly in the red dust at her feet, she saw an expedition of black ants, many thousands of them, extended in a winding caravan. She saw the porters stumbling under their loads, the shining bellies of their attendant askaris, and the solitary scouts which they had thrown out on either side. She could not guess where they had come from or where they were going, but the way which they had chosen, and from which no obstacle could dissuade them, happened to lie over the ragged edge of her skirt. She dared not move, for she feared that if she disturbed them they would swarm upon her with innumerable stings; so she lay very still and watched their column move past until the head of it wheeled away beneath a fallen bough; and the thought invaded her brain, now so perilously clear, that she and M'Crae, in their long adventure, had been no less tiny and obscure in comparison with their surrounding wilderness than this strangely preoccupied host. In all her life she had never been given to such speculations; but that was how it appeared to her now. "We are just ants," she thought. "God cannot see us any bigger than that." A strange business.... Very strange. It was hard to believe.

When, in another interlude of her dream, M'Crae arrived, the shadow of the acacia had moved away from her, and she found that she was lying in the tempered sunshine of late afternoon. He brought her water. That was the thing which mattered most. And when she had drunk she found that she was ready to tackle another plug of biltong. Little by little the dream atmosphere faded.

"I've been a long time," he said, "but I wanted to make sure of everything. I can tell you we're in luck's way. We slept within a couple of miles of water. To think of it! The railway lies over the brow of the hill on our right. I made a false cast for it at first. And there is not only the railway there, but a sort of station. Now you can be sure of safety. I can leave you happily."

Their eyes met, and both knew that he had not spoken the truth; but she also knew that his mind was already made up on what he still conceived to be his duty and that, however tragically, leave her he must.

"I found a man there working in the rubber. A Greek I took him to be. And I told him about Godovius and his levies at Luguru. They can't send help from here: but the stationmaster has sent a wire through to Kilossa. Probably they thought I was mad. He was old and very fat; but I saw his boys washing a woman's clothes, so I think you will be safe. So now I shall take you to the edge of the bush above the station. After that you will fend for yourself. It may be difficult... but I know how brave you are, you wonderful child."

"It is only a little way," he said, "and you must let me carry you. I know that you're done, my darling. No other woman could have stood what you have stood already. If I put everything else aside I should have to have loved you for that. You know how I love you?"

"Not well enough. You must keep on telling me.... But now," she said, "I can walk. Do they know that I am coming? Does that Greek woman know?"

"They know nothing. Only that a madman out of the bush has brought a message from Luguru and has gone again. When you get there you know that you will be a prisoner."

"But the Germans are not at war with the women," she said.

"No..." he said. "I am sure that you will be safe. A white woman is safe anywhere in Africa with white men. If it were not so it would be impossible for women to live here at all. But we must not waste time. You'll put your arms round my neck and I shall lift you."

"I will put my arms round your neck, and then I will kiss you; but I shall not let you carry me. You must be more tired than me. I've been resting all day."

"Then you shall try," he said solemnly.

He lifted her to her feet and the trees swam round her. She clutched at him, and it seemed as if he too were part of the swimming world.

"Now you see . . ." he said.

"It was getting up suddenly. Now I'm better," she protested; and so he let her have her way, and they set off slowly together in the cool evening. For a little way she would try to walk, and then, having confessed that she was tired, she allowed him to take her on his back and carry her.

In this way they passed through a narrow belt of bush and descended to a valley. Here, marvel of marvels, ran a little stream, where water, coloured red with the stain of acacia bark, flowed over a sandy bottom. They halted there for a moment, and Eva bathed her face, her arms and her bruised feet. In all her life she had never known water so wonderful; but they could not linger there, for already the sky was beginning to darken. So at length they came to the edge of the bush, and saw beneath them the valley in which the railway ran, an ordered green plantation of rubber, some fields of sisal, a cluster of homely, white-washed houses, and a little compound in which stood a group of paw-paw trees burdened with gourdlike fruit.

"Now you have only a little way to go," said M'Crae.

There, on the edge of the dry bush, they said good-bye. In the story of their strange courtship I have imagined many things, and some that I have written were told to me, so that I know them to be true. I have imagined many things . . . but for this unimaginable parting I have no words; for, as you may guess, they never met again.

II

This, too, is the end of Eva Burwarton's story. I can see her painfully making her way towards the station buildings and the compound in which the paw-paw trees were growing, turning, perhaps, to look once again at the dusty figure of M'Crae, clear at first, but in a little while becoming merged into the ashen grey of the bush and the bistre of burnt grasses. Perhaps it is true that they have never been more to me than figures of this kind, very small and distant, struggling with feeble limbs upon a huge and sinister background. One is content to accept them as this and as no more: for an action of mere puppets in surroundings so vast and so sombre were enough to arouse one's imagination and to claim one's pity. Of all the actors in this lonely drama it was never my fortune to know more than one: and it seems to me that the rest of her story matters very little. If you would have it—and for those who are in search of further horrors there is horror enough—it is all written in the Bluebook, or White Paper, or whatever it is called, which tells of the persecutions and indignities of the English prisoners at Taborah. One heard enough of these things at Nairobi in the winter of ; one heard them with pity and with admiration, but never with the thrilling sense of drama, remote and intense, which underlay Eva's story of the months before. She didn't stay long in Nairobi. For a week or two they warm-douched her with sympathies and chilled her with prayer meetings, and then they sent her down the line with her unfortunate companions, and shipped her home by the way of South Africa. That, for me, was the end of her story. Perhaps she returned to Far Forest. I don't know; but I imagine that this was unlikely; for, if I remember rightly, there were no more of her family left, unless it were an aunt to whom she used to write from Luguru, an aunt who lived in Mamble—or was it Pensax?—some place or other not very far away.

In those days it was my business to visit German prisoners who were confined in the camp on Nairobi Hill near the K.A.R. cantonments, a happy and well-fed company, very different from our famished and fever-ridden spectres who had lain in prison at Taborah. From time to time large batches of these civilians were sent away to be repatriated in Germany; and when others came to take their place, my curiosity would always make me ask them if they knew anything of Luguru or of Godovius, for, whether I would or no, my mind was occupied at that time by Eva's story. Many of them had heard of Godovius. The story of the woman who had been killed by the mamba was popular; any lie in the world was popular that might serve to ingratiate them with the hated English. A poor crowd . . . a very poor crowd! But nobody at all professed to be acquainted with James. I suppose he had not been long enough in the colony.

One day my luck turned. It was my business to treat a new arrival who went by the name of Rosen—something or other. A Jew at any rate. He had been left behind somewhere in the neighbourhood of Morogoro, had been taken unarmed, had claimed to be a missionary, and had been treated as such. Personally I am convinced that he was a waiter, and an appalling specimen at that. When he discovered that he was on the point of repatriation, he remembered that he had been born at Kalisch, in Poland, and was therefore a Russian. Anything in the world to keep out of Germany. You see, the papers were full of the stories of bread riots and fat tickets, and, for all his religious protestations, his only god, as far as I could gather, was his belly. When the day came nearer he sprung an attack of fever. I'm prepared to admit that it was genuine enough, but he certainly made the most of it.

"Herr Doktor," he said to me, clasping his hands in front of him, so that I could see no less than ten black finger-nails, "it is probable that the next attack will kill me. I have had blackwater fever five times. I understand this disease. I have been for many years in Africa, and if you will pardon me saying so, I understand myself."

So did I; but although I hadn't any possible use for the swine, the mere mean ingenuity which he showed in his attempts to avoid returning to Germany amused me, and so, sometimes, I let him talk. He had lived in England. I must confess that for a missionary he was pretty well acquainted with the least reputable bars and lounges of the West End. Of course he was a waiter . . . or perhaps he had been a steward on a British liner. He was great on idiomatic English and the slang of the nineties, and from time to time he would trot out the names of Englishmen whom he had befriended or whose lives he had saved in German East. One day he startled me with the remembered name of Bullace. "Bullace?" I said. "Yes . . . I knew him. Tell me about him."

"Ah, Herr Doktor," he said, "then you knew, no doubt, my old friend's failing? A sad thing for a brother missionary. Twice I nursed him with what you call the jim-jams."

I questioned him about Luguru, about Godovius, about James. He shook his head.

"But do you not know what happened at Luguru early in the war?" he said.

At last he had found a chance of entertaining me without so much painful effort. He settled down to it. He was charmed to tell me everything he knew.

It surprised him that we, in British East, should have known nothing about it. Quite a sensation, he said. At the time when it all happened he had been in Kilossa. He was at great pains to explain that his mission lay near to that place. Those were early days of the war, and all his community had volunteered for work—noncombatant work—in the field. They were all gathered together at Kilossa, waiting for orders.

And then, one day a message came over the wire from a small station near M'papwa. The stationmaster, a fool of a fellow, had been given a message about some native rising at Luguru. He hadn't had the sense to detain the messenger. Madness . . . but the Germans were such a simple, trustful people. A rising at Luguru, where the levies of Godovius were believed to be in training; where, only a few days before, a caravan of rifles and ammunition had been sent. Still, the news was definite enough, and there was no time to be lost. Volunteers were asked for. Ober-Leutnant Stein, a planter himself, was put in charge. "And I offered to go with them," said the little Jew.

"But you are a missionary. . . . You cannot carry arms . . ."

"I know it," says my friend, "but there is also a mission at Luguru, and the missionary there, even if he is an Englishman, is my brother. It was my duty to go."

They shook their heads, he said; they tried to dissuade him; but in the end he had his way. Had he not held the Englishman Bullace drunk in his arms? Had he not, very nearly, succeeded in reforming him?

He wept for Bullace.

They left Morogoro the next day at dawn. Twenty whites, a hundred askaris, Wanyamweze, trained men. Stein in command: a man who had been long in the colony, who had known Africa in the Herero campaign, one of Karl Peters' men. "He knew how to deal with these black devils."

They moved quickly; and indeed the story went too quickly for me. I asked him about Godovius. "A Jew," said he, shaking his own undeniably Semitic nose, implying that no more need be said. "A Jew . . . and a very strange man. You know the story of the mamba? A fine organiser, and greatly respected by the Waluguru. Rather too catholic in his taste for women . . . there were other funny stories about him . . . but then, we are not in Europe; we must not be too hard on the sins of the flesh. The tropics, you know . . ."

On the third day they came to Luguru. The people were very quiet, cowering in their villages. Perhaps they knew what was coming. The column marched in pomp through the forest to Njumba ja Mweze. A pitiful sight. It had been a fine house for the colonies, well built of stone, almost like a one-storeyed house at home in Germany—in Poland. Burnt. Absolutely gutted with fire. He remembered the pathetic appearance of a grand piano, crushed beneath a fallen beam, worth, he supposed, as much as three thousand rupees, worth half that second-hand, now only a twisted tangle of strings and a warped iron frame. No trace of Godovius or of his servants. No trace of anything in the world but ashes. Stein said nothing. It was a dangerous thing when a man like Stein, a man of deep feeling, remained silent.

Next they went to the mission. They had expected to find the same sort of havoc, but, strangely enough, the house was standing. "I went into the house myself and there everything was quiet. I thought: 'God is great. This is a miracle. They have spared the holy place!' I offered up a prayer. It was most touching. There, in the kitchen, was a table and on it a piece of woman's sewing and a work-basket. In the bedroom, the very room where I had saved the life of Bullace, another table on which there was an open Bible. But I saw that the spinners had hung their webs across the room. I saw a great big spinner [gesture] fat as a black chief, sitting in the middle of the web. Ugh! . . . No man had lived there for days. I thought of the woman whose work was in the kitchen. I went to Stein. 'Look,' I said, 'there has been black work, black work. . . . These devils have killed them.' Stein said nothing:

"I thought, 'These people, the missionary and his wife, had gone to Godovius for protection. Alas! they have shared his fate. Now there are three white people to be avenged.' Stein told the askaris to load their rifles. He himself walked behind the machine-gun porters. 'Now we will see to these Waluguru swine,' he said. Stein was a man of few words but a colossal courage. Later he was killed, up on the Usambara line. 'Come, you,' he said . . ."

They went down through the bush to the forest. There was an askari who knew the Waluguru villages, and he showed the way. "We marched past the church, and I thought to myself: 'It is right that I should go in there, to the place where my friend Bullace worked and prayed. I will go in and offer a prayer myself.' I opened the door. . . . Pff! . . . But the stench was too much. 'My God!' I said. 'What is this?' . . .

"You are a Protestant. You do not know . . . If you had been in the Roman Catholic churches in Poland [he got it right that time] you would have seen the human-size crucifixes which frighten the children with a big dead Christ. It was on the pulpit. They had hung him there on the pulpit with big nails. Through his neck was a carpenter's chisel. The nails and the hammer were lying on the floor. In his black coat he hung with his feet tied together. He was far gone, as you say. Pff! . . . Oh, it was very bad. And the black swine had mutilated him in the way that Africans, even our own askaris, use with their enemies. You know . . . Pff! . . . It was too awful. I tell you I could not stay there to offer up the prayer that I had intended in that place. I went out. I could not bear the sight of that crucified man. I ran after them. I was afraid to be alone. You will understand; I was not allowed to carry arms . . .

"I told Stein. Stein said nothing: but I know that his blood boiled nobly. Then the firing began. It was just. Never was there such a revenge. We went from village to village. Everywhere the fires crackled up. Everywhere they ran screaming, the black pigs, women and all. Stein had the machine gun. The askaris knew what had to be done. By evening that forest was cleansed. I do not think the Waluguru will trouble us again. There is only one way of teaching savages.

"That night we slept in the mission. There was not room for all of us and so I and another gentleman went to rest in a little banda in the garden on a heap of sisal. There, too, the woman had been. It pained our hearts to think of that woman. But we knew she had been avenged. We had done our duty, even for our enemies. The place was full of whisky bottles. Worse luck! [idiom] they were all empty.

"That was the end of it. Next day we left Luguru. We never found the woman. I expect she went to Godovius. Trust Godovius for that. But one more thing we found. It was the body of another man, or as much as the hyenas and the white ants had left. No doubt he was an Englishman, though we did not know there was another there. He had a rifle with him, a Mannlicher, which I should have liked myself if I had not been forbidden to carry arms. The white ants had eaten most of his clothes and some wild beast had carried away one arm: but he had on him a little packet of letters, or rather notes. I picked them up and put them in my pocket, thinking there might be paper money therewith. If I had taken money it would not have harmed him. When I began to examine it I found that it was all written in English. He wrote badly, like a child, that man; and you may believe me or not—it was all notes on places in our colony: on good water holes and winter streams and things of that kind. It was an affair for the General Staff. You see he was a spy . . . an English spy, who had been killed by thirst or sickness and had his arm carried off by the hyenas. A brave man, perhaps. So . . . it was the right death for a spy. See, this was in the early days of the war, and already your spies were near Luguru!

"And now, Herr Doktor, you see how weak I am. You see how this simple story had tired me? Ah . . . this accursed climate! It weakens all of us. I think you too are pale. It will be a long time before I am fit to travel . . . the strain of a sea voyage. Is it not true? How can I thank you for all you have done for me?" He would have pressed my hand.

I left him. It seemed to me that the day was heavier than usual. I wished that the rains would come and have done with all this alternating oppression and boisterous wind. I left the camp. I went past a little garden where the children of some prisoners, little creatures with flaxen hair and blue eyes, were playing at soldiers, and walked due south until I came to the escarpment of the hills. Below me the levels of the Athi plains stretched without end, dun-coloured and dappled with huge shadows like the upper waters of the Bristol Channel, or rather of some vaster and more gloomy sea. It was an impressive and wholly soothing scene. I sat there until the sun had set, and on the remotest horizon the shadow of Kilimanjaro, a hundred miles away, rose against the sky. I sat there till it grew dark, and the great plains faded from me, thinking of the three men who died at Luguru: of James the martyr predestinate; of Godovius consumed in the flames which he had kindled; of M'Crae whom Eva Burwarton had loved. It was very still. All the shallow life of Nairobi might have been as far away as the great mountain's filmy shadow. And then, when I turned to make my way back in the darkness to the club, a sudden sound startled me. It was the beating of a drum in the lines of the King's African Rifles. I stopped. In that moment I knew that for all our pretences of civilisation I was still living in a wholly savage land. I looked up to the sky, to the south with its strange spaces and unfamiliar stars. I saw Orion, the old hunter, stretched across the vault. The beating of the drum awakened some ancient adventurous spirit in my blood. I knew that this was the land above all others which men of European race have never conquered. It was a strange moment, full of a peculiar, half-bitter ecstasy. I gazed at the stars and murmured to myself: "This is Africa. . . . This is Africa."

Printed in Great Britain
by Amazon